THE IMMORTAL CANCER

THE FIRST HUNGER

THE IMMORTAL CANCER
BOOK 1

ANDY DANGVU

ASH MERIDIAN PRESS

Published by Ash Meridian Press

Ebook ISBN: 979-8-9943552-0-6

Print ISBN: 979-8-9943552-1-3

First edition

Printed in the United States of America

CHAPTER 1

It was a cold November night in downtown Los Angeles. The dampness clung to her skin, especially after the sun had dipped behind the skyline. Here on Skid Row, the air carried a little more weight, and always filled with desperation, but she knew these streets better than most.

Amelia Devereux just started handing out sandwiches when she spotted the two twitchy guys on the edge of the block. They weren't part of the regular crowd. You could tell by the way everyone else steered clear. One of them knocked over a woman's cart just to steal a can of something he probably wouldn't eat. His buddy scratched at his neck like his skin didn't fit right. Their menacing laughs blanketed the air, and they lingered in the shadows too long. Finally ducking down a side alley.

She didn't say anything, not yet. But she made a mental note. Junkies like that never leave quietly.

People glanced twice when Amelia walked by. Not just because she was tall and moved like she owned the sidewalk, but because something about her didn't seem...temporary. Her almond-shaped eyes caught the streetlights like polished obsidian, unreadable and unhurried. She was the kind of beautiful that made people think twice about messing with her and three times about why they ever had. Her dark, straight hair flowed to the middle of her back like silk, catching the moonlight as she moved. She's lived over three centuries as a vampire, and she was still struggling to make sense of it.

Walking along the wet streets, this wasn't her first night on Skid Row. Not even close. For the last few years, Amelia had come here weekly. Sometimes more. Learning names, checking in, and making sure they knew someone saw them. She moved from person to person with a quiet familiarity. She was one of them.

"Hey Lisa," she said, crouching next to a woman wrapped in three coats. "Any luck finding Peanut?"

The woman shook her head, tears glimmering. "No... he's still missing."

Amelia touched her arm gently. "I'll keep an eye out."

Lisa nodded. Amelia smiled with sympathy.

Further down, she leaned into a man slumped against a crate, his foot wrapped in a filthy towel. "That still infected, Manny?"

He nodded slowly. "Hurts like hell."

"I'll bring antibiotics soon," she promised. "You sure it's not just an excuse to get me to come back?" she teased.

Manny laughed, a wheezy, honest sound. "You'd come back anyway. You like us too much."

She smirked. "Don't push your luck, Manny."

A gray-bearded man with wide, grateful eyes clutched the sandwich with dirt-stained hands she had just handed him. "Thank you, dear. You always do such nice things for us. Most people just look right through us, but not you."

She smiled softly. "Think nothing of it, George. Everyone needs a little help now and again."

Each exchange chipped away at the weight of her own centuries. Helping the helpless wasn't just charity. It was the closest she ever got to feeling human again.

She rolled up the now-empty bag and tucked it under her arm. "I'll be back soon to check on everyone, don't let them push you off this block, okay?" She said, waving off a few final thank yous.

As she walked away from the encampment, the buzz of downtown began to fade behind her. She turned down a dim side street, toward the quiet where she'd parked her bike, a vintage 1964 Honda CB77. It wasn't vintage when she bought it.

I've lived so many lifetimes, everything feels like a hand-me-down.

The air grew colder. Streetlights flickered uncertainly, and the foot traffic thinned to nothing. The deeper into the side streets she went, the quieter it became. The city's pulse softened, but her senses stayed sharp. Her boots echoed with a steady rhythm against the pavement until she heard it, two sets of footsteps pacing behind her. They were distant at first, but their pace quickened. Faster, closer. She didn't need to turn around. Her enhanced hearing picked up every word.

"Grab her from behind, knife to her throat. Real quick," one man muttered.

"Yeah. We'll fuck her up. No way she's talking to anyone after this," the other replied, voice twitchy, desperate.

Amelia slowed her pace slightly, listening. The voices were slurred, full of tension. She caught the sound of them scratching their arms, their necks jittery with withdrawal.

Oh, joy. PCP and testosterone. The world's deadliest cocktail of dumb, she mused to herself.

"You got the gun?"

"Yeah."

"I got my blade. Let's do this. I need a fix, bad."

She glanced back just enough to catch a glimpse of their outfits. They had on ripped hoodies, sagging jeans barely clinging to their hips, stained tank tops, and sneakers that had seen better days. One had duct tape wrapped around his shoe like a sad badge of honor.

Ah, yes, the unofficial uniform of poor life decisions.

Amelia's eyes narrowed. She hadn't felt fear in centuries. Combat was second nature, honed over hundreds of years. She'd trained with warriors, soldiers, and assassins. Being immortal gives you time. Being immortal made it easy to accumulate wealth, and being wealthy meant access to the best. When restlessness crept in, when the weight of centuries pressed too hard, she turned to danger like it was an old lover. It reminded her she was still alive.

They were only a few feet behind her now. She could feel the charge in the air. Her predator's sense tingled. She kept walking.

Let's play a little game.

As the two men crept closer, she threw a glance over her shoulder to make sure they saw her, with wide eyes and a flicker of pretend fear, she bolted down the street.

"She saw us!" one man barked. "Cut her off! Get around the other side!"

The second man took off at a sprint, knife in hand, trying to flank her.

Amelia ducked into a dark alley where she knew there were no working lights and a dead end. It was exactly what she wanted. The first attacker entered, stepping cautiously. The alley reeked of piss and rotting trash. Fire escapes cast long shadows like prison bars. Then a rat scurried past him, and it made him flinch.

"Come out, sweetheart," he crooned in a singsong voice. "We just want your cash. Then we'll leave."

"Please...just leave me alone," Amelia whimpered, her voice trembling with theatrical fear.

"Come on, baby, be smart. We'll make it quick," as he passed the knife from one hand to the other.

Quick? Honey, you're already dragging this out. She mused.

The second man reached the alley just in time to hear, *THUMP! THUMP!.* It sounded like a baseball bat slamming against a sandbag. Then silence, it was deafening.

"Yo?! Where the fuck are you?" he called out, gun raised and panning back and forth in the dark alley. From the darkness, a knife skidded across the pavement, stopping at his foot. He kicked it to the side. His fingers tightened around the trigger. Beads of sweat began building over his brow.

"Real subtle," Amelia muttered from somewhere in the dark. "Just gonna leave evidence lying around?"

"Don't mess with me, bitch," he whispered, stepping into the gloom. His nerves were raw. He jerked at every creak and every gust of wind. From the shadows, his partner lunged with a bloody lip and his eye swelling. The smell of urine was so strong in the air that when he looked down to see, he uncontrollably pissed himself.

"Get outta here... she's not...she's not..." He whimpered.

"Oops. Someone's leaking," she laughed.

The second man shoved him to the ground. "You're pathetic. I'll finish this myself!" He stepped forward, shouting into the black. "Where are you, you psycho bitch? I'm gonna kill you!"

A voice floated down from above. Calm and mocking.

"Well, that sounds like a lot of work."

He whipped around. A dark figure crouched on the fire escape above, two glowing red eyes piercing through the dark.

Seeing the eyes and trying to shake off what he thought he was hallucinating, "No... no, that's just the drugs..." he muttered. He fired.

BANG!

"Nice shot. You hit...ummm, probably a rat." Then the figure vanished.

"Are you sure you're even aiming? That was awful," her voice teased, now behind him. "You can do better than that?"

"Fuck you!" He turned and fired twice

BANG! BANG!

Bullets cracking bricks. A trash bin ricocheted with the force and then silence.

"That wasn't even close," she mocked. "I'm over here."

She darted past him like a shadow, the wind of her speed spinning him. She laughed.

"I'm getting my workout in. You boys ever consider cardio, or you more into pilates?"

He spun again just in time for Amelia's elbow to smash into his jaw. He staggered, dazed with stars dancing in his vision. At the mouth of the alley, the wounded junkie struggled to his feet, grabbed the discarded knife, and shouted, "Kill her!"

Amelia moved so fast between both men, appearing between

them like a shadow rising from the earth. Eyes glowing like burning coals, a smile spread across her lips, exposing her long fangs glimmering in the moonlight. The gunman's eyes opened like saucers.

"Now. Where were we?" She started.

"Freak! What the hell are you?!"

"You wouldn't believe me if I told you."

Raising his gun, shaking, he shouted, "You're dead, bitch!"

"I've been dead, sweetheart. Try something original."

He fired. Too slow. She twisted, the bullet grazing her denim jacket.

"Damn it!. I liked this jacket. It's finally vintage."

With practiced speed, she hurled a throwing knife. It struck his hand with brutal precision. The gun fired wildly, and a bullet pierced straight into his partner's kneecap, dropping him to the ground.

"What the f... " he stammered, staring at his friend as he fell.

Before he could react, Amelia was on him. She grabbed his wrist, knocked the gun free with a twist, and spun to drive her elbow into the side of his head. His eyes rolled back as he crumpled to the ground. She looked over at his partner as he screamed while holding his bleeding knee. Looking up at her, he yelled, "What the hell are you..."

But before he could finish his sentence, she rushed at him and struck him under the chin with her knee, knocking him out quickly.

She stood over them; they were bruised, bloody, but breathing. She could've ended them, but they were still human. They still had a choice. Vampires didn't.

"You'd think after 300 years I'd get bored of this. Nope, idiots keep lining up."

She glanced toward the sky, hearing sirens in the distance.

"Cue the boys in blue."

*Two junkies knocked out from a drug-fueled fight...*she thought, stepping over their bodies and pulling her knife from the unconscious attacker's hand. *At least that's what the police will think.*

"I helped the forgotten. Got in a workout, and now it's time for a drink," as she kicked up the stand and mounted the bike. "Not bad for a Tuesday."

The engine growled. A blur of taillights and black hair vanished into the city, leaving only the echo of gunfire and the smell of fear behind her.

CHAPTER 2

Amelia guided her motorcycle into the private underground garage of her high-rise, the echo of the engine fading into polished silence. She parked in her reserved corner marked not by signage, but by an aura of wealth and stepped into a private elevator accessible only via biometric scan.

The elevator hummed softly as it lifted her to the top floor, her sanctuary in the sky. She leaned against the wall, arms crossed, letting the night fall off her shoulders like an old coat. Another night, another round of borrowed humanity. She could still hear Manny's laugh, feel the dirt of the street on her boots. The doors opened directly into her penthouse.

A soft click greeted her, the security system recognizing her presence, unlocking the heavy door with its usual obedient sigh. She stepped into the circular foyer, where a marble table sat at the center like a relic, untouched except for a crystal vase of lilies and white peonies.

They were already wilting. They always did after a few days. Even beauty died eventually, unless you cheated time like she had. As she dropped her keys on the silver tray, the sound echoed like punctuation as she moved down the corridor. Empty rooms, spa bathrooms, and the office passed by in silence. She had built this place for comfort, for armor, not for company. Her feet carried her to the door at the end, her training room.

Inside, the scent of oiled metal and rubber mats greeted her. The space was pure function, weights on one wall, sleek equipment on another, and a wide MMA mat stretching across the center. A mirrored wall faced her, full-length and still.

How many hours had she bled into these mats? How many times had she cracked bones just to remind herself she could still feel?

She walked to the mirror and pressed her palm to the hidden sensor. The lights pulsed beneath her skin, then soft rings of light spiraled outward. The mirror split open with its usual hush, revealing the weapons vault behind it.

Rows of guns gleamed on one wall, carefully maintained and sorted by era and caliber. On the other wall, her real treasures, blades of every kind. Katanas, Roman gladii, medieval broadswords, Persian daggers, throwing knives, and shurikens. Weapons of kings and assassins alike.

Each one had a story. Some forged in war, some stolen in silence, but none forgotten.

She stared at the trench knife. The handle still bore a crack near the base. It had split the skull of a boy, maybe seventeen, who'd tried to rob her during a riot. She hadn't needed to kill him, but she did it anyway. Afterward, she'd stared at his body in the mud, surrounded by broken pots, and felt nothing but an ache that wouldn't go away.

That night, she'd sworn off killing humans. Not because they were good, but because she wasn't God. It wasn't her decision who lived and who didn't. Not anymore. No one else remembered him, but she did. She remembered. Blood banks had opened not long after, and medical refrigeration changed everything. She didn't need to feed on people anymore.

Not that she didn't miss it sometimes. There was a rush in it. The drumbeat of a heart as it slowed under her mouth, but she'd learned what that cost, too.

She pulled out the knife from tonight's fight, finished cleaning the blade, and set it back like an artifact on a shelf.

Satisfied, she sealed the vault and headed for the kitchen. The penthouse opened up before her with glass walls framing the city like a living mural. Los Angeles glowed beneath her, pulsing and restless.

She pulled two blood bags from the fridge, type O, chilled, and poured them into a crystal glass. The color, deep and rich, was almost beautiful, but it still tasted like regret. No matter how clean the source, it always did.

She stepped up to the window, drink in hand. The city stretched for miles, cars streaming like blood cells through concrete arteries. It was alive, loud, and fleeting. She'd seen cities burn and rise again. Watched empires fall, lovers age and die while she remained. A constant. A ghost.

She sipped the blood, letting it settle in her veins. Not fresh, but enough. She sank onto the couch, pulling off her boots. The chill of the marble floor bit at her bare feet. She welcomed it. Even now, she craved sensation. Some reminder she hadn't gone completely numb.

The room around her was a museum of the life she'd lived, paintings from a long-ago salon, a Ming dynasty vase, a violin gifted by a composer whose name had vanished from history. All dusted, arranged, and perfectly preserved. Sometimes she wondered if she collected these things to honor the past...or just to pretend she still had one. These were pieces of a world that no longer existed, just like her.

She didn't belong. Not to the humans, whose patterns she could predict in her sleep. Not to the vampires, who had traded purpose for politics. They had become cowards. Brokers. Obsolete in their ambition. They called it evolution, but she called it rot.

She'd spent centuries chasing meaning. Lost friends and lovers. Lost herself a dozen times over. Some nights, the silence was unbearable. The ghosts came back in laughter and in names she hadn't spoken aloud in a hundred years.

She'd been a queen's assassin, a painter's muse, a war medic. Worn crowns and shackles. Held blades and babies. Every era had a version of her, and none of them stayed.

How many lives does it take before one finally matters?" She thought.

Now, she haunted the world of the rich like a well-dressed phantom. A woman of mystery. A patron of causes but not truly seen. Not truly known. To humans, she was a symbol. To vampires, a nuisance. To herself?

Just tired. Not broken or weak. Just worn down by the weight of time.

And here she was again, pretending a wine glass full of blood made this all feel normal. She stared out over the city. The centuries kept piling up like ash. And still, she waited.

Then the call came just after midnight. Of course it did. Nothing good ever came after midnight. Not with Sebastian Voss.

CHAPTER 3

S he didn't answer the phone right away. Considered ignoring it, just staring at the screen while the seconds ticked by. But curiosity had always been her worst habit, right behind a soft spot for old monsters who thought they were still charming. The name on the screen didn't surprise her: Sebastian Voss.

Sebastian never called unless he wanted something, and when someone like him wanted something, she had to weigh whether it was worth the cost. She let it ring until the last possible second, then picked up.

"Amelia," he said smoothly, his warm and calculated voice like velvet draped over a loaded gun. "I wasn't sure you'd answer."

"Sebastian," she replied, leaning against the counter. "You say that like you haven't been waiting for me to pick up."

He laughed softly. "Still quick. I admire that about you."

She rolled her eyes. "I'm sure it's somewhere on your list, right between 'difficult' and 'dangerous.'"

"I wouldn't dare reduce you to something so predictable."

She could hear him smiling, the way he always did when he thought he had the upper hand. What most people didn't realize was that Sebastian didn't smile for amusement. He smiled when he was calculating, setting the pieces in motion.

He always did this, wrapped inquiries like blades under soft silk before you realized they'd drawn blood. She'd seen assassins with more restraint.

"What do you want, Sebastian?"

"A conversation. That's all."

"That's never just it with you."

He paused. A subtle beat.

"Darling, tell me, have you been hiding? Los Angeles has been dull without your usual presence. I was beginning to think you were avoiding me."

"Now, why would I do that? That would imply you're worth the effort. If you're calling just to flatter me, I'm hanging up. My ego doesn't need the boost, and I highly doubt you care about the state of LA's nightlife."

Then there was another pause. Not long, but just enough to register that he wasn't here to waste time.

"Things feel...tense lately. Don't they?" he asked. "Even you must sense it."

"Well, that's a vague and ominous statement. Are we skipping straight to the riddles tonight?"

"Only if you insist. But I'm not the only one who's noticed. The city hums differently now, it's a different kind of electricity."

"Maybe you're just bored."

"Perhaps. Or perhaps something is shifting. Slowly and imperceptibly...until it's not."

"Shifting? That's a delicate word."

"Delicate, yes. Also accurate." He let the silence stretch again. "You've felt it, haven't you?"

He let it hang there, waiting for her to fill in the silence.

"The only thing I've felt lately is tired of having this same cryptic dance with you."

He chuckled. "Amelia, come now. We've danced far less than we should've, but if it helps, I'll be direct."

"That would be new."

He let out a soft sigh. "You're still spending time in Skid Row?"

There it was. The shift. The first tug of the thread.

"Observant as ever. Yes, I am." She kept her tone neutral. "Why? Looking to expand your real estate portfolio again?"

"You misunderstand me," he said. "I just find it curious. It's a strange habit. For someone like you."

"Feeding the forgotten offends your sensibilities?"

"It surprises them," he said. "You walk among the discarded like one of them. They see a savior. I see a contradiction."

"Of course you do." She sipped from her glass. "You only value people if they have power to trade."

"I value purpose," he corrected. "Even yours, though you've been avoiding it for quite some time now."

She let the silence stretch now. He always dangled philosophy like bait, hoping she'd bite. "I'm not interested in purpose," she finally said. "I'm interested in peace. Which, if I recall correctly, is the one thing you're allergic to."

He chuckled again. She imagined him leaning back in some overpriced leather chair, swirling a glass of something that wasn't wine, watching the city through his mansion's sprawling windows like a child playing with ants.

"And yet, you're still in the city," he said softly. "Still in the thick of things. You haven't left, which makes me think...you're waiting for something."

Her grip on the glass tightened. "Don't project your obsessions onto me, Sebastian."

"No projection," he replied. "Just observation. You've always been drawn to moments of transition. You hate the status quo almost as much as I do."

"You hate not being in control. There's a difference."

He didn't deny it.

"Anyway, I'll be throwing a fundraiser in a couple of weeks. For a city initiative called 'Everyone Deserves a Home.' One of those large, expensive displays of generosity for the less fortunate. I thought this would interest you. You know, important people with loud intentions. Let's just say it's the kind of evening where people reveal themselves. You've always been good at spotting cracks in pretty façades."

"Sounds nauseating."

"I thought you might enjoy the guest list."

"You're inviting me to a party?" She raised an eyebrow. "You think I care about champagne and hollow speeches? Why don't you just donate to the local food bank?"

"It's not about champagne or speeches, Amelia. It's about...watching. Seeing who turns up. Who tries too hard not to."

"Is there someone I should be watching?"

"Always."

He didn't elaborate. Just left it there like a trail of breadcrumbs.

"You're still as vague as ever."

"And you're still tempted. I can hear it."

She didn't answer right away.

"Anyway, I thought you'd enjoy the view," he added.

"I usually prefer my views from rooftops or battlefields."

He chuckled again. "Then think of it as reconnaissance, then."

Sebastian never made idle suggestions. If he wanted her there, it meant something or someone was important enough to risk the bait.

"Is there someone you're worried about?" she asked.

"Isn't there always?" he admitted. "But I'd be careless if I didn't say your presence changes things. It always has."

"I'm flattered. Now I definitely won't come."

More laughter. "You will, because curiosity is your drug of choice. You love circling the flame, Amelia. You always have."

She leaned back against the marble island and stared out across the dark skyline. The city glittered with secrets. Some hers, some his, and he was right.

"I'll think about it," she said.

"I know you will."

"And if I don't show?"

"You will," he said smoothly. "Because you want to be there and because you know, sooner or later, I always find a way to pull you into the fray."

She let the silence stretch, pretending to weigh the decision. She wouldn't give him the satisfaction of an outright acceptance.

"I'll think about it," she said again.

"I'd expect nothing less," Sebastian murmured. "I'll send you the invitation, Amelia."

There was a pause. Then the line went dead.

She stood at the window a while longer, glass still half full in her hand, the city glowing beneath her like a dying ember trying to catch flame. Sebastian never said everything. He left holes on purpose. Enough rope to tie a noose or pull someone in.

Something was happening. Something big. And if Sebastian Voss wanted her at that party, it wasn't just for the ambiance.

The question wasn't whether she'd go.

It was whether she'd go as a guest...or as a threat.

CHAPTER 4

Two weeks later, Sebastian Voss stood atop his modern fortress in the Hollywood Hills, a sprawling mansion of glass, steel, and shadow. The architecture was sharp and calculated, jutting like bones from the hillside. Below him, the city of Los Angeles pulsed like an open vein.

Armed guards with automatic rifles and trained German shepherds moved along the perimeter, their silhouettes slicing through moonlight and motion sensors. Inside, priceless art adorned the walls, but only in shades of black, silver, and blood-wine red. His vampire staff and familiars moved like ghosts, humans bound by blood and greed, serving their vampire master.

A young vampire approached with a crystal glass of thick, velvet-red blood.

"The biometric upgrades are complete, Master Voss," the young vampire said, head bowed. "Voice ID is live on all entry points."

Sebastian took the glass and sipped, slow and precise. "Excellent. I prefer my peace to be absolute."

He turned back to the window, the glass wall swallowing the view. Behind him, the house thrummed like a machine, efficient and just dangerous enough to keep everyone sharp. Exactly the way he liked it.

They think this city belongs to its people. To politicians and protestors. It doesn't. It belongs to those who understand systems. Those who know when to pull...and when to cut.

He didn't want to own Los Angeles. Ownership was for men with inferiority complexes. He preferred influence, quiet, and permanent. Voss Enterprises was the perfect mask, a ghost ship drifting across biotech, real estate, defense, and pharmaceuticals. It was run by a boardroom of puppets whose strings he had long since coiled around his fingers.

They worship visibility, but true power doesn't shout; it rewrites.

And tomorrow night, the game advanced. The fundraiser would serve as more than a spectacle. It was a litmus test. A pressure point.

Control the board. Predict the sacrifice and never forget who you are in the endgame.

He allowed himself a small smile. Not smug or amused, just the quiet confidence of a man who already knew the outcome.

Walter Billings was the easiest piece to move, L.A.'s mayor, his familiar, his puppet. The man had once imagined himself a lion. These days, he barely manages to act like a house cat. Sebastian had plucked him from the gutters of obscurity and draped him in power, just enough to make him dance. A leash disguised as a legacy.

Ambition makes such a lovely collar.

He turned away from the window. Tomorrow night wasn't just a fundraiser. It was the beginning of a new plan. The vampire network in L.A. was splintering, and Sebastian had no interest in preserving the past. He had bigger plans that would change everything. Plans that could make him something no other vampire could ever imagine.

Why should gods dress like mortals? Why should predators apologize to prey?

But even gods need allies, and some storms are better harnessed than ignored. He picked up his phone and tapped a number without needing to glance. Billings would answer on the first ring. That's what good pets do.

The line clicked.

"Master," Billings answered, voice tight with anticipation and fear. "Everything is set for the fundraiser. Just as you asked."

"Good," Sebastian said, his voice a practiced drawl of command. "Walk me through it."

"The guest list is clean," Billings replied quickly. "Some local politicians, corporate reps, light media presence. Nothing too invasive. The donation announcement for Dr. Lee's foundation is set right before dinner, just like you requested."

Sebastian swirled the blood in his glass. "And Dr. Lee?"

"He thinks it's just a charitable grant," Walter said. "No clue about the...broader interest."

He wouldn't understand it even if he did. Sebastian suppressed a laugh.

"Keep it that way."

"Yes, Master."

Silence stretched, and Sebastian didn't fill it. Power didn't need to. It waited, like the loaded chamber of a gun.

"And what about the protestors? They're always an inconvenience."

"They'll be kept at a distance. LAPD's been told to contain without escalation. For optics, obviously..."

"Oh, Walter," Sebastian interrupted with a low chuckle. "I don't care how it looks. I just care that it doesn't interfere."

A beat of hesitation. Then, "Of course, my master. It won't."

"See that it doesn't. I'll be watching."

He ended the call.

Somewhere downtown, Walter Billings exhaled for the first time in minutes. "I've got to get out from under him," he muttered, wiping sweat off his brow.

Sebastian knew the Mayor would sleep poorly tonight, if at all. The leash may be invisible, but it left a mark. Immediately, Billings dialed a number and waited. The line picked up without a word.

"Is everything in place for the fundraiser?"

"Yes," the voice replied. "As long as you hold up your end."

"I told you, he'll be there," Billings said angrily, then ended the call.

Sebastian moved through the corridor with quiet purpose, the soft click of his polished shoes echoing faintly off marble floors. He entered the library, an immense chamber two stories high, wrapped in shadow and elegance. Dark oak shelves lined every wall, packed tight with leather-bound books, ancient grimoires, and first editions that spanned a thousand years of obsession. The scent of parchment, aged ink, and faint incense lingered in the air, like the breath of forgotten centuries.

He approached the far wall, his fingers drifting along the spines until they landed on a worn leather-bound copy of *The Wicked Bible*. A first pressing, one of only eleven to exist. He tugged it out halfway. A soft mechanical hiss answered him.

A narrow seam of light appeared, and a small panel slid open with a whisper of pressurized air. Embedded in the wall was a concealed biometric scanner, rimmed in steel and lit with a faint crimson glow.

Sebastian placed his palm over the panel.

A pulse of light traced the shape of his hand. Then came the quiet chime of access granted. With a muted rumble, a section of the bookcase slid inward, revealing a narrow passage descending into darkness.

Not even the library was just a library.

He descended into the bowels of his estate, a corridor of stone and shadow hidden beneath the glamour of his glass-and-steel fortress. The temperature dropped with every step, but it wasn't the cold that made this place feel inhuman. It was the silence between screams.

The dungeon lights buzzed overhead in a sickly fluorescent hue. The scent was a cocktail of antiseptic, dried blood, and burning flesh, an odor that clung to the walls like a memory no one asked for.

Inside a reinforced cell, a vampire prisoner was a mess of torn skin, cracked bone, and blood-slick restraints. His face looked like it had been run through a concrete mixer, swollen shut in places, slack-jawed and broken in others. But the damage was temporary. Already, deep red muscle was stitching itself back together. His fractured arm had started to realign with a wet pop.

Sebastian's human familiar, a thick-necked man named Garrison, leaned on a steel baton glistening with fresh gore. His face glistened with sweat, his knuckles split from repetition.

"He keeps healing," Garrison muttered. "I've shattered the same rib four times."

Sebastian gave a faint nod. "That's the problem with resilience. It breeds confidence."

The vampire's good eye opened at the sound of Sebastian's voice. He slurred through mangled lips, "You can't stop us. You're rotting from the inside."

Sebastian crouched, calm and curious, as if observing an insect trying to grow wings. "So poetic. Do all your friends talk like that before they die, or are you trying to impress me?"

The prisoner sneered, coughing up black blood. "I'd rather burn than give you a name."

"Oh, don't tease me," Sebastian said, eyes glittering. "You might just get both."

He stood, walking slowly around the prisoner. "The problem with old methods is predictability. Beat a vampire hard enough, and sure, you'll get a scream. But we heal. We adapt. Pain's just a phase for us."

He stopped beside a metal cabinet bolted into the wall. With a flick of his hand, Garrison stepped up and opened it. Inside sat a compact case, gleaming black with hazard markings.

"That's where innovation comes in."

Sebastian put on gloves and opened the case, revealing a sleek, silver-plated rod. At the push of a button, it activated with a low hum, casting a steady ultraviolet glow.

The vampire tensed.

Sebastian twirled the device casually between his fingers. "This little marvel burns at 400 nanometers. Focused, precise, and most importantly, permanent. No regenerative cheat codes this time."

He held it to the prisoner's cheek. The hiss of burning flesh was instant. The vampire convulsed, snarling as a strip of his face blackened and peeled like scorched paper.

"Now," Sebastian said gently, "let's try again. Which faction sent you?"

The vampire heaved against his restraints, panic overtaking pain.

"I don't know their name. Just a job. No names. Orders through drops. Always encrypted."

Sebastian arched a brow. "And yet, here you are. Disposable."

"They said you'd fall. That your time was over. They want open rules. No councils. No hiding."

"Of course they do." Sebastian stepped back, deactivating the UV rod. "Children always mistake anarchy for freedom."

He leaned close, "One last time. Who are 'they'?"

A pause. "They are inside your circle."

That stopped him. Sebastian's expression darkened just slightly.

He gave a thin smile. "Thank you."

He handed the UV weapon to Garrison. "Make it slow. Then ash him."

Sebastian turned and walked toward the stairs. As the screaming began, the steel door groaned and shut behind him.

Inside my circle. A traitor among the loyal. Good. Let them play their hand. I've never lost a game I finished.

He didn't flinch. If anything, his mind had already moved on to Amelia Devereux.

She was older than most. More powerful than she admitted, even to herself. Independent, cautious, and infuriatingly ethical. Sebastian had studied her for decades.

She's chaos wrapped in silk. A storm that doesn't know it's a hurricane. But even chaos has a frequency.

He didn't want to dominate her. That would be a fool's

errand. No, he wanted to align her. All it would take was the right temptation.

Purpose is the leash that doesn't feel like one.

She'd be at the fundraiser. She'd said she wasn't sure, but curiosity was her fatal flaw.

She thinks she's circling the flame. She doesn't realize she's the match.

Sebastian smiled. He finished the last of the blood, savoring the quiet. Below him, Los Angeles buzzed with its usual cocktail of delusion and decay. It thought itself untouchable.

It's almost cute how hard they fight with one another when the real game is just beyond their comprehension.

Tomorrow night, Sebastian would move another piece on the game board.

CHAPTER 5

Meanwhile, across town in Santa Monica, the air inside the surveillance van was thick with tension, the kind that always came before a hunt. The glow from the monitors painted the faces of Reece Drake's team in shades of blue and green. Their eyes locked on the live drone feed of the abandoned building. It was an old warehouse, nestled between rows of dilapidated structures that served as the perfect hiding place for the creatures they hunted.

Reece stood at 6'3", his presence commanding without a word. Years in special forces had carved his body into lean, precise muscle built for efficiency, not show. Faded scars crossed his torso and arms, each one a quiet testament to survival. They didn't mar him; they defined him. He was sharp, unflinching, and always calculating.

Vampires always thought places like this would hide them. Urban decay, forgotten neighborhoods with no security patrols, but the silence always gave them away.

"Target confirmation?" Reece asked, his voice even, controlled.

"Sonar signatures inside match vampire activity," said Lisa "Hot Shot" Gonzales, their sniper and recon specialist. She was small in stature but deadly accurate with any weapon and even better with tech. She watched the live feed from a rooftop a block away, her rifle already assembled. "Movement patterns indicate at least six."

"That sounds like a standard nest," Cole Burns, the team's second in command, muttered. At 5'11", his agility matched his sharp features, which were set in a scowl as he checked the magazine of his modified rifle. "Let's clear them out." Cole, ever the soldier, had been with Reece since the beginning.

Reece exhaled slowly, surveying his team. They were the best of the best, ex-military, elite operatives who had seen war and bloodshed before taking on an enemy most people didn't even know existed. Then there was Marcus Johnson, their heavy hitter, standing at 6'5", who lived for the thrill of a fight and often did.

Just behind them, Skylar "The Kid" Bowers. He had traded in a promising special forces career for a fight that felt like it actually meant something. Hunting vampires, he once said, was the first time he'd felt like he was on the right side of a war. He checked his sidearm with a speed that came from routine, not nerves. At twenty-six, he was nearly a decade younger than the rest of them, still wiry in build but sharp as hell and quick with both a blade and a comeback.

"We move in, silent," Reece instructed, clicking the safety off his weapon. "Keep it clean. Keep it fast."

The van doors slid open, and the team dispersed into the night. Reece led the way, his movements fluid and practiced.

Skylar was the first to stack up behind Reece, itching to be point. He always was. Not out of recklessness, but because he needed the team to know he belonged, especially Reece. They moved through the darkened alleyways, their bodies hidden beneath the weight of tactical gear and the confidence of experience. They had been tracking this nest for weeks, waiting for the right moment to strike. Now, with the intel confirmed, there was no hesitation.

They had all bled. All buried people who shouldn't be dead.

"Remember," Reece's voice was calm but firm over the team's comms, "standard sweep. Engage and eliminate only if necessary. We take no risks."

Cole gave a dry chuckle. "Boss, these bloodsuckers are always a risk."

Marcus, the most aggressive of the squad, tightened his grip on his rifle. "Agreed. No mercy."

From her overwatch position, Hot Shot checked in. "Perimeter is clear. No signs of movement outside."

Reece signaled forward, leading the team into the abandoned warehouse where the nest was hiding. They moved in calculated silence, their boots barely making a sound against the concrete. It was a well-rehearsed maneuver, refined through fire and repetition.

They worked in perfect sync, ghosting through the shadows until they reached the warehouse's side entrance. The door was rusted, but it wasn't locked. That meant one thing: the vampires inside felt safe.

Big mistake.

Skylar took point, easing the door open just enough for Reece to peek inside. The warehouse smelled of old blood and rot, an unmistakable stench that confirmed their intel. The vampires were careless, lounging in makeshift nests of broken furniture and discarded blankets, their laughter low and guttural. They didn't expect company.

Reece lifted his fingers, signaling the attack.

The breach was swift. Silver bullets, UV grenades, and coordinated strikes eliminated most of the targets within minutes. One vampire tried to escape, but Skylar was faster, intercepting and driving a silver dagger into its chest. It let out a strangled gasp before collapsing into ash.

"Don't worry, old man," Skylar said over the comms. "I'll save some action for you."

"Talk to me after your knees start popping, Kid," Cole muttered.

They moved like a well-oiled machine into the next portion of the warehouse. Cole and Marcus took the left flank while Reece and Skylar swept right. Suppressed gunfire whooshed through the air. Another vampire lunged toward Marcus, but he caught the creature mid-air, slamming it to the ground before driving a silver stake into its chest.

Reece turned, firing two rounds into another vampire's head and one through the heart. It dropped instantly.

The team pressed forward through the abandoned space, their boots crunching softly against shattered glass and debris. The stale air was thick with the scent of decay and old blood, but beneath it, Reece caught something fresher. The unmistakable iron tang of spilled human blood.

"Stay sharp. One left, and he's fresh off a feed," Reece murmured into the comms.

Cole swept his rifle's muzzle across the vast, dark space. "Copy that. Expecting enhanced speed and strength."

They advanced cautiously. Reece signaled Hot Shot to take position on the catwalk above. She moved like a ghost, her rifle settling against her shoulder.

"I think I got something...moving fast," she said over comms.

Then, a sudden blur of motion. The last vampire exploded from the shadows, a streak of unnatural speed. One moment, he was crouched over a slumped human body, blood still dripping from his lips; the next, he was gone.

Skylar moved first, fast, clean, and low to the ground with his blade drawn. He landed the first cut before the creature even registered the ambush. Still, the vampire batted him away, sending him tumbling across the floor.

"Still good!" he called, voice strained.

Then the vampire was on Marcus. Fangs bared, strength amplified by the feed. Marcus was hurled backward, crashing against a rusted metal beam. The impact reverberated through the warehouse.

"Shit, he's fast!" Marcus growled, rolling onto his feet.

Cole fired first. The bullets hit, but the vampire barely flinched. He twisted, evading the worst of the damage, and was already on Cole before anyone could react.

Reece surged forward, drawing his combat knife. With a swift motion, he slashed, the silver-laced blade cutting through flesh.

The vampire hissed and recoiled. Marcus recovered and unloaded another round into its stomach.

Still, the creature wouldn't go down. It weaved through their attacks, forcing them onto the defensive.

"Hot Shot, now!" Reece barked.

A sharp crack echoed from above. The sniper round punched clean through the vampire's knee. He staggered.

Reece lunged, driving his blade into the vampire's chest and twisting hard into its heart. The creature let out a strangled gasp, eyes flashing with rage before dulling. It slumped to the ground, twitching, then disappeared into ash.

The warehouse fell silent except for their heavy breathing.

Marcus wiped blood from his brow. "Damn. That one put up a fight."

"I could've taken him," Skylar said sarcastically.

Marcus rolled his eyes. "Sure, Kid."

Reece yanked his blade free and wiped it clean. "That's what happens when they feed on fresh blood. We got lucky. Next time, we assume the worst."

"Clear up top. No more movement," Hot Shot reported.

The team regrouped. Reece crouched beside a pile of vampire ash and brushed something metallic from the collar of a burned shirt. A chain with a crest.

He recognized it. His blood ran cold.

"What is it?" Cole asked, stepping up beside him.

Reece hesitated, then shook his head. "Nothing. Just some junk."

Cole didn't push. He trusted Reece, but even trust had limits, and lately, Reece had been keeping too many secrets.

"We're done here," Reece said, standing. "Burn the clothes. Let's go."

As they exited the warehouse, flames licking at the sky behind them, Reece clenched his jaw. He knew that crest. He'd seen it before on the dagger buried in his wife's chest the night she and their daughter were slaughtered.

That had been years ago. And if this vampire had worn the same emblem... he didn't believe in coincidences.

He would find the truth. No matter the cost.

The memory hit him like a sledgehammer, as it often did after a hunt. He imagined the screams of his wife and daughter, still echoing in his mind.

Years ago, Reece had been one of the military's finest, top of his class in special forces, an expert in tactics, hand-to-hand combat, and tracking. But none of it mattered when he wasn't there to protect his family.

He had been overseas on a mission when it happened. A home invasion, the police had called it. His wife, drained of blood. His daughter, lifeless and empty as well. A ceremonial dagger with an unfamiliar crest was left behind.

When Reece returned and saw the scene for himself, something in him snapped.

That's when he met Jonathan Smith, head of a special FBI task force handling paranormal crimes. A quiet government intervention. An offer. A choice.

Reece left the military. Formed his own team. Handpicked those who had seen the impossible and refused to ignore it.

"No more," he had sworn. "Not while I'm alive."

From that moment on, his life had one mission: vampire extermination.

Reece exhaled sharply, pushing the memory aside.

His phone buzzed. No Caller ID.

He answered. "Go ahead."

Agent Smith's gruff voice came through. "Reece, I need your team at a fundraiser Saturday night. Beverly Hills Hotel. I'll get you in as staff."

Reece frowned. "What's going on?"

"Intel says a large vampire attack. Possible assassination attempt on the Mayor. I'd rather not take chances."

"Any other details?"

"The Mayor's the one raising red flags," Smith said. "Find out what he knows and who wants him dead."

Reece's grip tightened. Reece leaned back against the wall.

How was the Mayor connected? If vampires were targeting him, there was more going on.

"Okay," he said. "We'll be there."

He ended the call, his mind already working.

Skylar stepped beside him. "If they're planning something big, I want to be first through the door."

"You'll be in the fight," Reece said. "But we're going in undercover."

CHAPTER 6

Inside a decrepit lab in Burbank, the hum of outdated equipment filled the stale air. Overhead, flickering fluorescent lights buzzed, casting a cold, bluish glow across cluttered workbenches. The scent of chemicals and burnt-out circuits lingered, a testament to the countless hours spent within these walls.

Dr. Andrew Lee sat alone at the main workstation, his back hunched in concentration. His fingers absently tapped against a vial he had just pulled from the centrifuge, a pale amber serum that shimmered under the artificial light. Holding it up to eye level, he scrutinized the liquid for any breakdowns in its composition.

His mind drifted.

He'd been fourteen when he watched his mother wither away, her body eaten alive by cancer. He remembered how frail she had become, her voice barely above a whisper as she tried to comfort him, when it should have been the other way around. There had been no miracle, no last-minute experimental drug to save her. Just death. And then, the cold, impersonal foster system had swallowed him whole. Orphaned, alone, passed from one facility to another.

His grip tightened around the vial.

"Mom, I'm so close," he whispered under his breath. "If only you could see what I'm trying to do... what I *could* do once this is complete."

That promise, the one he had made to himself as he stood at her bedside feeling helpless, was the only thing that had kept him going. He would make sure no one else had to suffer the way she had. That no child would have to watch their parent slip away while doctors stood by, offering nothing but apologies and false hope.

He had dedicated his life to that mission.

Andrew had once been at the pinnacle of his field, a rising star in cancer genetics. The research center he had worked for had been well-funded, backed by government grants and private investors. But limitations, ethical red tape, and bureaucratic delays had shackled his work. They had wanted slow progress, incremental advancements that fit neatly within the parameters of publishable results. He just wanted a cure. So he walked away from it all.

Now, his research was entirely his own. No oversight or rules. Only the work. He wasn't just trying to eradicate cancer cells; he was trying to reverse them, to reprogram them back into normal, healthy cells. If he could succeed, he could change everything. He was skipping meals, forgetting to sleep for days just for one more serum, just one more simulation, but success still eluded him.

A soft beep from his monitor jolted him back to the present. His gaze flickered to the screen; it was another failed result. The serum wasn't stabilizing. The cells were rejecting the treatment, mutating instead of healing. His shoulders slumped.

Across his desk, a stack of unopened mail loomed. He already knew what was inside: late notices, overdue bills, more reminders that he was running out of time. The lab's lease, the equipment costs, the utilities, everything was bleeding him dry.

Then the melodic ring of his phone cut through the silence. Andrew glanced at the screen: No Caller ID.

Bill collectors usually had their names displayed, or at least a recognizable number. This was different. He hesitated for only a second before answering.

"Dr. Lee speaking."

Dr. Lee, just the man I was hoping to reach." The voice was smooth and practiced. "You haven't forgotten about tonight's fundraiser, I hope?"

Andrew pinched the bridge of his nose. He had, in fact, nearly forgotten.

"I've been busy," he admitted. "I was just…"

"Yes, yes, your research. Important work, no doubt." Billings cut him off, his tone dripping with forced patience. "But tonight isn't just about you, Doctor. It's about your charity. The people who depend on you. The donors who make your work possible."

Andrew sighed, already feeling the weight of obligation settle onto his shoulders.

Billings took the pause as an opening to press further. "I've arranged for you to meet some very influential people tonight. They're eager to contribute, you know, philanthropists with deep pockets who just love a good cause." He chuckled. "And, of course, the cameras will be there. These sorts of things look excellent for PR, and well, you know how these people are. They love a good photo op."

Andrew barely heard him. His eyes had drifted back to his workstation, fingers itching to adjust his latest calculations and run another test. The work always felt more pressing, more important than these tedious social obligations.

"Doctor?" Billings' voice sharpened. "Tell me you'll be there."

Andrew exhaled slowly. There was no avoiding it. The charity and the homeless shelters he had founded depended on donations to stay operational, and as much as he despised playing the game, he needed these people.

"I'll be there," he finally said.

"Good man," Billings replied, the charm sliding back into place. "Dress to impress, Doctor. I'll see you soon."

The line went dead before Andrew could respond.

He tossed the phone onto the desk and ran a hand through his already-messy hair. This was the one extracurricular activity he allowed himself, the only thing that pulled him away from his research because he knew what it was like to have nothing.

When he had aged out of the orphanage system, he had ended up on the streets. No safety net, no family to turn to. Just the raw, brutal truth of survival. He had clawed his way out of that life, had fought for every inch of success he had achieved. And now, he gave back whenever he could, ensuring others didn't have to suffer the same fate. His true nature was to help, help the helpless.

Glancing at the clock, he realized it was already past 6 PM. With a reluctant sigh, he pushed away from his desk. His eyes lingered on the vials and screens, the unfinished calculations still blinking on screen, like they knew he'd failed, but tonight, failure had to wait.

Grabbing a suit jacket from the back of his chair, he gave it a quick shake in a futile attempt to smooth out the wrinkles. It would have to do. It was one of the few suits he owned that he purchased from a 75% off Macy's sale. It wasn't much to look at, but it would do. He slipped into the jacket, grabbed his keys, and headed for the door.

The fundraiser awaited, and with it, the next step in a game he didn't even realize he was playing. He didn't know who would be watching tonight, only that it might cost more than time.

CHAPTER 7

Amelia stood by the floor-to-ceiling window of her penthouse, the city sprawling beneath her like a kingdom of broken glass and golden light. It had been a couple of weeks since Sebastian called to invite her to the fundraiser. The sun had just slipped behind the skyline, racing long shadows across her marble floors. In her hand, the invitation felt heavier than paper should.

What are you up to, Sebastian? she wondered, her gaze distant. *You never invite anyone without motive... especially not me.*

The fundraiser was an elaborate affair hosted under the guise of charity, a benefit for the city's growing homeless crisis. A cause that, unlike most among the elite, actually stirred something in her. She'd spent enough nights in alleyways and forgotten corners of cities across the world to know what survival without shelter felt like, even if it had been centuries ago.

They're the canaries in the coal mine, she thought. *When the vulnerable are abandoned, rot spreads through everything. The humans just haven't realized it yet. But he has. That's why he's interested, I'm sure of it.*

She sighed, the weight of her years pressing briefly against her spine. *And maybe...maybe there's something in me that still wants to care.*

She turned from the window and walked into her bedroom,

dimly lit by warm amber sconces. A row of sleek black garment bags hung neatly along one wall like soldiers waiting for command. She unzipped one and pulled out a long black Tom Ford gown, backless, with high slits along both sides that would reveal her toned legs, honed through decades of training and combat. It clung to her like black ink.

Her fingers brushed over her earrings, diamond-studded and subtle. Then she selected a small Alexander McQueen clutch. The brass knuckles affixed to its handle brought a smirk to her lips.

Elegant... but still a weapon. Just like me.

She stepped into sharp Christian Louboutin stilettos, the crimson soles catching the light like blood beneath her feet. Her reflection in the mirror was stunningly sleek and deadly. But behind the eyes was a weariness that never quite faded.

Well, you never know what the night will bring, she thought.

Before leaving, she made a detour to the training room. Her footsteps echoed softly against the mat-lined floors and mirrored walls. With practiced motion, she opened the hidden weapons cache, selecting two custom daggers. They were balanced, razor-sharp, etched with sigils from another lifetime. She holstered them high on each thigh, hidden beneath the fabric but always within reach.

Just in case...It's always "just in case," isn't it? She thought, staring at her reflection.

The world had a way of turning glamorous evenings into battlegrounds. She'd learned long ago that danger didn't RSVP.

In the garage, her red 1956 Mercedes 300SL Gullwing waited, polished beneath the lights. A relic of another era, just like her.

The straight-six engine roared to life. As she pulled out into the dusky glow of downtown, the wind teased through her hair, and the horizon opened up in front of her. The sky melted into twilight, an edge between day and night where monsters and martyrs crossed paths.

Let the games begin, she thought, pressing the gas.

· · ·

The evening air in Beverly Hills carried a warmth that hinted at the lingering autumn heat. Golden light bounced off polished cars easing up to the grand entrance of the Beverly Hills Hotel.

A reporter stood poised before a camera crew, microphone in hand. "We're here at the Beverly Hills Hotel for the city's highly anticipated fundraiser for the 'Everyone Deserves a Home' charity. Tonight, some of the most influential figures in Los Angeles are gathering in an effort to combat homelessness, an issue that has reached crisis levels in our city. We're expecting to see key political figures, philanthropists, and celebrities all in attendance. But not everyone is thrilled about this evening's event. Just beyond the barricades, protestors have gathered, demanding real solutions rather than lavish parties."

The chants of the protestors grew louder, their voices clashing against the hum of the arriving guests. Signs bobbed above the crowd: "Housing, Not Parties" and "Real Change, Not Empty Promises." Police officers held the lines firm, their radios crackling. Interspersed through the crowd, shadowy figures watched each vehicle pull into the hotel.

A black Rolls-Royce Phantom glided to a stop. Before the valet could react, the driver stepped out and opened the rear passenger door. Sebastian Voss emerged.

His tailored Italian suit hugged his tall, lean frame. His dark brown hair was slicked back, accentuating the sharp line of his jaw and the striking clarity of his eyes. Eyes that didn't just look, they dissected. Conversations faltered. People adjusted their postures without realizing why.

To Sebastian, this wasn't just a fundraiser. *So many pawns in one room,* he mused. *Money, politics, and public sympathy all dancing in one gilded ballroom. And they still think they're the ones in control.*

Trailing him, a statuesque blonde in a midnight blue gown clutched his arm. She laughed too loudly at something he hadn't said. Sebastian offered a bland smile.

She'll be useful for the evening. Jealousy is a crude but effective tool.

Then, a red vintage sports car purred up to the curb. A young valet nearly stumbled getting to the door.

The gullwing door rose like a bird spreading its wings. A long, sculpted leg extended, followed by the effortless grace of Amelia Devereux.

Her black silk gown clung to her lithe frame, a glimmer of a holstered blade visible in the slit, just enough to hint at danger. At six feet two in heels, she towered over many of the men present. None could look away. Her raven black hair cascaded down her back, catching the breeze.

To Amelia, the hotel felt like a stage. A mask. A memory.

This city still stinks of false promises, she thought. *So many pretending to care, pretending they can fix a system designed to break people. Still, if even one life changes tonight... maybe it's worth it.*

Her eyes flicked to the protestors beyond the barricades.

At least they're honest. Anger is real. Louder than champagne toasts and photo ops.

As she passed under the hotel's striped entrance, Sebastian turned slightly, offering a smirk. "Nice to see you, my dear," he murmured.

Still radiant. Still untouchable, he thought. *But you came. Curiosity means you're not done with us.*

Amelia barely glanced at him. "Is it?" she said, smooth and teasing, but not an invitation.

Sebastian chuckled to himself. "It is," he murmured.

The blonde on Sebastian's arm stiffened, her grip tightening. Amelia didn't notice, or maybe she didn't care.

Inside, Amelia felt the prickle of Sebastian's attention.

He wants something. He always does. But I'm not here for him. I'm here for the ones without a voice. And if he's manipulating this...I'll find out.

Turning back to his date. Sebastian cupped her chin gently.

"You," he said, "are the most beautiful woman here."

Her earlier jealousy melted. She beamed. Sebastian smiled, satisfied, and followed Amelia inside.

But his mind had already returned to the game.

The doctor will be here. All eyes are watching. Amelia complicates things, but she also reveals them. Let's see what truths shake loose tonight.

Outside, the protests surged.

"Your donations won't house us!" a woman yelled. "We need real solutions, not another night of champagne and cameras!"

Then the crowd shifted.

A battered sedan screeched to a stop.

Dr. Andrew Lee stepped out, disheveled and breathless. His hair was unkempt, and his glasses askew. His shoes didn't match his belt. The suit hung awkwardly on him, but his focus was clear.

Tonight could change everything. Raise enough money, and maybe we can keep everyone housed. Maybe we can get more off the streets. Just stay focused.

The grand doors closed behind him, muffling the noise.

A police officer barked, "Back behind the barricades! I won't tell you again!"

The protestors shouted louder.

Then, a towering figure stepped through like a battering ram in a tailored coat. Protestors parted instinctively. Behind him, Kellin moved with the calm assurance of someone who expected the world to move around him.

His eyes pulsed red beneath his hood.

Tonight won't just shift the order, he thought. *It will leave blood in its wake.*

CHAPTER 8

The Beverly Hills Crystal Ballroom shimmered under the warm glow of ornate chandeliers. The air carried the scent of fresh floral arrangements, a subtle mixture of roses, lilies, and expensive cologne. Gold-accented tables were dressed with crisp white linens, fine china, and crystal glasses reflecting the candlelight. Guests milled about, exchanging pleasantries, laughing lightly over delicate hors d'oeuvres, while waiters weaved through the crowd with trays of champagne flutes.

After meeting with the Mayor, Reece's team was scattered throughout the ballroom, disguised as staff. He stood behind the bar, expertly mixing drinks while keeping his sharp eyes on the guests. Marcus moved smoothly through the crowd, carrying a tray of appetizers, blending in as a waiter. Cole, equally disguised in a server's uniform, emerged from the kitchen carrying another tray, though his scowl suggested he would rather be anywhere else. The Kid was busy sweeping up in hotel overalls.

"This is a damn waste of time," Cole muttered under his breath, adjusting the tray in his hands. "A PR stunt. We should be out hunting real vampires, not babysitting socialites."

"At least you guys are in tuxedos. I'm cleaning up trash in the corner. Pretty sure nobody puts Baby in a corner," Skylar muttered through the comms.

Reece, stirring a martini, responded through their concealed comms. "Stay sharp. We don't have solid intel, but something's off about tonight. Just do your job and Kid, no more pop culture references for the rest of the night."

"Copy that."

Upstairs, their sniper, Hot Shot, was stationed in a private suite directly across from the ballroom's towering windows. One eye remained pressed to her rifle scope while the other flicked between multiple camera feeds from hidden surveillance equipment placed strategically around the room. Her voice crackled through their earpieces, calm and professional. "I got eyes on the floor. No red flags yet. Heads up, doors are about to close."

Across the room, Sebastian had separated from his date, speaking quietly with Mayor Billings near a gilded pillar in the corner. Billings, the outward picture of confidence in public, was anything but when in the presence of Sebastian. While his tuxedo fit him perfectly and his smile never faltered, his hands trembled ever so slightly as he straightened his cufflinks. He listened attentively, nodding as Sebastian outlined the evening's timeline.

"You'll introduce Andrew after the first toast about what has been raised for the charity thus far," Sebastian instructed smoothly. "He's to be presented as the face of the homeless initiative. Then you'll announce that my company will donate a one-million-dollar check to ensure his work continues and to make sure we make an impact to his cause."

Billings swallowed. "Yes, of course. Everything's set." He hesitated before adding, "although he still hasn't arrived."

Sebastian's expression darkened, his piercing gaze making the mayor's stomach churn. "That's unfortunate. I wanted time with him before the announcement." He took a measured sip from his glass, then let the weight of silence settle between them. "You've disappointed me before, Walter. I trust you won't do so again."

A bead of sweat slid down Billings' temple. He forced himself to nod, his throat tight. *I need to get out from under him...* the thought flickered across his mind, though he dared not let it show on his face. *Let's see if he'll make it through the night,* finishing his thought.

Hot Shot's voice came through their earpieces again. "Ballroom doors are closing."

Reece exhaled slowly, shifting behind the bar. "Copy that. Everyone, focus up."

At one of the VIP tables near the front, Amelia sat, gracefully engaged in light conversation with the city's elite. She was a fresh face in the charity circuit, an enigmatic presence wrapped in wealth and mystery.

Her laugh was effortless, just the right volume to charm but not command. Yet even as she entertained the people around her, her mind wandered. Another gala. Another night of pleasantries, empty toasts, and under-the-table deals disguised as philanthropy. She had perfected the role of the beautiful distraction, and yet it was a performance that had long since dulled her. Still, this place had its uses. Sometimes, amid the glitz and noise, truth slipped free from gilded tongues or monsters revealed themselves in tailored tuxedos.

Sebastian soon returned to his seat, his human date draping herself over his arm, though she paled in comparison to Amelia's effortless allure. Amelia barely acknowledged his presence, offering a fleeting smirk before turning back to the conversation at hand.

Still circling the same orbits, are we, Sebastian? she mused, sensing the undercurrent of tension between him and the mayor from across the room. Even without supernatural senses, she could smell the predator in his poise.

Then, the ballroom doors suddenly swung open, and Dr. Andrew Lee stumbled in, slightly breathless, scanning the tables for his name card. His sandy brown hair was disheveled, his glasses askew, and his suit, while meant to be formal, was wrinkled from his rushed dressing. He drifted from table to table, his awkwardness growing with each missed name card.

"Late arrival. We got a nerd with a briefcase," the Kid sparked on the comms from the side of the room before the team turned around.

"Checking..." Hot Shot spoke up, "Dossier says he's Dr. Andrew Lee, the head of the charity."

Amelia's gaze drifted to him, expecting just another late arrival, a social climber or misguided donor, but something about him tugged at her. He looked...real. And real out of place.

Not polished like the others. No sheen or no practiced charm. He was just raw nerves and a tattered tie. There was a spark of something sincere in the clumsy urgency of his movements, the way he clutched his briefcase like it held something important or something *personal*.

And then there was the smell. Not his cologne, which was faint and utilitarian at best, but the unmistakable scent of exhaustion. Of long nights, of sterile clinics and city streets. Of work. *Real* work. He was helping the homeless, wasn't he? She had heard his name earlier in the evening, tossed casually around champagne flutes, but she hadn't made the connection until now. A flicker of curiosity bloomed low in her chest.

Okay, who is this guy? What are you doing here? She thought, her eyes narrowing slightly. *And why do you feel...familiar?*

It wasn't recognition. She had never seen him before in her long life. But something about his presence stirred an old, restless place in her. The part of her that still remembered causes, and hope, and the strange ache of connection.

She tilted her head subtly, studying him in profile. There was an unguarded awkwardness to him that struck her as rare in this room full of polished lies.

He's either lost...or he doesn't care if he fits in. Maybe both.

Then, a hand waved him over. Sebastian, a devilish smile curving his lips, beckoned him. "Dr. Lee, I believe you're sitting next to me."

Andrew hurried over, adjusting his glasses. "Thank you, I was pretty lost there. I didn't get your name?" He dropped into the chair, setting his briefcase beside him.

Sebastian chuckled, studying him. "My name is Sebastian Voss. I've been looking forward to meeting you."

Amelia caught the faint edge of calculation behind Sebastian's smile and filed it away.

Before he could continue, a chime echoed through the room,

and the evening's host took the microphone. "Ladies and gentlemen, please take your seats. The event is about to begin."

Amelia didn't move immediately. Her eyes lingered on Andrew a moment longer.

There's something about you, she thought, lips curving ever so slightly. *And I intend to find out what it is.*

CHAPTER 9

The soft clink of glasses and hushed murmurs faded as the fundraiser's host, a striking woman in an emerald-green gown, glided onto the stage. Her voice rose above the crowd with practiced poise, warm and commanding.

"Good evening, everyone. I want to thank you all for attending tonight's benefit for the 'Everyone Deserves a Home' Initiative. Your presence here tonight is a testament to the compassion and unity of our city."

A polite round of applause followed, accompanied by the faint rustle of gowns and suits shifting in their chairs. Amelia barely moved. She sat at her VIP table, chin resting lightly on her hand, legs crossed beneath her gown, gaze angled just past the stage. Her mind wasn't on the host's carefully curated speech; it rarely was during these things. She had heard versions of this speech a hundred times in a hundred cities. Polished, hopeful, and overly sanitized. The same vague language, community, responsibility, dignity, and always a call for change, and yet tonight, she couldn't quite zone it out.

Because of him. Dr. Andrew Lee.

She flicked her eyes across the table again. He was seated beside Sebastian, still a touch disheveled, still mildly out of sync with the cadence of the room. And yet he didn't seem to care. That intrigued her.

She was trying to figure out why. Was it the way he didn't preen under the chandeliers like the others? Or maybe it was the fact that Sebastian had gone out of his way to introduce himself. That never happened without an agenda because Sebastian had many agendas.

What do you want from him, Sebastian? she thought, her fingers subtly drumming against the stem of her wine glass.

The host's voice continued. "As many of you know, Los Angeles has seen a record rise in homelessness over the past five years. We face a crisis that doesn't just belong to politicians or nonprofits, but to every one of us who calls this city home."

Amelia shifted in her chair. *There it is. The guilt pitch.* She smiled faintly to herself, not unkindly, but more out of familiarity. She'd watched cities rise and fall, promises made and broken. And yet here she was, still attending the parties.

"Now, please welcome a man who has served this city tirelessly. A native son of Los Angeles, and our partner in this vital cause, Mayor Walter Billings."

Applause swelled again as the mayor stepped onto the stage from behind velvet curtains. He adjusted his tie as he took the microphone, smiling like he hadn't just been scolded by a thousand-year-old vampire minutes earlier.

"Thank you, thank you," he said, waving modestly. "You know, I grew up just a few blocks from MacArthur Park. It didn't look then like it does now. I remember walking past folks sleeping in stairwells, pushing carts, waiting in line for meals. I thought, even as a kid, *how did we let this happen?*"

Amelia sipped from her glass. Her gaze wandered. She didn't doubt his sincerity, not entirely, but the man standing on stage now was deeply compromised. She had seen Sebastian whisper to him. She had seen the tremble in his hands.

"We've spent decades avoiding this problem, passing the buck," Billings continued. "But tonight, I'd like to introduce someone who didn't just talk about change, he acted."

That drew Amelia's attention.

"Dr. Andrew Lee," the mayor announced, motioning toward

the table, "has taken time from his groundbreaking cancer research to build a foundation that gets people off the street and into shelter, job training, and health programs. And let me tell you it's working. Tonight, thanks to your generosity, we've raised nearly $133,000 for his foundation." The spotlight hit different donors in the room as the Mayor read their names off.

The applause came again, louder this time.

Amelia's gaze settled fully on Andrew now. He looked...mildly uncomfortable with the praise. Embarrassed, even. He ran a hand through his hair and gave an awkward smile to someone across the table. There was no smugness. No expectation of applause. He was just happy the money would continue to help others. She tilted her head slightly. *Interesting.*

Everyone else in this room puffed up like peacocks the moment a spotlight landed on them. Andrew shrank a little. And for the first time in a long while, something stirred inside her, something quiet, almost forgotten. Curiosity...and the beginning edge of admiration.

You don't know who he is, she reminded herself. *And yet...*

"Please join me in welcoming the man of the hour to the stage, Dr. Andrew Lee," the mayor said, gesturing broadly.

Andrew stood, gave a bashful nod, and made his way up the steps. The applause followed him, but he didn't bask in it. His stride was clipped, adjusting his jacket, his eyes scanning the audience only once before settling awkwardly to the floor beside the mayor.

Billings clapped him on the back. "Ladies and gentlemen," he continued, "great work like this doesn't happen without support. And thanks to the generosity of one of tonight's biggest sponsors, Voss Enterprises is pledging an additional one-million-dollar donation to Dr. Lee's foundation."

A hush swept the room for half a second, then the applause swelled to its highest yet.

Amelia didn't clap. Her eyes snapped to Sebastian.

He sat there, hands folded lightly in his lap, lips curled into a small, pleasant smile. But she knew that smile. It was the smile of a wolf who'd just tossed a bone into the pen to see which dog would bite first.

You're buying him. Her eyes narrowed. *And he has no idea what the cost.*

On stage, Andrew looked stunned.

His mouth opened slightly, then shut again. He turned toward Sebastian, as if checking to make sure it wasn't a mistake. The vampire gave him a graceful nod.

The mayor beckoned Sebastian up. "Let's bring the man behind this incredible gift to the stage."

Sebastian rose smoothly, fixing his cufflinks as he ascended. The crowd adored him. Of course, they did. He walked like power wrapped in a tailored suit.

Andrew, still stunned, stepped forward to meet him. He extended his hand, and Sebastian took it in a firm shake. "Thank you," Andrew said, leaning in. "Really, thank you so much."

Sebastian leaned closer, speaking low enough that only Amelia's sharp ears could catch it.

"I understand you've been working on reversing cancer cells," he murmured. "I believe I may be able to help with…"

A comm crackled in Reece's earpiece. Hot Shot's voice snapped through it.

"Protesters breaching the courtyard. One just made it past the outer line. Headed for the main doors."

Amelia's enhanced hearing heard it too; she stiffened.

Another crackle, faster this time. "Something's not right. I count five no, seven no… ten vamps mixed in. Hoodies, black armor. They're hiding, intermixed in the crowd."

Her breath caught.

"Chaos's comin' your way," Hot Shot said coolly. "Buckle up, buttercup."

Reece tensed and in a split second, he shifted his eyes to each of his team, "Get Ready!"

Was it the vibration in the air? A distant echo of memory? Amelia didn't know. She just knew something was wrong as she jumped out of her chair and looked out the window. Reece somehow sensed this, too, from behind the bar.

Glass shattered. A police officer came crashing through the ballroom window, scattering glass and screams as he slammed into a dessert table.

The room exploded into mayhem. Glass rained. Screams erupted, and in an instant, the ballroom became a war zone.

CHAPTER 10

The double doors of the ballroom exploded open with a thunderous *bang*. Protestors surged in like a tidal wave, fists flying, voices raw and furious. The air went sharp with shattered glass. Smoke grenades were thrown in and detonated throughout the ballroom.

LAPD officers at the entry tried to intercept the growing crowd, grabbing wildly, but they were shoved back, some flung into tables and pillars by the black clothed protestors who moved with unnatural strength. Reece's team moved instantly without hesitation.

"Grab the gear," he muttered into his comms.

In that moment, ten figures entered through the smoke, seven men, three women, moving with military precision amongst throngs of protestors. They scattered throughout the room, blocking exits like trained wolves penning in sheep. Black hoodies cloaked their faces, but their eyes, those glowing, demonic red eyes, cut through the haze like laser sights.

"Vamps," Reece growled.

"Multiples," chimed Cole.

"Copy," Skylar and Marcus repeated.

The tallest among them, thick-necked, square-jawed, built like a wrecking ball, was Luther. He stood beside Kellin, the clear leader, who issued silent orders with quick, practiced signals.

Smoke erupted across the floor with a metallic *pop-pop*, making everyone cough and squint. Panic grew. Screams multiplied. Tables were overturned. The glittering gala had become a battlefield. Then the vampires moved, coordinated and swift, straight toward the stage.

Amelia saw it first. The vampires weren't feeding. They were scanning the crowd, looking for their target, until they zoned in. They were going straight for Sebastian.

At the back of the room, Reece was mid-grapple with a rioter when he saw it too, those red eyes slicing through the fog.

"I see one," he said into his comms while throwing off a protester.

Cole and Marcus dropped their fake server trays, reached into the planters, and pulled out hidden Glocks. Red dots cut through the smoke like sharks moving beneath waves. Skylar drops the broom and reaches into a utility bag for his weapons.

"Can't see shit with this smoke," Hot Shot called from overwatch. "No shot yet."

Reece lunged at the first vampire he made out in the smoke. His silver stake sank deep into a vampire's chest with a *wet crunch*. The creature's scream was sharp, guttural, then it burst into ash, collapsing like a pile of charred leaves.

Across the room, the other vampires stopped. Red eyes snapped toward Reece. Fangs flashed. Rage immediately spread across their faces.

Two vampire women rushed him with terrifying speed, hands pulling out their sidearms.

But laser sights danced up their bodies. *BANG. BANG.* Marcus and Cole didn't miss.

The bullets blew clean holes in their foreheads, then through the chest, sending them sprawling and disintegrating into ash.

"Two down," Cole said. "We're moving."

Gunfire cracked through the ballroom, rattling chandeliers and walls alike. The Kid was moving so quickly through the flood of protesters as vampires were dispatched to ash while screams and glass exploded. He was truly a part of his team, dealing death to the undead, and Reece felt pride in the chaos.

Andrew stood frozen near the stage, still gripping Sebastian's hand. His mind reeled. *What is this? Who are they?* Then he saw them. The red glow of eyes, the long fangs bared. *Those aren't humans, those eyes, those teeth.*

Kellin's eyes, now blazing, looked directly at the mayor, but not with hunger; it was recognition. The Mayor stared back. A subtle nod passed between them before the chaos swallowed it, although not subtle enough that Sebastian saw everything he needed to see.

Reece and his team were now dodging bullets and bodies while trying to reach any vampire still standing and heading towards the stage.

"I got a few cornered!" Reece barked halfway towards the stage.

"We're on you," Cole replied.

Three more vampires from across the room bolted for the stage.

Amelia spun around like a storm towards the incoming evil. She pulled back the slit in her gown, revealing two 6-inch blades strapped to her thighs.

Her eyes glowed crimson as she whispered:

"Let's dance."

With a blade in each hand, she leapt, spinning through the air like a high diver and landing like a gymnast. Her blade sang through the throat of the first vampire before his brain could register movement.

Blood sprayed like a fan across the smoke. He staggered, still healing too slow.

The second vampire paused, confused by the speed of the attack. Well, that was a big mistake. Amelia didn't stop.

"Who's next?" she smirked.

The vampires turned, sensing her now. They were engaged with an equal, another predator. From across the chaos, Kellin watched Amelia with a flicker of recognition in his eyes.

So the rumors were true, he thought. *The stray still bites.*

On the stage, Andrew's instincts kicked in; he snapped into motion, guiding guests out through any break in the chaos, but a female vampire lunged forward, past Amelia, straight for Andrew.

She grabbed his throat, lifting him off the ground. Andrew's mind couldn't keep up. *Eyes. Teeth. Strength. This isn't real. This isn't...*

"What... are you?" Andrew gasped, eyes wide with terror and disbelief.

Amelia didn't hesitate. She spun, threw her dagger.

Thunk.

The blade slammed through the vampire's back. Ash exploded from her chest. Andrew dropped, coughing, staring at the pile of dust where a monster just stood.

From across the room, Cole saw it. So did Reece.

Amelia's eyes were glowing. Her strength was inhuman. Her presence...undeniable.

"Vamp!" Cole barked, raising his gun. The red dot landed on her chest. Reece noticed something too. She had protected Andrew without hesitation.

"Wait!" he shouted, slapping Cole's hand aside just as the trigger went off.

BANG.

The bullet punched through Amelia's side, missing her heart by inches. She twisted, grunted in pain, and dropped to one knee. Her eyes flickered.

"What the fuck is wrong with you!?" Cole shouted.

"She saved him!" Reece yelled. They didn't have time to argue.

"They're heading for the stage," Reece called. But his eyes caught the truth; they weren't after the mayor. They were coming for Sebastian.

Amelia collapsed, blood soaking through her dress. Her mind spun. Her limbs were numb. Everything faded to black.

Andrew's mind screamed to get down, to run, to get out. This wasn't his world, but then he saw her fall. Saw the way she didn't flinch from danger, and something inside him, something deeper than fear, moved. He wasn't a soldier. Not a hero. Just a man who couldn't let her die.

Andrew hopped off the stage and ran, scooping her up. "Hang on, hang on. I've got you," he whispered, bolting toward the exit.

Just offstage, Sebastian's date screamed and turned to run.

Luther caught her mid-sprint as she headed for an exit. "Not so fast, bitch," he snarled, yanking her hair back, fangs descending.

Her scream cut the air. "Sebastian, help..."

But he didn't move. Luther sank his teeth in. Her body twitched, then stilled. Her eyes went glassy. Sebastian's gaze was cold. Detached. When she went limp, the vampire dropped her like garbage. He locked eyes with Sebastian. The fury in his eyes. The hunger and power pulsing through his veins.

Sebastian raised a brow. "I'm waiting," he whispered, almost bored.

From the side of the stage, The Kid witnessed everything. He moved fast, recklessly, and brave. Still trying to prove he belonged.

Hopping over broken tables and shattered chairs, pulling out his Ka-bar combat knife, he plunged it into Luther's shoulder blade. Looking towards Reece, he gave a quick glance for approval.

Luther let out a deep guttural groan, grabbed the Kid by the leg, and threw him into the open hands of Kellin.

Without a moment of hesitation, Kellin snapped his neck, Skylar's body instantly went limp and fell to the floor like a sack of bricks, and everything stopped.

"Noooooo!!!!" Reece screamed. He's lost teammates in battle before, but this hit differently; this was deeper.

Cole froze for a second, unsure of what he witnessed before snapping out of it.

"The Kid's down, repeat the Kid's down!" he yelled.

"Take 'em out!" Marcus shouted back.

LAPD officers charged Kellin, but they were too slow. The vampire leader swatted them like flies. They hit walls. Unconscious and laid lifeless.

"The smoke's clearing," Hot Shot chimed in, then, seeing Skylar's limp body on the ground, wiped away a quick tear, zeroed in on targets. "Line of sight, coming in hot, watch for debris."

BANG!

A sniper round shattered the ballroom window. One vampire turned to ash instantly.

BANG! BANG!

Two more down. Dust clouds where monsters once stood.

Reece sprinted at the vampire leader, slid under him, and fired up between the legs.

Perfect hit. A bullet right between the eyes.

The leader stumbled but didn't fall. The wound quickly began to seal. He grinned.

"Cheap trick, human."

Just as Reece regained his footing, Luther's large hands grabbed him by the shoulders and threw him across the room into the broken stage.

But before Luther could turn, Cole and Marcus rushed in from the front of the stage with silver stakes drawn. They struck each stake, jamming into his shoulders, pinning him briefly.

"FUCKING DIE!" Cole roared.

BANG.

Another sniper round blew the top of Luther's skull wide open.

Still not enough.

Reece wedged his foot against the stage and lunged at the monstrous vampire from behind, his silver stake stabbing straight into the heart.

The vampire gasped. Time froze. He turned to ash, falling backward as Cole and Marcus shoved with all their strength.

They all quickly scanned for Kellin, but he was nowhere to be found. As the remaining guests and protestors escaped from the ballroom, silence fell. Only the broken chandeliers swayed overhead, creaking in the smoke-filled quiet.

Sebastian stepped forward, brushing ash from his jacket. "Thank you, gentlemen," he said calmly. "Your service is exceptional."

The team stared at him, confused. He wasn't fazed. He wasn't scared. Reece narrowed his eyes. "You knew what they were? You knew about the Mayor's assassination attempt?"

Sebastian smiled. "Let's discuss how we can eliminate more of these creatures...together. I think your team may be more useful than even you realize."

Reece blinked. "Our intel was an attack on the Mayor, not you."

"Hmmm." Sebastian turned to the Mayor, who now looked like a puppet with cut strings. His mind was putting together the events of the evening with the vampire attack. Sebastian leaned close, "I think it's time we left," he whispered to the Mayor.

"Yes, my master," the Mayor muttered. His security detail swarmed in, and within moments, they vanished into the night escorted by the LAPD.

Did I really hear that? Or the grief of losing Skylar playing tricks on me, Reece thought.

Meanwhile, in Andrew's arms, Amelia's wounds began to seal. Her vision flickered. She saw through blurred vision, looking up at Andrew while he ran through the banana-palmed, wallpapered walls of the hotel...fading to black, then flickering visions of Andrew as he screamed at bystanders to move out of the way. He was sweating, shaking, his suit soaked with her blood.

"I've got you. I've got you, please don't die," he said to her.

She heard a car door open and felt him place her down. Amelia stirred with a slight moan. Then her vision suddenly came back with a whoosh, and she sat up in the backseat of his car. She looked out the front window to see Andrew at the valet stand searching for his keys. Her vampire senses, all rushing back to her.

I gotta get outta here, now!" she thought.

Slipping out of the back seat, she gathered up her bloody dress and, with the speed of a 300-year-old vampire, she vanished into the night. Gone in a blink. Just wind where she once was.

Andrew turned. Saw the open car door. The bloody seat and nothing else. He just stood there, stunned, as sirens wailed and ash drifted from the broken ballroom windows like dark snow.

CHAPTER 11

Acouple of hours have passed, and the flashing of camera lights turned the hotel's grand entrance into a blinding gauntlet of questions and disorder. Mayor Walter Billings stepped up to the makeshift podium, the polished front of his tailored suit glinting under the harsh lights. His smile was tight and calculated. Behind him, the LAPD Chief and a string of aides flanked the backdrop of a hastily thrown-up barrier. The noise from the crowd surged forward with questions flying from every direction.

"Mayor Billings! Was this a terrorist attack?"

"Eyewitnesses saw things they can't explain. Do you confirm the reports of...unnatural violence?"

Billings raised his hands with practiced calm. "Ladies and gentlemen, please. One at a time."

The reporters didn't slow down; they smelled blood. Someone shouted, "Is it true that several bodies were turned to ash?!"

Billings barely blinked. "Tonight's chaos was the result of known gangs hijacking peaceful protests. These individuals incited panic inside the ballroom, leading to the regrettable injuries of both guests and protestors."

He spoke slowly, smoothing over every rough question with carefully chosen words. There was no mention of fangs or of glowing eyes. No mention of bodies turning to dust.

A second reporter pressed harder. "There are witnesses

describing things no 'gang violence' can explain, Mr. Mayor. Are you denying this?"

The mayor's smile tightened just slightly. "I understand tensions are high. It's natural after a traumatic event, but I assure you there's no conspiracy. No hidden threat. LAPD has the situation under control." He deflected with reassurance, soothing the crowd of reporters like a snake charmer with a flute.

Another aide touched his arm discreetly, signaling it was time to exit. Billings gave a few more rehearsed lines about public safety, donated funds, and "not letting fear win", before nodding gravely and stepping back. He handed the wolves off to the Police Chief, who looked like he'd rather be anywhere else.

Waiting near the curb, Sebastian Voss sat in the back of his black Rolls-Royce, legs crossed, fingertips tapping against the armrest. Through the tinted glass, he watched the mayor give his performance.

Theatrics and scrambling. He's sweating more than the cameras show.

His driver sat rigidly still with eyes forward. His familiar knew better than to interrupt the predator's thoughts.

The rear door opened, and Mayor Billings climbed in, adjusting his tie with shaking hands. Sebastian didn't immediately acknowledge him. He let him stew. Let the mayor imagine every way he'd disappointed him.

As the Rolls began to pull onto the busy street, Billings cleared his throat. "I...handled it. The press. The gangs are being blamed. No mention of anything...unnatural."

Sebastian finally turned his head, gaze heavy and unblinking. "You're getting better at lying," he said smoothly. "Almost convincing."

Billings gave a nervous laugh. "It's necessary, given tonight's...situation."

Sebastian studied him. The man reeked of fear. It was in his clenched jaw, the way his fingers twitched against the door handle, like he wanted to bolt.

"Convenient," Sebastian murmured. "How quickly you diverted the blame."

Billings bristled, a flash of offense crossing his face before he swallowed it back down. "I did what was necessary," he said stiffly. "The city needs stability. You...need stability."

Sebastian's smile was a bare curve of teeth. "Careful, Walter. You almost sounded like you believe you're protecting *me*."

Silence pulsed thick between them. The mayor shifted. "Should we move forward with Dr. Lee? Set up the next meeting?"

Sebastian let the moment hang just a little longer before nodding. "Yes. Dr. Lee must be brought in closer. Quickly."

Billings exhaled in relief. That was a mistake. Sebastian's mind ticked over the deeper layers. Billings was hiding something. Something more than nerves. Something dangerous, but not yet. Not tonight.

Better to let him think he's still winning.

The car slowed. It was the mayor's stop. Sebastian leaned in slightly, his voice dropping to a soft, predatory murmur. "Keep your secrets if you must, Walter, just remember when the house burns, I won't be the one who chokes on the smoke."

The mayor paled but said nothing. He exited quickly, the door shutting with a muted thud. The Rolls-Royce pulled away, the city lights bleeding into a cold blur behind them. Alone on the sidewalk, the mayor lingered a moment too long, staring after the car as if it might turn around and devour him.

I have to get out from under him, he thought bitterly. *Soon. Before he figures out what I'm working on. What I've set in motion.*

Inside his head, the words echoed like a prayer and a death sentence.

Across the city, Dr. Andrew Lee gripped his steering wheel tighter than necessary, guiding his battered sedan through the empty streets. The night blurred around him, red lights, green lights, the endless stretch of asphalt, and none of it seemed real.

All he could really think about was *her*.

The woman who had appeared from nowhere. Who had saved

him? Who had bled out in his arms, only to vanish before he could even breathe her name.

Andrew stared at the spot where she'd been, pulse hammering in his ears. He wasn't sure what he'd just seen. Not just her disappearance, but the woman who tried to kill him, turning to ash. Instantly. Like something out of a horror movie.

He blinked. Then again, maybe it was adrenaline or trauma. Maybe he'd imagined it all.

People didn't just disintegrate like that. Right?

He pressed a hand to the blood still soaking his shirt. *She was real.* He'd carried her through the hotel. Felt her weight, her warmth. That was what kept circling in his head.

Is she alive? Knuckles whitening on the steering wheel. *Is she dying somewhere because of me?*

The questions followed him back to the lab. They stayed with him through the dead hours of the night, and when the sun finally clawed its way over the skyline, he was still asking,

What really happened last night? Who was the woman who saved my life?

And why did every cell in him feel like she was the only one who could answer them?

CHAPTER 12

The city buzzed around her obliviously, but she was alive. She crouched low between two ruined dumpsters, the stench of piss and old smoke curling into her lungs. Dried blood stuck against the torn slit of her dress. Pain blurred the edges of her thoughts, but rage carved them clean again.

They didn't even hesitate, she thought. *One second saving their lives, the next...pulling the trigger.*

She'd once taken a musket shot shielding a French noble's child, only to be hunted by that same family weeks later. Called a monster, spat on, and hunted. Those old wounds hurt worse. Not the ones in her flesh, but the ones that echoed centuries deep.

You don't belong anywhere. Not to them. Not to anyone.

She pressed trembling fingers to the hole near her ribs; she felt the tissue already beginning to knit under her skin. Her healing was slow, but faster than any human. Her heart battered against her ribs, each beat a furious drum. Across the skyline, lights danced and glittered, mocking her with life.

They'll never know what you are. They'll never want to.

Amelia pushed off the wall, unsteady but alive. For now. Her lips curled into a blood-smeared smirk as she whispered into the dark, "Fine. I don't need saving anyway," as she disappeared into the city's hungry night, a shadow swallowed whole.

·   ·   ·

Across town, inside a dim safehouse, Reece Drake's team gathered around a battered metal table scattered with weapons, surveillance footage, and cooling coffee. The mood was ugly. Skylar was gone, and grief, especially for warriors like them, always found its way out sideways.

Cole slammed his palms down onto the table hard enough to rattle the mugs.

"You *pushed my hand*, Reece!" he barked. "I had a clear shot at that vamp bitch, and you blew it!"

Reece stayed seated, unmoving. His steel-blue eyes pinned Cole with calm fury. "She wasn't attacking civilians," Reece said, voice low. "She saved them."

Cole shoved away from the table, pacing like a caged wolf. "She's still a vamp! You don't get to rewrite what that means because she played hero for five minutes."

Hot Shot leaned back in her chair, arms crossed. "He's got a point, Cole. We've never seen one of them protect humans before."

Marcus, looming near the corner, grunted. "Maybe she's different, or maybe she's just smarter. Wolves wear sheep's clothing, too."

Cole whipped around. "And you're willing to bet lives on that? You willing to let one of us die like the Kid? Or is she just another woman you can't see straight around?"

The room froze. Even Cole looked like he wished he could suck the words back in.

"Say that again."

No one did.

The room crackled with tension. There it was. The thing no one wanted to say out loud. Grief didn't show itself easily, but once it cracked through...it drowned everything.

"Alright, that's far enough." Hot Shot piped in. "You know that could've happened to any one of us."

Reece clenched his jaw, the image of Skylar's limp body flashing again. He pushed the grief down like he always had with focus and not feeling. Reece finally stood, the chair scraping back against the concrete.

"I'm not betting anything," he said. "I'm *watching.*"

He stepped closer to Cole until they were nearly chest to chest.

"I don't trust her, but something else went down tonight. Something bigger than a rogue attack."

Cole's jaw flexed, his hands clenching and unclenching.

It was Hot Shot who broke the standoff.

"What about the Mayor and that Sebastian guy?" she asked sharply. "How the hell did he know about the vampires? Why wasn't the LAPD briefed properly? They both knew something."

Marcus nodded. "And he lied to the press so fast he barely blinked."

Reece's gaze hardened.

"Yeah, Billings knows more than he's saying," he muttered. "I'll dig a little deeper on the Mayor. Hot Shot, let's dig into this Sebastian guy. We need to keep an eye on him too."

"Got it, once I know where he's at, I'll get a drone on him," Hot shot replied.

The team fell into grim silence because if the Mayor of Los Angeles was playing games with vampires, and them, they were in a hell of a lot deeper than they thought. And trust, what little they had left, was already bleeding out. Somewhere out there, the one person who helped them might already be their biggest threat.

CHAPTER 13

The hum of lab equipment was usually enough to center Andrew. The rhythmic churn of centrifuges, the soft beep of monitors, the familiar scent of antiseptic and cool metal all formed a kind of controlled cocoon around him. This morning, none of it was working.

He leaned over the microscope, fingers adjusting the focus, eyes locked on a new slide, a genetic material from one of his most promising cellular mutation studies. It should have excited him. Two days ago, it would've consumed him.

Instead, all he could see was her.

The woman from the ballroom. The one who moved like smoke and struck like lightning. The one who had bled out in his arms and vanished like a ghost before he could even get her name.

She wasn't just beautiful. She was something else. Something *impossible*. No human being moved like that. Survived a shot like that. Dissolved into the night like vapor.

Andrew shook his head and leaned back in his chair, scrubbing a hand over his face. "Focus," he muttered to himself. "You're not writing a damn vampire novel."

His phone buzzed, cutting through the silence.

NO CALLER ID

He hesitated, then swiped to answer.

"Dr. Lee speaking."

"Dr. Lee," came the unmistakably smooth voice of Mayor Walter Billings. "I hope I'm not interrupting anything urgent."

Andrew hesitated. The mayor sounded calm, persuasive as ever, but his mind kept circling back to that night. The fundraiser. The gunfire and the moment that woman turned to ash right in front of him. No one mentioned anything like that on the news. He hadn't told anyone either, and who would believe him?

He sat up straighter in his chair, forcing his voice into something closer to composed. "Not at all, Mr. Mayor. I wasn't expecting your call."

"I imagine not," Billings said, chuckling lightly. "I just wanted to personally check in with you after...well, the unfortunate incident at the fundraiser."

Unfortunate. That was one way to describe it.

"I'm fine," Andrew said. "Just...shaken, I suppose. I didn't expect to be dodging bullets at a charity event."

"None of us did," Billings replied, voice laced with the well-practiced sympathy of a seasoned politician. "Truly tragic. A few agitators can ruin the goodwill of hundreds, but you handled yourself with admirable composure."

Andrew didn't respond to that. He didn't feel admirable. He felt confused, haunted, and useless.

"I do have some good news, though," the Mayor continued. "Despite the...chaos, Mr. Voss has confirmed that his donation to your homeless initiative will go through as planned. One million dollars."

Andrew blinked. "That's...incredibly generous."

"Yes. Sebastian is nothing if not committed to causes that matter," Billings said. "And I think he sees the potential in what you're building. Which brings me to the reason I'm calling."

There it was. The favor.

"I'm listening," Andrew said cautiously.

"Mr. Voss would like to meet with you personally. He has a private project he's hoping you might consult on, something biomedical in nature. The details, I'm not entirely briefed on, but he was quite insistent that it aligns with your expertise in genetic research and rare cellular disorders."

Andrew leaned back in his chair again, frowning. "Mayor Billings, I'm already stretched with the trials for my cancer reversal therapy, not to mention the homelessness initiative. I'm honored he wants to involve me, but..."

"I understand," the Mayor cut in. "And I wouldn't ask if it weren't a rare opportunity. From what I've gathered, Mr. Voss is offering full laboratory support. State-of-the-art equipment, an unrestricted research budget...the kind of resources that could fast-track *all* of your projects, not just his."

Andrew hesitated. That was the problem. It *was* tempting, too tempting.

"And what exactly is this project?" he asked, cautiously.

There was a pause on the line.

"All I know," the Mayor said carefully, "is that Mr. Voss suffers from a rare genetic condition, an extreme form of polymorphous light eruption. Sunlight causes rapid epidermal deterioration. He's hoping you might help him...improve his quality of life."

Andrew sat in silence, running that over in his mind. It wasn't unheard of, rare, yes, but not impossible. But something didn't sit right.

"And he wants me to come to him?" Andrew asked, finally.

"Yes. Tuesday night. 8 pm. His personal lab, mid-Wilshire. He'll have everything ready."

"I'll... consider it," Andrew said, unsure of whether he meant it or not.

"Just show up," Billings said gently but firmly. "Talk. That's all he's asking."

Andrew could hear the veiled urgency in the mayor's voice. Not a request, but a directive. He sounded friendly, yes, but it was laced with expectation.

"Ok, I'll be there," he said finally. "But only to hear him out."

"Of course," Billings said, smooth as ever. "Thank you, Dr. Lee. I know you won't regret it."

The call ended.

Andrew stared down at his phone, still cradled in his hand. A lab with no budget limits and unlimited access. All the tools he needed to finish what he'd started. A man like Sebastian Voss offering to open every door, but something told him this wasn't just science, and he'd seen that look in Voss's eyes at the fundraiser. The look of a man who knew how to move people like pawns. He didn't know what game he was stepping into, but he had a feeling it had already begun. Andrew swallowed.

Maybe this meeting would give him answers, or maybe it would confirm the part of him that still wondered if he was losing his mind.

He set the phone down gently beside his microscope. The hum of the equipment continued around him, the steady buzz of refrigeration units and centrifuge drums a comfort once, now drowned in distraction.

He leaned back in his chair, staring at the samples he'd been analyzing before the call. His mind refused to return to work. The mystery woman, the way she'd looked at him. The way she'd vanished. He ran a thumb along the side of the microscope slide, grounding himself in the tangible, trying to anchor his thoughts. There were too many questions, and now a personal meeting with Sebastian Voss, the man who was already funding his homeless initiative? The timing wasn't a coincidence. He wasn't sure if he was walking into a partnership...or a cage.

CHAPTER 14

I *hadn't heard from Sebastian Voss since the fundraiser exploded literally, and part of me assumed he'd crawled off to whatever silk-lined tomb he called home to lick his wounds. Another part of me? The one who knew how inconveniently unkillable he was knew better.*

So when her phone buzzed and his name lit up the screen like a bad omen, she stared at it for a good three seconds before answering. Not because she didn't want to hear what he had to say, but because she didn't want to give him the satisfaction of thinking she did.

She tapped the screen and brought it to her ear.

"Well," she drawled, "either this is the ghost of Sebastian Voss calling to haunt me, or hell has better reception than I thought."

His voice poured through the line like aged scotch, smooth, warm, and absolutely hiding a knife.

"Charming as ever, Amelia. I'm glad to hear your voice."

"I'd say the same, but I was kind of hoping you didn't make it out of the ballroom."

A pause. "Shame."

"I'm touched," he said. "Truly. I was worried about you, too. But then I remembered you've always been good at disappearing."

She could practically hear the smirk in his voice. He was sitting somewhere high and sterile, undoubtedly in one of his brutalist lairs, sipping something expensive and blood-based. Probably staring out at the skyline like he owned it. Which, in a way, he did.

"So," she said, pacing her penthouse, "what's the occasion? Just calling to reminisce about the worst fundraiser in modern history, or is there an actual point?"

"There's always a point," Sebastian replied. "I've done some digging. The attackers "

"Were after you," she interrupted. "Not the mayor or the humans. You."

He went quiet for a breath. Calculating, probably.

"Yes," he said. "They were. And you noticed that."

"I'm observant like that. Comes with the whole not-dying-for-centuries thing."

"They were part of a new faction. Young and volatile. No respect for the Old Code, the rules that kept us hidden. They want no hierarchy. Just chaos dressed up as freedom."

She rolled my eyes, even though he couldn't see her. "Sounds like every twenty-year-old in a Che Guevara shirt. What do they actually want?"

"An end to the masquerade. No more secrecy. No more structure. They believe we should dominate openly, treat humans like cattle, erase the lines. They call it...liberation."

"And you call it what? A threat to your little empire?"

"I call it short-sighted. Brutal and yes, dangerous for everyone."

He let the silence stretch for a moment, letting it get heavy.

"They've put a bounty on you."

She stopped pacing.

"That so?" she said, keeping her tone light even as her stomach twisted.

"Yes. You've been a problem for them. A symbol of restraint. They think if they take you out, they make a point."

"And you're telling me this... why?"

"To help you," he said, with that perfect, elegant lie.

She didn't respond right away...because he *was* lying. She could feel it through the phone, but the problem with Sebastian

Voss was that even his lies were dressed in truths, and right now, part of her knew this was how the game worked.

"I want to meet," he continued, soft, coaxing. "Face-to-face. I have more information."

"What's the catch?" She said, dry as sandpaper.

"None," he said, far too quickly. "Just...come to my office. I've taken over a biotech facility. It's secure and clean. You'll like it."

She laughed once. Sharp. "You think I'm going to walk into your den because you hung up a few UV lights and stocked the fridge with O-negative?"

"I think you're going to come because you're curious."

And damn him, he was right.

"Also," he added, far too casually, "I'd like to introduce you to someone."

She froze. "What kind of someone?"

"Dr. Andrew Lee."

The name hit like a dropped match in dry grass. Her silence was deafening. Even he couldn't miss it.

"The man you saved. He's...impressive. Brilliant and driven. Passionate about healing the broken."

He knew exactly what he was doing. Her weakness wasn't bloodlust. It was always the idea that things could be better.

"And?" She asked, carefully.

"And I think you two might find each other...enlightening."

She scoffed. "Is this matchmaking now? I thought you were more the puppet-master type, not a Tinder algorithm."

"Why not both?" he said smoothly. "Think of it as...mutually beneficial. You protect him. He grounds you. And, I gain a better understanding of what's at stake in the war ahead."

"Very altruistic of you," she said. "Trying to keep me close through the man you plan to own."

Another pause. Just long enough to confirm the hit.

"You see too much," he said, not quite smiling anymore.

"You hide too much," she replied.

"So? Will you come?"

She let the silence hang for a moment longer. The idea of

seeing Andrew again stirred something in her she hadn't felt in a long time, something infuriatingly close to hope.

"Fine," she said. "But if you try anything, I'm putting a stake through your heart and blaming it on youthful rebellion."

"I look forward to it," he murmured, satisfied. "Tuesday, 8 PM."

She hung up before he could say anything else. Her reflection caught in the window, her hazel eyes stormy, mouth curved in something between a frown and a smirk.

Whatever he was playing at, I was walking straight into it, but I wasn't walking blind, She thought.

CHAPTER 15

On Tuesday evening, Sebastian Voss stood by the floor-to-ceiling windows of his private study, one hand tucked into the pocket of his charcoal vest, the other swirling a crystal glass half-full with a viscous, near-black liquid. The filtered sunlight bathed the room in golden haze, soft and harmless behind layers of custom-engineered UV glass.

The last light of day. A beautiful lie.

Behind him, the city bloomed with electricity, restless and blinking beneath him like a grid of mortal distraction. He didn't watch it for the view. He watched it for leverage.

A soft knock at the door.

"Enter," he said without turning.

His home assistant, Viktor, a gaunt familiar with immaculate posture and an even more impeccable fear of disappointing him, stepped into the study. "The call with Mayor Billings went as expected. Dr. Lee agreed to the meeting."

Sebastian allowed himself a small smile. *Of course he did.*

"Did he sound wary?"

"Very."

"Good. Curiosity is more useful than obedience. It breeds dependency."

Viktor nodded once, as though agreeing with a line in scripture.

Sebastian finally turned from the window. His eyes glowed faintly in the dimming light, not the unnatural red of the younger vampires, but something more subtle. More *refined*. His power didn't announce itself. It simply took root.

"Has Amelia confirmed?" he asked.

"Yes, sir. She should arrive at the same time as Dr. Lee."

He set his glass down, slow and deliberate. "Excellent."

He walked to the chessboard at the side of the room and slid the black queen into position beside a white knight.

"I'm offering her the illusion of choice. That's all anyone wants, isn't it? To feel like their cage was handcrafted."

Viktor hesitated. "And if she senses what you're doing?"

Sebastian's smile sharpened into something almost fond. "She already does, but she's tired. Worn. She wants a reason to stop running, even if she won't admit it."

He paused, tapping a finger thoughtfully on the edge of the board.

"Dr. Lee, is that reason, or he could be. He burns with idealism, like a candle flickering in a cave full of shadows. He thinks he's saving people. What he doesn't realize...is that he's saving her."

Viktor gave the smallest frown. "And if he doesn't?"

"Then he burns out, and she watches another good man die. Either way...she stays close."

Sebastian turned back to the window, watching the city lights flare brighter now that the sun was gone.

"Love, Viktor...is the oldest leash. Even for immortals."

CHAPTER 16

S unset was crawling over Los Angeles like a slow spill of honeyed blood across the skyline, and she was already regretting saying yes.

Sebastian Voss. Of all the devils in all the cities, she had to entertain a meeting with the one wrapped in designer suits and riddles. Two days ago, she might've let his call go to voicemail and left it there to die like a wilted flower, but now...now he claimed someone had put a price on her head, and as charming as that threat was, it wasn't what gnawed at her.

It was him. The human.

Dr. Andrew Lee.

That flash of something she hadn't felt in a long time, something delicate, inconvenient, and ridiculous, had lodged behind her ribs like a splinter. she'd saved him, and bled out in his arms, and vanished before he could say thank you or scream. Now she was being offered a second chance, and she hated how much she wanted to take it.

Wanting is the first step toward loss. And loss? That's something I learned to bury a long time ago, but here I was, digging it up.

She slid another dagger into the holster strapped beneath the slit of her dress. Yes, it was another black dress, always black. Nothing hid bloodstains better. If someone was foolish enough to try collecting on her bounty tonight, they'd find out just how bad an investment that was.

They always do.

The penthouse had been unusually still these past few days. she'd kept to herself, no late-night Skid Row visits and no fights picked in alleys. Just silence. It was the kind of silence that got dangerous if left unchecked.

Amelia told herself she was weighing Sebastian's offer, but really, she was replaying a moment. A glance. The way Andrew had looked at her. He was confused, terrified, maybe in awe. He didn't know what she was, but something had passed between them, something...very human. And she hadn't felt like that in longer than she cared to admit.

Hope is the worst kind of addiction. The funny thing about being immortal is that time bends. Seconds feel like hours when you're bored, and decades pass like whispers when you're in love, and this...this anticipation was sharp. It had edges.

She checked the time. Two hours to go.

Of course Sebastian had been vague. He was always best at the bait.

It wasn't just him she'd be seeing tonight. He knew exactly what he was doing. If he dangled Andrew Lee in front of her like some fragile, brilliant carrot, she'd come running. That man was building homes for the homeless and still found time to chase a cure for cancer, and somehow, he hadn't turned into a cynic.

Part of me wanted to protect that, like I did the people in the streets. Another part wanted to see if someone like him could look at me...and not flinch.

She smirked at her reflection in the mirror, pulling her hair back with a practiced flick.

"I'm not doing this for him," she told herself aloud. "I just want to know if this price on my head is real."

The mirror didn't have to respond. She could already hear Sebastian's voice in her head.

Of course it's real, darling. When has danger ever not followed you?

She grabbed her coat, slipped the second blade into her boot, and stepped out onto the balcony. The air smelled like heat, jasmine, and inevitability. Time to see what game Sebastian was playing and maybe, just maybe, she'd get another glimpse of the man who still haunted the space behind her ribs.

CHAPTER 17

Sebastian stood near his obsidian desk, sipping blood from a wine glass like it was a merlot. His silhouette cut a clean, elegant shape against the sleek office interior. He was still immaculate and, of course, still theatrical.

His assistant, Evelyn, led Amelia into his office without ceremony.

"Thank you Evelyn, that will be all," as she stepped out and closed the door behind her.

"I see your décor is still 'Bond villain meets biotech start up,'" Amelia said dryly, crossing her arms.

Sebastian turned, smiling like he'd been waiting centuries for her. "And you're still the dark queen of sarcasm. I was starting to think I'd have to bribe you with a blood bag and a sonnet."

She ignored the chair he gestured toward and remained standing. "Cut to it. You said I have a price on my head."

"Ah, yes. Straight to the blade." He set down his glass. "A young faction. Impulsive and undisciplined. They believe structure is a cage and humans are livestock, not a shared ecosystem. They call their movement 'the Reign.' How poetic."

"And how convenient," she muttered. "So now I'm a liability because I don't fall in line?"

He raised a brow. "You don't fall in line with anyone, Amelia. That's what makes you dangerous...and useful."

She narrowed her eyes. "There it is. The ask."

He gave a light chuckle. "No ask, just a gentle suggestion. Keep your eyes open. Word on the street is your haunts may be crawling with whispers. Someone like you...might hear things the rest of us can't."

"You want me doing your recon?"

"Remember, someone's put a price on your head, Amelia. You might want to watch your back. I want you alive." His smile thinned. "And I know you. If someone's stirring the waters in this city and threatening the fragile balance, we both know you won't just walk away."

He was right, and she hated that. So she said nothing. Just stared at him, searching his expression for the thing he wasn't saying.

Then she felt it, the shift. The softening around his eyes, the tiny flicker of amusement that meant he was about to change the game.

"I have one more surprise for you," Sebastian said smoothly. "I believe you two have crossed paths."

He gestured toward the far door as it opened, and there he was.

Dr. Andrew Lee.

He looked less frazzled than he had at the fundraiser, though still slightly disheveled in that endearing professor way, collar uneven, a pen tucked behind his ear, and that same look in his eyes. The one she hadn't been able to shake.

He froze when he saw her.

"I, wait... you..." He stammered, taking a step forward, his brows knitting in disbelief. "You're okay? I thought..."

She cocked her head. "You thought I bled out in your arms? You're not the only one full of surprises. My name is Amelia Devereux. It's a pleasure to thank my knight in shining armor in person."

He let out a breath that was halfway between a laugh and relief. "Uh, hi Amelia, I'm Andrew Lee. Although I'm not sure about being 'the knight in shining armor,' you disappeared. One second you were unconscious, and then...gone. I thought maybe I imagined all of it."

"If you imagined me throwing a knife into someone's chest, taking a bullet, and then vanishing into the night, I'd be concerned about your hobbies."

His mouth twitched into a sheepish smile. "I don't usually hallucinate knife-throwing vigilantes."

"Good. One of us should be stable."

They stood there for a beat, the silence not quite awkward, just charged. Then she glanced at the file in his hand.

"So, you're the doctor everyone was clapping for at the fundraiser. The one trying to fix the world with a clipboard and good intentions."

His cheeks flushed slightly. "I run a program housing transition, skill development, and addiction support. We try to get people back on their feet."

She raised an eyebrow, genuinely intrigued. "You're actually getting people off the streets? Not just throwing checks at the problem?"

"It's more than just checks," he said, the conviction creeping into his voice now. "It's time and patience. Showing up when no one else does."

That made her pause. She felt it, a flicker of warmth behind her ribs. This was dangerous territory.

"You're idealistic," she said, soft but not unkind. "And a little foolish."

His smile widened. "Maybe, but foolish people build the things that last."

"I'll drink to that," she murmured, not expecting him to hear it.

Then she stepped closer, reached in, and wrapped him in a light hug. He tensed at first, then eased into it.

Before she pulled back, she leaned in close, her lips near his ear.

"Not everything here is what it seems," she whispered. "Be careful, Dr. Lee."

His expression shifted, the weight of her words settling behind his eyes.

Before he could ask what she meant, she stepped away and gave Sebastian the kind of nod that said *'we're done here.'*

"Don't keep your doctor waiting," she said with a wink. "I hear he's brilliant."

Sebastian's voice followed like velvet. "I'll be in touch, Amelia."

"I'm sure you will," she called over my shoulder. "You always are."

The room seemed colder the moment she left.

Andrew stood in the middle of Sebastian's office, pulse still unsettled. The scent of her perfume lingered in the air, a strange blend of ozone and sandalwood, ancient and familiar at once.

"She's... remarkable," Andrew said quietly.

Sebastian offered a nonchalant nod, as though Amelia wasn't the most extraordinary thing in the room. "She's effective and has her principles, in her own way."

Andrew turned to face him, curiosity beginning to override nerves. "Why did you want me to meet her?"

Sebastian folded his hands behind his back and stepped closer to the wall of security monitors overlooking the lower levels of the lab. "Because I believe in collaboration. Amelia represents a different angle of the problem we're all trying to solve, and you, Dr. Lee, are the key to our next step."

Andrew hesitated. "Look, I appreciate the donation. What you've done for the charity...it's more than anyone's done, but I have my own research. My own goals."

"And I'm not here to derail them," Sebastian said smoothly. "In fact, I want to accelerate them."

Meanwhile, outside Sebastian's office building, a small drone closes in on his penthouse window. Hot Shot guiding the drone just out of sight of the occupants inside, with the team watching on the monitors, as the camera focuses in on the two men.

"Ok, there he is. Is that the doctor with him?" Hot Shot asked.

"Yep, I guess when you donate all that money, you expect them at your beck and call." Cole sparked.

"Can we hear what they are saying?" Reece asked.

"Nah, we just have visuals," Hot Shot replied.

Back inside Sebastian's office, Andrew continued, "There's... something else."

His eyes drifted, not sure if he should say anything, but he committed. "At the fundraiser. I saw someone...she turned to ash. Right in front of me. No one's mentioned it. Not the news, not the reports. Did that... actually happen?"

Sebastian didn't miss a beat. "Trauma does strange things to the brain, Dr. Lee. You might have been confused and surrounded by chaos. Memory bends under pressure."

"But I remember..."

"Bodies were recovered," Sebastian cut in, already walking toward another glowing display. "Gunmen, mostly. What you saw wasn't ash, just smoke and adrenaline. The perfect storm for confusion." He turned back with a small smile. "Now. Let me show you the sequencing suite. This, I think, you'll find far more grounded in reality."

He moved toward a sleek panel and tapped it. A schematic of a state-of-the-art genetics lab blossomed into view, equipment Andrew had only dreamed of. Entire sequence machines, AI-driven CRISPR designs illuminated on screens, and the unlimited resources the mayor mentioned.

"I want your help with a condition," Sebastian continued. "A rare one. An extreme form of Polymorphous Light Eruption. Direct sunlight causes my skin to blister within seconds. Doctors don't know how to treat it, but you and your gene reversal model? It could change everything."

Andrew stared at the display. "And I'd be free to continue my cancer research?"

"Unrestricted," Sebastian said. "You'll be fully funded and staff supported with full autonomy."

It sounded too good to be true, but something in Andrew,

some deep, desperate belief in doing more good, made him say, "I'd need a week to evaluate your condition. Maybe more."

"You'll have all the time you need," Sebastian said.

Andrew nodded slowly. "Then...I'm in."

Sebastian's smile was slow and satisfied. He pulled out a necklace, a gold pendant with a crest embossed on it. "Wear this at all times while you're in my building, and you'll have access to every room in the lab. The sensors will activate every door. You won't need anything else," he said.

"That's an interesting symbol, does it mean something?" Andrew asked.

"It's just a family crest, and since you'll have full access to my laboratory," Sebastian said smoothly, fastening the chain around Andrew's neck like a quiet crown. "I'll consider you as close to family as it represents."

Back at the safehouse, Reece pointed to the monitor. "What's that he's putting on him?"

"It looks like some sort of necklace or keyfob," Cole replied.

"Probably to let him in places. How loving of him." Hot Shot sarcastically said.

"There's nothing here. Just some rich guy donating money to a scientist and now givin' him a job." Marcus shot out.

"You're probably right, but Sebastian knows about vampires and he wasn't afraid at all at the fundraiser. Let's keep and eye on him and if anything changes keep me updated. I'll keep focusing on if or how the mayor's involved," Reece sneered and walked away.

Back in Sebastian's office, Andrew stood gripping the necklace for a moment, looking at the luminous lab schematics, when two striking members of his staff walked into the room. A man wearing a lab coat and striking Asian woman in a long red dress who looked straight off a Milan runway except for the katana strapped to her back.

"Perfect timing," Sebastian said smoothly. "This is Elis, your lead technician. Whatever you need, equipment, access, answers? He'll get it for you. Now this is Camille Tanaka, she is head of security. After what you went through at the fundraiser, I want you to know that your safety is paramount to us, to me. So please don't hesitate to reach out to Camille if you ever feel unsafe."

"Ah...should I feel unsafe?" Andrew questioned.

"Just if you do," Camille cut in with a rehearsed smile.

As Andrew followed the two, something flickered in the glass wall beside him. Just for a second.

Sebastian's eyes were glowing red.

Andrew blinked and quickly turned, but Sebastian's gaze was calm, his irises the same pale blue they'd always been. Maybe it was a trick of the light or fatigue. Or something else, but as he followed the assistants out of the office, a chill threaded in his guts. Something was off, and it wasn't just the lab or Sebastian, but something deeper, and he was just stepping into it.

CHAPTER 18

Dr. Andrew Lee followed the pair down a long, dim corridor. The deeper they moved into the office compound, the more clinical everything became. Ornate office finishes gave way to surgical sterility. Each door they passed had no handle, only palm-sized scanners embedded into the wall, glowing faintly with biometric access indicators. It wasn't just state-of-the-art. It was beyond government grade.

Beyond anything Andrew had ever seen outside of defense contracts and theoretical black-budget projects. This wasn't just a lab. It was something closer to a temple designed not just to discover truth, but to worship it. The lab technician, Elis, tall and sharply built, with glacier-blue eyes and a voice like polished stone, turned to him with a flawlessly rehearsed smile. "Dr. Lee, welcome to your new research facility."

The final set of doors hissed open. Andrew stepped into a sprawling lab bathed in soft white light. Floor-to-ceiling glass divided rooms with specialized equipment: one held genomic sequencers that made the university's look like toys, another was filled with cryogenic storage, a third lined with AI-assisted analytical rigs humming quietly beneath pristine surfaces. Above them, reinforced panels glowed with an ambient daylight hue replicating circadian light without the heat or UV radiation. The whole place pulsed with precision. Money had not just been spent here; it had been poured like a river.

He turned slowly, overwhelmed. "This...this is incredible. You could cure everything from ALS to hemophilia down here."

Sebastian's voice floated in like a silk ribbon through smoke, smooth, but invasive. "That's the idea."

Andrew turned to see him strolling into the lab with effortless grace, his expression calm. "You wanted freedom, didn't you? To chase real answers without budget restrictions, red tape, or university politics?"

"I did," Andrew admitted. "But I never imagined..."

"You'd be offered paradise?" Sebastian smiled. "It's yours. The lab, the team, the resources. I only ask for one thing in return, discretion and, of course, results."

Andrew nodded slowly, still in awe, but then he saw them.

Technicians moved through the corridors with quiet precision, young men and women in white coats, all beautiful in that hyperreal way that seemed more airbrushed than genetic, just like Elis and Camille. Not just attractive, but symmetrical. Glossy-eyed with skin like porcelain or bronze, flawless in every angle of light. They glided rather than walked, each motion measured and disturbingly perfect. They were too perfect. He watched one woman input data at a glass panel. Her hands moved mechanically, her face set in a serene half-smile like it had been painted there. A twist of unease bloomed in his stomach. He couldn't place it yet, but it itched at something primal, the part of him that didn't think, just warned. Not just the appearance, but the uniformity of them. Like dolls lined up behind scientific instruments.

Sebastian followed his gaze. "Ah. Yes. You'll find my staff efficient. Many of them are the best minds in their respective fields. Some...have unique advantages."

Andrew turned back to him slowly. "What kind of advantages?"

Sebastian's smile didn't reach his eyes. "Let's just say I recruit globally. Exceptional people with exceptional minds. A few quirks, maybe, but you'll adjust."

Amelia's voice whispered through his memory like a breeze through a half-open window.

Not everything is what it seems...be careful.

He rubbed the back of his neck, trying to ground himself. "They seem... unusual. Are they part of a larger biotech initiative?"

Sebastian walked beside him now, hands clasped behind his back. "They're not part of any publicly funded programs if that's what you mean. Everything here is private and proprietary. We like to keep things...contained."

'Contained.' That word thudded like a weight in his chest.

Andrew tried to shake it off. "It's a little overwhelming. I'm not used to this level of..."

"Power?" Sebastian offered with a glint in his eye.

"I was going to say opportunity."

Sebastian gave a small nod. "Opportunity *is* power, Dr. Lee. The question is how you use it. I believe you'll use it wisely."

Andrew looked around again, trying to focus on the machines, the technology, the potential, but all he could see were the glassy-eyed stares of the staff. The way their smiles never quite faded. The way they moved in sync, without a whisper of exhaustion or error.

And the way Sebastian's reflection, just for a second, had flashed red in the glass wall.

He blinked, and it was gone. Sebastian's eyes were normal now. Piercing blue. Human. Maybe it was nothing, or maybe it was the stress. The trauma from the fundraiser. All the blood and chaos, but something deep in Andrew's gut whispered otherwise. Something wasn't right, and despite the white coats and warm smiles...he was already in too deep and the surface was disappearing.

CHAPTER 19

By the time she left the lab, the air had cooled, but she hadn't. As the elevator doors dinged behind her, she walked through the lobby and out into the night, the heavy glass doors hissing shut behind her with the finality of a vault.

The air was crisp, cooler than it had been all week, but the chill didn't bite the way it should have. Her blood was too warm and too loud. She could still feel Andrew's arms around her, the quiet tremble in his chest when she whispered in his ear. The way his pulse kicked up when he saw her. Not out of fear, but something else. Recognition and relief. It was a connection.

Damn it. I should've walked away the moment I stepped through Sebastian's door. Should've told him to shove his half-truths and veiled threats somewhere unpleasant, but then he dangled Andrew like a ribbon, and just like that, I was grabbing at it like I didn't know better. Because I do know better. Hope is dangerous. It's the sharpest blade of them all, beautiful, seductive, and always pointed at the heart, she thought.

As she crossed the courtyard of Sebastian's private complex, the sound of her boots echoing against the manicured stone like a countdown to her next mistake. Somewhere in the distance, she heard the low hum of a security drone overhead, and cameras tracking her every move.

I was already in the web and who was the spider? He was sipping blood behind office windows, smirking like he'd already won, but he hadn't. Not yet.

He thought pairing me with Andrew would soften me. Open some doors he hadn't been able to pry loose on his own. He wasn't wrong, but he wasn't ready for the version of me that door might unlock. Because I felt something tonight. When Andrew looked at me, it wasn't just attraction. It was trust. Blind, unearned trust, and that terrified me more than a stake through the chest.

What if I wasn't worthy of it? What if, for the first time in a hundred years, I wanted to be seen for something more than what I am?

She reached her car, the engine still warm from the drive over. She didn't get in right away. Just stood there, staring out at the flickering lights of Los Angeles below, wondering how far down she'd already fallen.

Sebastian was playing a game, and maybe, just maybe, she was finally tired of surviving alone. She slid into the driver's seat, turned the key in the ignition, and shifted into 1st.

Whatever came next, chess match or war, she'd be ready, and God help the bastard who thought she could be controlled.

CHAPTER 20

The air outside the warehouse was thick with the scent of oil and rust. Reece's boots echoed against the cracked concrete as he stepped out into the night alone, the metal door clanging shut behind him. His team's argument still simmered in his ears. Cole was pissed, and he had every right to be, but Reece didn't have time to explain instinct to a team trained to follow orders, especially not when grief was already twisting into revenge.

This wasn't just a vampire problem anymore. It was a cover-up, and somehow, the mayor and Sebastian Voss were involved. Reece didn't believe in coincidences. Especially not ones wrapped in Armani suits and silver smiles.

He slid into his black Dodge, factory standard on the surface, armored like a tank underneath, and slammed the heavy door shut. Silence enveloped him, save for the hum of the engine and the tap of his fingers against the steering wheel.

How the hell did Sebastian know? Why wasn't the Mayor rattled? And who the hell was feeding them intel?

He pulled up the encrypted contact hub on his tablet, dialing one of his lesser-known local informants on his phone. A former city clerk, now deep in debt and deeper in Reece's pocket.

The line picked up after a few rings.

"Yeah?" rasped a tired voice.

"It's Drake," Reece said, low and sharp. "I need access to any communications linked to Mayor Billings over the last seventy-two hours, private or city-issued."

"That's suicide," the man hissed. "You know how locked down his digital is? Everything's rerouted through third-party filters. Firewalls like Fort Knox. Half of it doesn't even touch city servers."

"You've got six hours. Start with whoever called him before the fundraiser."

A long pause. A sigh. Then the line went dead. Reece tossed the phone onto the passenger seat and leaned back.

He stared up through the windshield at the stars, what little of them could be seen past LA's light pollution. His mind circled the same questions like a wolf pacing a cage.

How was Billings involved? He saw the vampires, but knew what to say to the press. That meant one of two things: he was in bed with the vampires or he was playing both sides.

Reece's jaw clenched. He needed answers, and if Billings wouldn't give them willingly, there were other ways.

CHAPTER 21

Mayor Walter Billings closed the door to his office with a quiet click. The room was dark except for the low golden glow of the desk lamp, casting long shadows across the polished mahogany and the framed photos of political handshakes and award banquets. He locked the door, pulled the cord on the heavy blinds, and crossed to his desk. With deliberate precision, he opened the lower drawer and retrieved a burner phone, an unregistered flip model he kept for only one kind of call.

He dialed. It rang once. Then again. The line clicked. A voice answered, smooth and sharp like broken glass. "You're calling me? After that disaster?"

Billings didn't sit. He stood behind his desk like a general surveying a losing battlefield.

"Let's skip the righteous indignation," he said, tone clipped. "You told me you'd bring enough. You didn't. I gave you the time, the place, and even told you Sebastian would be vulnerable. You failed."

A beat of silence. Then, a low growl. "You didn't tell us Amelia Devereux would be there."

"I didn't know," Billings snapped. "I don't track rogue vampires handing out sandwiches in Skid Row. That's your job."

"She cut down three of ours before they touched the stage.

And Voss? That arrogant bastard barely blinked. My people weren't ready for that."

Billings pinched the bridge of his nose, trying to keep the heat out of his voice. "That's not my problem. I held up my end. You blew it."

The voice hardened. "Careful, Mayor. You're not untouchable."

Billings barked a cold laugh. "Really? Because from where I'm standing, you're the one licking your wounds. You want to test me? Go ahead. I'll march straight into Voss's office, show him the time-stamped messages, the audio files, and your name. He'll wipe your little faction off the map before nightfall."

Silence. Then a longer beat.

Then, the voice shifted, more cautious now, more calculating. "You wouldn't survive the fallout."

Billings leaned against the desk, his expression unreadable in the dim light. "No. But I'll make sure your little uprising dies with me."

A pause, then the voice grumbled. "What do you want?"

"Voss has a new toy. Dr. Andrew Lee. You might've seen him, sweet, awkward face, the guy running the homeless initiative."

"Not our concern."

"It is now," Billings said, too calm to be casual. "He's working for Sebastian. Full access to a new state-of-the-art lab. All funded by Voss Enterprises. You know what that means?"

A pause.

"They're experimenting again," the voice said.

"Exactly," Billings replied. "And I guarantee you this one isn't just about blood banks or immunity boosters. This one's deeper. Voss is planning something."

"And you want us to do what?"

"I want pressure. Surveillance. Maybe a break-in, a scare. Nothing traceable. Just...make sure the good doctor knows he's being watched and if we're lucky, maybe Voss bleeds a little."

"You're playing a dangerous game."

"I always do," the mayor said with a pause," and keep an eye on Amelia Devereux. She can't be trusted to stay out of our plans."

Then the line went dead.

Billings snapped the burner shut and slid it back into the drawer. He exhaled, long and low, then straightened his tie in the dark reflection of the window.

Two sides. One gameboard. And as long as they both kept underestimating him, Walter Billings planned to win.

CHAPTER 22

Kellin stood at the center of the room, jaw clenched, eyes flickering with rage. He was young for a vampire, just over a century old, but he had ambition that burned like sunlight in his veins. And now, that fire was aimed squarely at Mayor Walter Billings.

"That human," he growled, pacing. "That *pet* dares to threaten us after *he* failed to warn us about Devereux?"

A soft click of heels echoed behind him. Syla, slightly older, and infinitely more patient, leaned against a pillar of exposed steel and concrete. Her blonde hair gleamed under the flickering red light. Her nails, painted the color of blood, tapped once against the steel.

"He didn't fail to warn us," she said. "He just didn't think we mattered enough to warn. There's a difference."

Kellin spun toward her, fangs bared. "You think this is a game?"

"I think," she replied coolly, "you rushed the board without knowing all the pieces. You attacked Sebastian Voss with just your attack dog and barely trained recruits, hoping chaos would win the day. Now they are all dead."

"Don't you think I know that?! I was there! We *had* him," Kellin snapped. "Until Amelia fucking Devereux showed up and a bunch of fuckin' vampire hunters. He was supposed to be unprotected. Alone. He fed us lies and said the protest would give us cover. He said Voss would be exposed, but what do we find?"

He stopped and slammed both fists into the metal table. "Devereux was already there, and then vampire hunters were waiting for us? That wasn't a coincidence; it was an ambush."

Varek stepped from the shadows. He was bald, and built like a wrecking ball. He was easily the oldest in the room. He'd fed in the trenches of World War I and survived every power shift since. He was their leader, and his gravelly voice cut through the room. "That's the part I don't like. The hunters. That wasn't part of the plan."

"You think Billings double-crossed us?" Syla asked, eyes sharp.

"I think," Varek said, "He handed us a map straight into a firing line."

Syla folded her arms. "So we were bait. A disposable test run."

"And now, Sebastian's not only alive, we've got Billings breathing down our necks like he's in charge." His eyes flicked to Kellin. "You brought him into this. You gave him leverage. Now he wants us to spook the scientist."

"Dr. Lee," Kellin said, eyes narrowing. "He's a geneticist. A human with a clean record. Until last week, he was just another bleeding-heart altruist. Now he's Voss's pet project."

"A pawn," Varek muttered. "Or a weapon."

Kellin slammed his hand into the metal table, leaving another dent. "So what do we do? Cower because a mayor and a lab rat might be threats? We're vampires."

"No," Syla said, stepping forward. "We remind them we bite. We go in quietly, strategically. You want to play Billings' game? Fine. We'll watch the lab. Apply pressure and stir some fear."

"And the doctor?" Kellin said with a sneer. "What's he supposed to be, leverage?"

Varek grunted. "Nah, we make him a liability. Whatever Sebastian sees in him, we sever it. Rip it out."

"Not just kill him," Syla said, her voice smooth and dangerous. "We use him. Make him afraid. Shake him until he realizes who really runs this city. If Sebastian wants something from this man, we make sure he never gets it. Kellin, we'll give you another chance to get your revenge."

Varek grinned. "A little pressure and a little blood. Maybe we pay the good doctor a visit and we get Tadgh to shadow Devereux so we can keep tabs on her."

Syla walking slowly, like a predator circling wounded prey. "Maybe it's time we apply some pressure of our own. Billings thinks he can command from both sides. Let's see how well he does when *both* sides are watching."

"And the hunters?" Kellin asked. "We kill them?"

"Eventually," Varek said. "But not just yet."

Syla smiled, dark and slow. "We let them see shadows move. We let them *feel* us. Make them wonder who's watching whom. Let them shoot at ghosts until they beg to know what's real. Let them squirm." Syla's smile returned, slow and cold. "We'll remind them there are other monsters in Los Angeles. One's not wearing suits. Ones who don't need grants to draw blood."

Kellin's fists unclenched slightly, but the fire in his chest didn't fade. "Fine, but if Sebastian makes another move against us..."

"He won't," Syla cut in, "because he thinks we're licking our wounds." She smiled. "Let him believe it."

CHAPTER 23

The streets outside smelled like oil and wet pavement. The city kept moving on without her, cars idling at lights, and strangers crossing in tight packs. As she walked, letting the noise chew in her head, she kept hearing Sebastian's voice.

"Someone's put a price on your head, Amelia. You might want to watch your back."

His voice was too calm for it to be a threat. Too casual for it to be a lie. Or maybe that was exactly the point.

I could have gone straight back and got more answers about this price on my head. I should have. Every step away from that lab felt like one more chance for whoever Sebastian was talking about to close in. And if it wasn't true? Then why tell me at all?

She was nearly there, the bar was tucked between a pawn shop and a boarded-up pharmacy. No sign, just a door the color of old pennies and a security camera that followed her as she approached. She knocked twice, waited, then once more. The lock clicked.

Inside, the air was thick with the tang of something almost coppery, teasing her nostrils. Low light bled from red-shaded lamps, while vampires from different eras spoke to each other in hush voices as they sipped their blood-filled glasses. Rubied-eyes glanced her way, but quickly averted back to their conversations. Ronan was behind the counter, polishing a glass like the cliché he enjoyed being. His smile showed just enough fang to remind you not to forget what he was.

"Well, look who wandered into my little hole in the wall." He leaned his elbows on the bar. "You're a long way from home, Amelia."

"I need information." She grabbed a stool and discreetly slid a gold coin across the bar top. They didn't speak loudly. Too many ears, even here. She told him what she'd heard that someone wanted her dead, and waited.

"You'll need to speak with the sisters," he said.

"Uggghhh, they're so weird," she reluctantly replied. "Ok fine. Are they available now?"

"Haha," he chuckled softly under his breath. "Yeah, just head back," as he nodded to a side door off the bar.

As the door swung open into a gothic chamber styled in dark opulence, gilded frames with haunting art, and velvet drapes pooled on the floor. Lit by candles on bone candelabras dripping wax, and scattered gothic trinkets filled the room. A round table sat in the center with three identical sisters, Hecate, Circe, and Lilith. All three had long, raven black hair, dressed in what looked like black lace wedding gowns with veils covering their faces. They turned, looking as though they were expecting her, with their glowing red eyes. The sisters were old vampires, and they were in the business of knowing things. They had a strange mental connection when they spoke. Each saying the next sentence in the conversation, like they all shared the same brain. She took the only open seat at the table and sat down.

"Well, well, well," each sister said in a sing-song way.

"Amelia." Hecate started.

"The lost one." Circe continued.

"What graces us with your visit?" Lilith finished.

"I was told I have a price on my head," she started.

"For information, you know our payment?" Hecate replied.

"Is a favor," Circe seconded.

"When we most need it," Lilth finished.

Ugghhh, creepy.

"Yes, I know," she replied.

"It could be true," the sisters continued.

"We have heard many voices of a price on your head."

"But it also could be Sebastian winding you up to take advantage."

"Do you know which one it is?" Amelia asked.

"I know people have been asking about you," Hecate started again.

"Some of the new ones."

The kind with deep pockets."

"Nobody's saying a name, but the bounty's high enough to make every parasite in this town take notice," Hecate finished.

"How high?" She asked.

They tilted their heads, studying her like they were measuring how much to tell.

"Enough that even some of the disciplined ones might start thinking with their wallets instead of their brains," Circe continued.

"Who would put it out?" She asked.

"If we had to guess?" Lilith started as the sisters looked at each other.

"It could be one of Sebastian's rivals."

"It could be someone you pissed off without knowing it."

"Or it could even be..." Lilth paused to look at her sisters.

They let the pause hang.

"The one who made you. Some old grudges don't die," they all spoke in unison.

A chill slid down Amelia's spine. "Why?"

"Why does a cat play with a mouse?" Hecate questioned.

Their smile was slow, deliberate. "Because it can," they all said again in unison.

Well, that wasn't annoyingly creepy, and left her with more questions than answers. She stood up, nodded to each sister and started to walk out when she heard Hecate speak.

"Remember our price, Amelia."

"Yeah, I remember," she replied reluctantly.

She left the bar with her coat pulled tight. It wasn't exactly what she wanted to hear, but it was a start. The night air was colder now, damp from a marine layer rolling in.

Halfway to the main street, the hairs on her neck prickled. Someone was behind her. Not close, but close enough. She didn't hear footsteps, just the faint shift of weight on concrete when she slowed.

Amelia glanced over her shoulder. A figure stood half in the shadows. They were tall and still. She couldn't make out the face, but the air carried something sharp and strange. A scent like cold stone after rain. It was faint but piercing enough to etch itself into memory.

Then a delivery truck roared past, and the space where they'd stood was empty.

She stayed in the pool of streetlight a few seconds longer than she needed to, scanning the dark. The scent still lingered, as if whoever it belonged to had been there a moment too long.

CHAPTER 24

The room was quiet, but not comfortable. The kind of quiet that sat too still. Reece stood at the center of the warehouse command post, arms folded. His eyes locked on the surveillance footage playing across a wall of monitors. It was the footage from the fundraiser, from street cams, from bodycams, and of Skylar's death. All of it told the same story: chaos, betrayal, tragedy, and something bigger brewing.

Cole leaned against a table, arms crossed, scowl set. "I still don't get it. The mayor was supposed to be the target, but it could've been that rich prick? Our intel was half-ass...and then they both just walked away clean?"

"It doesn't add up," Marcus muttered, loading a fresh magazine into his rifle. "Feels like someone lit the fire and watched from the crowd."

Hot Shot kicked her boots up on a nearby crate. "You're all thinking it, I'll say it, they knew more than he let on. Way more."

Reece didn't answer right away. He kept watching the screen, replaying the moment Billings nodded. Was it at the vamps, or someone else?

"I think he's connected to the vamps," Reece said finally, his voice low. "And I think it's time we stop waiting for answers."

The room went silent.

Marcus raised an eyebrow. "You mean..."

"I'm breaking into his office tonight," Reece said, pulling a black duffel from beneath the table. "I want to know what he's hiding."

Less than an hour later Reece arrived. The Mayor's office sat dark on the 19th floor of a secure municipal building, wrapped in glass and the arrogance of power. Security was thin, one half-asleep guard in the lobby. The motion sensors were easy to reroute.

Reece moved like a shadow, his black combat gear tight to his frame. He disabled the alarm with a custom scrambler and picked the lock in under thirty seconds.

The door opened into a cathedral of politics, an oversized desk, a cityscape view, and shelves stacked with law books no one had read in years. Reece ignored all of it. Using his blade, he went for the drawers first; the top held nothing but city permits and donor lists. The second, bingo! A cheap, unregistered burner phone with only one number stored. Outgoing. Reece pulled a wireless duplicator from his pocket, connected it to the phone, and copied the data. He tucked the burner back into the drawer when he heard it, voices down the hall.

"Shit," he whispered.

He moved fast, slipping behind the large desk and ducking low. Footsteps grew louder. Keys jingled. It was the janitorial staff. Laughing and too close. Reece waited, his breath still, until the voices passed the door. He stood, his heart steady, and with one last glance at the untouched desk, he vanished, silent as smoke.

Back at the safehouse, the team gathered around the table, the duplicator plugged into the console, downloading the data. Hot Shot whistled. "That's it? One number. That's not sketchy at all."

"Can we trace it?" Cole asked, leaning in.

"I can try," Hot Shot said, already working. "But if this thing was talking to someone important... they're gonna have good cloaking."

Reece watched the data transfer scroll across the laptop. "We don't need to call it. Not yet."

Marcus raised an eyebrow. "Then what do we do?"

Reece's voice was steel. "We find out who owns that number. Who's on the other end. If the mayor was talking to vamps, if *he* lit that match, we're not waiting for the next one to go off."

The team nodded. No more shadows and no more questions. This time, they wouldn't wait in the dark. They'd be the ones drawing blood.

CHAPTER 25

She wasn't going to see him. Not at first. That was the plan, anyway. But plans tend to bend when Sebastian's involved. Especially when he's playing his favorite game, the puppeteer.

She told herself she was going to the lab to follow up on the "so-called" bounty on her head and to keep tabs on what Sebastian was hiding behind all that glass and charm. The laboratory felt colder than she remembered.

She stepped through the sliding glass doors, the sleek hum of security scanners brushing across her body like a whisper. The Voss Research Facility gleamed with technological arrogance, polished floors, cold chrome, and spotless glass meant to impress and intimidate. She hated how sterile it felt.

Amelia's boots clicked softly against the floor as she walked. Her reflection stared back at her in the glass, but the second the receptionist smiled at her, she knew exactly what this was.

"Oh, Miss Devereux," she chirped, already standing from her sleek desk. "Mr. Voss said you might drop by. Dr. Lee is just finishing an experiment, and he'd love to see you."

Of course he would. She offered a polite smile, the kind that looked sweet, but meant *I see what you're doing and I'm not impressed,* then followed her through the sprawling hall of labs. They finally arrived at the last lab door. With a quick palm scan on the biometric scanner, the sliding door opened to a large laboratory.

Andrew wasn't alone; another lab tech looked up from one of the smaller workstations when she stepped in. He definitely looked like he hadn't left the lab in days.

"Excuse me, miss. I'll leave you two alone," as he slunk out of the room. There was a way he looked at her, it didn't sit right, but she was there for one thing.

That's when she saw him.

His coat was slung over the back of a chair, and he was hunched over a centrifuge, scribbling notes with the kind of distracted intensity that told her he hadn't eaten in hours. His brow was furrowed, his glasses slipping down his nose, and his hair slightly messier than last time. He looked...annoyingly endearing.

He looked up and blinked at her, and then smiled. It wasn't the kind of smile you practice in front of a mirror. It was soft and genuine.

"Hey," he said, standing a little too quickly. "I wasn't expecting...Well, I hoped...wait, let me start over. Hi."

She tilted her head, pretending to scrutinize the room. "So this is where the magic happens. Very clean. Very...ethically ambiguous."

He laughed, rubbing the back of his neck. "Yeah, well, I try to keep the human experimentation to a minimum. At least until after lunch."

"Good. I only came for the sandwiches."

He relaxed a bit, that smile still hanging around his mouth like it had nowhere better to be. She hated how much she liked it.

"I see you haven't been sleeping like your assistant. Who was that guy? He kinda gave me weird vibes." she said, arms folded.

He looked up, startled for a second. Then a smile bloomed. It was honest and unfiltered.

"Oh, that's Elis. He *is* a bit odd, but he's been very helpful. Anyway, you look...great."

She lifted an eyebrow. "Glowing review, Doctor."

Andrew chuckled. "Sorry, it's just..." He hesitated. "I still don't really understand what happened that night. But...I keep thinking about it. About you. What you did."

She arched a brow. "Saving your life or vanishing in dramatic fashion?"

"Both."

There was a beat of silence. It was heavy and charged.

"Yeah, I do that sometimes. You know. Dramatic exits. It keeps the mystery alive."

"But are you okay?" he asked.

It caught her off guard, how sincerely he asked. She tilted her head. "Fine enough. You?"

"Fine." He hesitated. "But I've been thinking about you. Wondering if you were alright. You saved my life."

She leaned on a counter, eyes scanning the machines. "And here I thought you only had eyes for petri dishes."

"They're not nearly as interesting."

She smirked, then looked away. Her chest felt tighter than she expected.

They moved through the lab together. He showed her some of his research, genetic pathways, immune responses, and cellular repair experiments. She understood enough to ask the right questions and enough to see the brilliance behind the rambling. His passion was magnetic and honest. The kind of truth that was hard to find in her world.

She found myself smiling more than she meant to. She had to change the subject before it got the better of her.

"So this is where Sebastian stashes all his brilliance?"

Andrew chuckled. "He's been...supportive. Very hands-off, surprisingly. He just wants me to solve his condition. Said something about extreme light sensitivity."

"Hmm. What a convenient medical mystery."

He looked at her. "You don't trust him."

She looked back. "Do you?"

That gave him pause. The silence stretched.

Then she stepped closer. Inches from him now. Her voice softer. "You really believe you can cure the world?"

"I want to try," he said, voice low. "Because someone has to."

That was it. That flicker in his eyes. That old, hopeless, beautiful kind of faith.

She should've turned away. Should've said something sharp and sarcastic to kill the moment. But instead, she moved closer. Because she wanted to know what it felt like to be wanted without fear.

She kissed him.

The kiss was unexpected. Gentle. No fireworks or swelling orchestra. Just soft lips, warm breath, and the quiet crack of something inside shifting. It wasn't planned. It wasn't slow. It was instinct. Her hand against his chest. His breath catching, and she felt it, sharp and real. She hadn't let anyone that close in a very, very long time.

When they finally broke apart, he was grinning. She rolled her eyes to keep from smiling back.

"Don't get used to it," she mused.

"Too late."

Before he could say anything else, one of the lab techs slid into the room. "Dr. Lee, the results from the CRISPR trial just came in. You'll want to see this."

Andrew's face lit up. "This could be it," he said to her, almost breathless. "Give me five minutes?"

She nodded. He reached for her hand again, then stopped himself and left with the tech.

As she watched him go, that old ache settled in her chest, the one she'd buried under centuries of cynicism and blood. Hope, she hated it, but she wanted more.

From a security feed, Sebastian watched, lips curved in quiet satisfaction. The next piece was in play.

Over the next few weeks, she found herself returning to the lab more than searching for clues about the vampires out to kill her. Not for Sebastian. Not even for the bounty the sisters claimed loomed over her head. It was Andrew. They talked. They laughed. They shared secrets in quiet corners, and every time she told herself it was the last time, something about him, his sincerity, his brilliance, the way he *saw* people dragged her back in. She was falling, and that scared her.

It was time to step back. To catch my breath before I fell too hard, too fast. Before hope made me reckless.

CHAPTER 26

The interior of the safehouse was quiet but charged with a low hum of tension. Reece sat at the metal table staring at the screen with the only number from the mayor's burner phone. The room was dim, lit only by a single desk lamp, casting long shadows across the walls. His team gathered in a loose half-circle, each of them armed, alert, and visibly itching for answers.

Cole leaned against the far wall with his arms crossed. "So you really broke into the mayor's damn office and just got this *one* number?"

Reece didn't answer right away. He stared at the screen, his jaw tight.

Marcus paced near the windows. "What kind of politician only keeps one contact in a burner? Feels like a message."

"Or a threat," Hot Shot added from her seat across from Reece. She had her tablet synced to trace any outgoing ping if Reece decided to make the call using the number.

"This is what we've got. Agent Smith tipped us off about a paranormal assassination attempt on the mayor, but we got more questions now about the mayor and how is this rich guy involved? Did the mayor know something was coming, or was he staging it?"

Cole pushed off the wall. "He knew, man. Come on. That wasn't some rando protest gone sideways. That was a full-on vampire hit squad, and we got played."

"We don't know who sent them," Reece countered. "We know the mayor is shady, hell, he *is* a politician, but if he was just trying to survive in a world full of bloodsuckers, maybe he's trying to keep the balance, or maybe he's just covering his own ass."

"Or maybe he's feeding both sides and betting on the winner," Hot Shot said dryly.

That got a grim chuckle from Marcus. "Classic Billings move."

Reece's thoughts churned as he turned his phone over in his hand. *Why just one number?* Whoever was on the other end had to matter, and if Billings had been in contact with someone tied to the vampires, that changed everything.

He pulled up his console and dialed the city clerk again, "Time's up. What did you find out?"

"Nothing suspicious other than numerous calls from that Voss guy, but that doesn't seem abnormal. He's been funding the Mayor's campaigns since he was in city council."

"That's it? What about emails or anything we can go on?"

"Well, he does have a secondary off-the-books office he sometimes goes to. That could have more intel for you."

"Okay, give me the address."

Reece hung up.

He looked back at the number on the screen, quickly entered it on his phone, and hit the call button. Looking quickly over at Hot Shot, and nodded as she started her tracing program.

The line clicked.

There was no voice at first, just breathing.

Then, "What now Billings? You got another tip or leading us to the slaughter?"

The voice was smooth, male, and dripping with casual confidence; it was almost familiar.

Reece's eyes narrowed. "Who is this?"

The voice laughed, low and derisive. "Ah, the mice came out to play. I think the better question is, how much do you know about your mayor?"

The team tensed. Marcus moved to the doorway, watching the

perimeter. Hot Shot twisted her hand in the air, signaling Reece to keep talking.

"We were told there might be an attack on him," Reece said. "Didn't say who. Didn't say why. What's your connection?"

"Oh, he's good. Told you just enough to keep your conscience clear and your guns ready. That's what makes him dangerous. You think you're protecting people. He's protecting himself."

"Who's Billings working for?"

"He's working with *whoever* keeps him on top. He's not loyal. He's not brave. He's a parasite in a custom-tailored suit, but you already knew that."

Reece's stomach twisted.

"And what about you?" Reece asked.

"I'm trying to see who bleeds first. You're poking around the edge of a war, soldier. You don't even know the battlefield."

Click.

The line went dead.

Cole muttered, "What the hell was that?"

"Misdirection," Reece replied. "He knows we're looking deeper now."

Marcus frowned. "You think it was one of the vamps?"

Reece shook his head slowly. "Not sure, it could be the vamps or someone in Billing's inner circle. The guy on the phone...he had his own play in motion."

Hot Shot's fingers flew across her keyboard. "The number rerouted through five cell towers, but the call was definitely from within the city."

Cole stepped closer. "So now what?"

Reece stared at the burner. "Now we find out if Billings is a middleman or a mastermind, and we start by figuring out who else he's talking to because the vampires are organizing, and someone's giving them intel."

Reece exhaled through his nose. "I think the mayor is a puppet. I want to know who's pulling the strings."

"So what?" Marcus asked. "We tap his phones? Interrogate his staff?"

Reece shook his head. "Not yet. We go in quietly. Break into the mayor's secondary office."

Cole whistled low. "You're getting bold."

"We're past bold," Reece said. "We're being played. I want to know who's got us on the board."

Silence fell over the room. Not of disagreement, but of focus. Of the mission.

Hot Shot closed her laptop with a snap. "I'll prep the drones. I want eyes on that building from every angle."

Marcus checked his gear. "We go in when?"

Reece looked down at his phone one last time, the number still glowing faintly on the small screen.

"Tonight."

But inside, his gut wouldn't settle.

Across town, a soft ping echoed in the dark office of Mayor Walter Billings. A security alert flashed on his screen. Unauthorized access to encrypted phone records and location logs. Someone was digging. He unlocked the second drawer to his desk and immediately knew the phone had been tampered with. He always made it a point to position the phone a specific way, and it was clearly moved.

He didn't need to guess who. He stood up and walked across the room. Behind a set of legal books on the bookcase, he pulled out another burner phone, thumb hovering over a single number. Then he pressed *call*.

"You still want that revenge?" he said. "I've got just the target."

CHAPTER 27

The night air downtown was thick with smog and tension. Reece crouched in the alley behind the mayor's unlisted office, a sleek glass box with no official records and no visible security.

Hot Shot's voice buzzed through the comms. "Drone coverage is up. There are four exits and one freight bay. Roof access locked. No signs of movement yet."

They moved like ghosts, slipping through the rear access door that Hot Shot had overridden the security panel ten minutes earlier. The corridor inside was sterile, cold with concrete walls, industrial lighting, and not a single camera in sight.

Reece looked over at this team and gave a nod. "Sweep the room. Find anything that proves the mayor's in bed with vamps or worse. No mistakes."

Marcus adjusted the strap of his heavy rifle. "You think we'll find anything?"

"We don't need much," Reece murmured. "A scrap of correspondence. A contact list or another burner. Something that connects him to the hit at the fundraiser."

Reece's boots barely made a sound as they swept through the first floor, clearing the main hallway and adjoining offices. The place was too clean, scrubbed down like it had something to hide.

"File cabinets are empty," Marcus muttered. "Even the trash cans are spotless."

"That's never a good sign," Hot Shot whispered from the other room.

Cole let out a low snort. "You think it's a trap?"

Reece glanced over. "That's supposed to be your way of saying you're nervous?"

"That's my way of saying I don't trust anyone anymore. Especially politicians who suddenly know about vampire attacks."

"Upstairs," Reece ordered. "Private elevator to the third floor. That's where the real office is."

They ascended in silence. As the elevator doors opened, the temperature dropped. Reece felt it first, an instinctive chill crawling up his spine.

"Something's wrong," he said, raising his weapon. "Eyes up."

Exit signs dimly lit the hallway, lined with multiple office doors. At the end stood a double-doored office with frosted glass windows. Reece started to approach slowly, Cole covering the rear. Hot Shot flanked the left wall. Marcus covered the right. Then the power went out. A subtle hiss cut through the dark, low like a serpent slithering by.

The hallway exploded with motion. Shadows erupted. Figures surged from side doors, six, maybe more. Fangs gleaming. Eyes glowing red.

"Contact! Two o'clock!" Hot Shot barked.

"Vamps!" Marcus shouted.

Gunfire erupted, flashes of muzzle light painting the corridor in harsh strobes. Reece fired two rounds into the chest of the nearest vampire, but it kept coming, snarling through the pain. Cole tackled it to the ground and jammed a silver stake through its ribs, twisting hard. The creature convulsed, then collapsed into ash.

"Fall back!" Reece ordered. "Regroup!"

They pushed toward the stairwell, fighting every step. Marcus dropped one with a shotgun blast to the face, but another leapt from above, knocking him to the ground.

"Get it off me!" Marcus roared.

Hot Shot spun and fired three rounds straight into the attacker's back. Silver-laced bullets. The vampire shrieked and burst into ash, coating Marcus in a fine layer of death.

Cole slammed the stairwell door open. "Go! Go!"

They tumbled down the stairs two at a time, but more shadows followed. A hand caught Reece by the collar and yanked him into the wall. He spun, blade flashing, cutting deep into the vampire's throat. The creature howled, but Reece didn't stop; he drove the blade upward through its jaw until the thing went limp and slumped to the ground.

They hit the first floor. The back exit was blocked by two more vampires waiting, one crouched on the wall like a spider.

"They knew we were coming," Hot Shot growled.

"Someone tipped them off," Reece hissed, heart pounding.

Marcus threw a flashbang. The explosion rocked the corridor, buying them seconds.

BANG! BANG! BANG! BANG! Bullets rang out as Cole and Marcus dropped the two vampires through the chest at the exit, turning them instantly to ash.

Reece kicked the door hard enough to break the latch, and they spilled into the alley.

They didn't stop running until they reached the van five blocks away, barely keeping the vampires at bay. Then they gunned it back to the safehouse.

The safehouse reeked of blood, smoke, and defeat. Marcus slammed the heavy metal door behind him, locking three bolts in quick succession. The team staggered in, battered and bruised, moving like beaten elephants in combat gear. Their faces told the story. Split lips, shallow cuts, bloodied knuckles, and a dull haze of adrenaline still hanging over their heads.

Reece ripped off his vest and dropped it onto the concrete floor. His shirt clung to his back with sweat and blood. He went straight to the small steel sink in the corner and ran cold water over his hands, staring blankly at the red swirling down the drain.

"Someone set us up," Cole spat. "We're hunting ghosts, and someone's feeding them our trail."

"Billings?" Hot Shot asked. "How'd he know we'd go to his private office?"

Reece didn't answer right away. His mind was still back in that dark hallway, in the flicker of red eyes and cold precision of the ambush.

"They were waiting," he finally said. "They didn't just know we were coming; they were expecting us."

"Who would do that?" Marcus asked. "Vampires don't coordinate like that unless someone's pulling strings."

Reece's jaw tightened. "Then it's time we start cutting strings. One by one."

But in the pit of his stomach, that same unease churned deeper. One question burned through the haze.

Whose side is Billings really on?

CHAPTER 28

"That was a goddamn ambush," Cole growled.

No one disagreed. Hot Shot hunched over the table, fingers trembling as she tapped her tablet. "Drones were jammed. We had clean eyes until the breach, then static. It was a complete blackout."

"They were waiting for us," Marcus said, pacing like a caged animal. "There's no way they just *happened* to be inside that building."

Cole turned to Reece. "You think we were followed?"

"No," Reece said, too quickly.

"Then explain it," Cole snapped, stepping forward. "Because I nearly got my throat ripped out tonight. Hot Shot almost got pinned, and Marcus took a fucking chunk of concrete to the ribs. Someone sold us out."

Reece shut off the water and turned, gripping the edge of the sink. "We've been careful. No leaks. The op was clean."

"Bullshit," Cole spat. "That office location, that fundraiser. You don't think it's a little convenient that whatever the mayor's involved with, so are the vamps?"

Hot Shot looked up. "He might have known about the vampires. That doesn't mean he's working with them."

"And if he's not?" Marcus asked. "Then who is? Because someone knew we were coming."

Reece's jaw clenched. He felt the pressure building in his temples, a slow burn of frustration he couldn't shake. The weight of command, of being wrong, pressed against his chest like a vice.

"We're all still alive," he said finally. "We adapt. We double-check every lead from now on. No more relying on anything without verification."

Cole let out a sharp laugh. "That's your big plan? Adapt? We almost died, Reece. You want to be cautious? Great. But caution doesn't help when the enemy's already inside the wire."

Hot Shot pulled her hands through her hair. "What if the mayor was alerted when you got that intel about him?"

"That would've been just long enough to set a trap," Marcus said quietly.

Reece moved back to the center of the room. "We've got two problems," he said. "A security breach and a vampire network that's clearly more organized than we thought."

Cole folded his arms. "Three problems. We've got a leader who keeps charging into the fire and calling it strategy."

Reece stared at him. The room fell silent.

Hot Shot looked between them, then stood. "Cool it. Both of you. We're not doing this. Not when we're bleeding."

Marcus grunted in agreement. "Tensions are high. Let's not splinter now."

Reece exhaled through his nose. His instincts told him Cole was lashing out because he was scared and still grieving Skylar's death. So was Reece, but he couldn't show it. Not yet.

"I don't have all the answers," Reece said finally. "But I'm going to find them. I don't care how deep I have to dig."

Hot Shot glanced down at the table, her voice lower. "Whoever was on the other end of that call...they knew too much about us. This is deeper than we thought."

Reece nodded. "And we're going deeper. No more favors and no more handouts. From here on out, we hit back."

There was a silence, a beat of mutual understanding, even if the unity felt fractured.

Then Marcus, standing by the gear bench, froze. He reached

down and picked up a small black device that had been tucked under one of the rifle cases.

"What the hell is this?" he muttered.

Reece stepped forward, his eyes narrowing.

It was a listening device. Tiny. Sophisticated. Embedded deep enough to have gone unnoticed for days, maybe even weeks.

Everyone stared.

Cole looked at Reece. "Still think we're not being watched?"

Reece said nothing because now, even he wasn't sure who to trust.

CHAPTER 29

Deep beneath Los Angeles, in the abandoned subway veins, the Reign gathered. Feral eyes gleamed in the half-dark as the low murmurs of dissent echoed through the tunnel chamber.

They were thinning. Fewer than before. Varek stood at the center, the flicker of a lone lantern casting long shadows against his angular, hollow-cheeked face. He didn't need to raise his voice; his presence did the work. Around him, his followers stood leaner, hungrier, more alert than they'd been weeks ago.

"Too many of us are ash," he said coldly. "Hunted, staked, and left to rot in the gutters by Sebastian's loyalists or those damn humans with silver bullets and earpieces."

He let the silence thicken.

"We've lost more than we gained. We've bled in alleys, sewers, and parking lots. And every time, the city just keeps turning."

Syla paced near the back, hands behind her back, jaw tight. "If we want to win, we need numbers. Now."

"We *will* get them," Varek said, pointing at the red chalk map scrawled across the crumbling concrete wall. Skid Row was circled. Not once, but several times with bold and erratic strokes.

"They're invisible to the city. No IDs. No family and no cameras. They are the perfect recruits."

A low growl rippled through the group.

"Turn the forgotten," Varek continued. "Offer protection.

Offer them purpose. Offer a new life. Turn one and they'll bring five more. We control the streets, we control the noise. Then we come back out of the dark."

Edin, A young female vampire, stepped forward. "What about Amelia Devereux? She's been patrolling those streets. Every time we move, she smells it before we finish the job."

She's not just a problem," Syla said. "She's a ghost in their streets. Four of ours are dead, and no one even saw her coming.

Varek's eyes narrowed. "She's a disruption because we don't know her limits yet. We know her reputation. Her power, but not her weaknesses."

He stepped closer to the map, dragging a long fingernail down from Skid Row to a circle marked Lee.

Out of the shadows, Tadgh spoke up, "She has a soft spot for the doctor. We saw it at the fundraiser. The way she looked at him, and we have it from our plant on the inside that they've been cozying up. Not sure to what extent yet, but it's definitely something."

"He's also Sebastian's pet now," Syla said darkly.

"Which makes him leverage," Varek replied. "But if we move on him too soon, she'll come for us. We need to separate them and turn her against Sebastian. Give the homeless something to fear and for her, someone to blame. While she's chasing ghosts in Skid Row, we move in on the doctor."

"And when she's distracted?" Edin asked.

"Then we strike," Varek said. "We turn the streets against her. We find the cracks in her. And when she realizes too late that she's been outmaneuvered, the doctor will already be ours or dead."

Murmurs rippled through the group again. Not of fear this time, but anticipation. He faced them once more.

"Recruitment starts tonight. No killing unless you have to. Convert and control. Spread fear where she once spread hope. Every soul she's saved is now a weapon we turn on her."

"And if they resist?" Tadgh asked.

Varek's eyes flared red. "Then we burn her world down, slow

and mercilessly. Until she begs and finds out that we don't forgive or forget."

Later that night, on the corner of San Pedro and 6th, the wind stirred the filth along cracked sidewalks. Skid Row didn't sleep. It watched. Quiet and waiting.

Tadgh stepped out of the shadows, his hood drawn low. Beside him, Edin moved like smoke, her pale face half covered by a black scarf. Neither spoke.

Ahead, sat a young man sheltered by a cardboard box underneath a flickering streetlamp. In his early twenties. He was gaunt and filthy. Wrapped in a torn blanket that didn't quite cover his legs. His arms were dotted with old track scars. He was one of the forgotten. Exactly the kind Varek wanted.

He tensed as they approached. "I don't want trouble."

From the shadows, other homeless faces turned and watched. Listening.

Tadgh crouched in front of the boy, voice low and calm. "Neither do I. What's your name?"

The kid blinked. "Luis."

"You hungry?"

Luis nodded. His stomach answered for him.

Edin pulled a foil-wrapped burrito from her coat and handed it over. "It's still warm."

Luis snatched it with both hands. "Why?"

Tadgh smiled. It wasn't a warm or cold smile, just steady. "Because someone once helped us, too. Sebastian Voss. Maybe you've heard of him."

He said it louder than he had to and just enough for the nearby tents to catch the name.

Luis froze, chewing. "Voss? The guy on the news? The rich one?"

Tadgh nodded slowly. "That's him. But he doesn't just throw money at problems. He sees people. Even down here."

Edin knelt beside Luis. Her voice was softer, more intimate. "He saw us. Now we're paying it forward."

Luis looked down. "My friend was beaten to death two weeks

ago. Cops said it was an OD. It wasn't." His voice cracked. "I saw what they did."

Tadgh met his eyes. "You're not crazy. And you're not alone."

Luis swallowed hard, burrito forgotten in his hand. "You believe me?"

"We do," Tadgh said. "And so would Voss."

Another pause. Just long enough for the name to settle again.

"He wants to help people like you. People nobody else sees."

Luis squinted at him. "This some kind of shelter?"

Tadgh chuckled. "Not a shelter. A new start. No more running. No more fear."

Edin added, just above a whisper, "No more being prey."

Luis stared, the burrito cooling in his grip. "So what do I do?"

Tadgh stood. His eyes caught the streetlight just enough to glow faintly red. "You say yes."

Luis's breath hitched. "To what?"

"To change your life," Tadgh said. "Forever."

CHAPTER 30

The soft hum of machinery was the only sound as Dr. Andrew Lee adjusted the microscope. His eyes burned from hours of staring through the lenses, but he barely noticed. On the monitor beside him, genetic sequences scrolled in dense lines of data, CRISPR patterns, protein markers, enzyme interactions slowly forming a puzzle that he was, for the first time in months, beginning to solve.

He tapped a few keys, overlaying his original notes from his cancer gene reversal project over the blood sample he'd pulled from Sebastian just days ago. He still wasn't sure how to classify Sebastian's condition. Sebastian claimed it mimicked a rare photo-dermatosis, Polymorphous Light Eruption, but it behaved more like a virus. Dormant until exposed to UV light. It was aggressive and reactive.

Andrew's serum was starting to suppress the reaction. At least in controlled trials. If it held, he might be a month, maybe just a few weeks away from a breakthrough.

He sat back in his chair and rubbed his temples, the tension in his shoulders slowly sinking into exhaustion, and yet, he couldn't shake the unease.

This lab, Sebastian's lab, was unlike any other he'd ever worked in. Fully automated systems, access to cutting-edge equipment, AI-enhanced diagnostics, and a staff of specialists that never tired, never left, and looked like they'd been selected from a modeling agency, not a research team.

They moved like a synchronized machine, polite, soft-spoken, and eerily perfect. Unnaturally perfect.

Andrew sipped from the coffee cup he'd been nursing for three hours, but it had long gone cold. He stood and stretched, glancing out the tall reinforced window that looked out over the city. It was night again. It was always night.

He checked his phone.

Amelia: *Midnight ramen? I know a place.*

He smiled. She always knew when to pull him away before he burned himself out. Their late-night meetups had become a ritual. Ramen, tacos, sushi, or walks through moonlit plazas and empty sidewalks when the rest of L.A. was asleep. Her laugh, dry and biting. Her stories, just vague enough to leave him wondering, and her eyes, which were unreadable golden brown, watched him like she already knew what he'd ask next.

They had kissed once. Just once. It had caught both of them off guard; it was quick, magnetic, and over before either could name it. She'd smiled coyly and changed the subject. He hadn't pushed.

But something lingered. Not just between them, but around her. It was gravity. A mystery.

Andrew walked to the storage unit and checked his latest cultures, carefully tagging the data for morning review. As he closed the cabinet, he caught his reflection in the glass panel opposite him and paused.

Elis was behind him, standing perfectly still. Andrew turned.

The man smiled without blinking. "Need anything, Dr. Lee?"

"No, just wrapping up."

Elis nodded and walked away...but his steps made no sound. Not even the soft scuff of shoes on tile.

Andrew's stomach tightened. The staff was always just there. Always ready and always...watching.

As he collected his notes, Amelia's warning echoed in his head.

"Not everything is what it seems. Be careful..."

At the time, he thought it was her usual sharp tongue, some private vendetta, or a distaste for the ultra-rich. But now?

Now he wasn't so sure.

Even the light cycle in the lab had been skewed. He hadn't seen daylight in three days. Meetings with Sebastian always happened after dark. Lab updates were scheduled at midnight. His meals came in just after sunset. He'd laughed about becoming a full-on nocturnal scientist, but the joke no longer felt funny.

He checked the time again. It was 11:48 PM.

Grabbing his coat, he stepped into the corridor, the echo of his footsteps the only sound as the sterile lights hummed overhead. Down the hall, two lab techs turned a corner and vanished, their silhouettes sharp against the glass walls.

He frowned. One of them cast a demonic face reflected in the mirror panel window.

He blinked and looked again.

Nothing.

"Too much coffee," he muttered.

Still, a chill crawled up his spine. As he walked toward the elevator, his phone buzzed again.

Amelia: *Booth by the window. I ordered for both of us. If you're late, I'm eating your dumplings.*

He smiled again, despite the tension. God, he needed her sarcasm right now.

As the elevator doors closed and he descended from the pristine lab built like a glass cathedral, the image of the lab tech's reflection, burned into his mind.

Something was wrong in this place, and if Amelia was right, Sebastian wasn't just the eccentric billionaire he pretended to be.

CHAPTER 31

The ramen shop was dimly lit, wedged between a shuttered bookstore and a flickering nail salon. Neon kanji buzzed above the door. Inside, the booths were old, lacquered black, and the smell of broth clung to the walls. It was perfect.

Amelia slid into the booth by the window, one leg crossed over the other, her dark hair falling like silk down the back of her leather jacket. She was early. She always was. It gave her time to scope out the exits, the clientele, and the emotional vibe of the room. A habit she never really broke, especially now.

She glanced at her phone. Andrew was only five minutes late. Technically still within the margin of punctuality, but she made a note to tease him about it anyway.

Then the door chimed.

He entered with his usual half-distracted, half-focused gait, the kind of movement that said his brain was still back in the lab while his body was catching up. A wool coat over a rumpled button-up, sleeves rolled, and those earnest eyes that always looked like they were trying to solve the world's problems.

He spotted her and smiled. It wasn't a big smile, but it was the kind that made her forget the years between heartbeats.

"Twelve minutes," she said as he slid into the booth across from her.

He blinked. "Only five."

"I operate on R&B time," she smirked. "Always on time," she sang.

Andrew laughed, low and genuine. "Wow, bringing back a classic Ja Rule song this late?"

"Just reminding you of a 2001 banger," she said, picking up her chopsticks. "But it's adorable that you know the reference."

He raised an eyebrow. "You really know your hits, don't ya?"

"Always," she said with a wink, "...on time," as they sang it together. Her heart filled.

Their ramen arrived, steaming and fragrant. The broth shimmered under the light, and she took a long breath in before diving in. They ate for a few moments in silence, the comfortable kind. The kind that hinted at intimacy without pressure.

Andrew was the first to speak again.

"So, how are things downtown? You haven't mentioned it in a while."

She wiped her mouth with a napkin. "Still messy. Still raw, but still worth it. A few people went missing last week, so I'm asking around. Seeing if anyone saw anything. Hearing some things that don't make sense, yet."

His expression darkened. "That's awful."

"It is, but you know how it goes. The world doesn't stop chewing people up. I'm just trying to keep a few from getting swallowed whole."

He looked down at his bowl, then back up. "I feel like I should be spending more time at the shelter myself."

She waved him off. "You're busy solving science. I get it, and I'm sure the people at the shelter understand."

"Actually," he leaned forward, excitement flickering in his eyes, "the donation from Sebastian helped a lot. I hired a full-time team to manage operations. Additional social workers, med staff, and volunteers. It's taken a huge weight off; it practically runs itself at this point. I can finally focus on my work."

"The gene project?"

He nodded, stirring his noodles absently. "Among other

things. I'm close to something...really close. I don't want to jinx it, but it's big."

She tilted her head. "You gonna make me guess or just bask in the mystery?"

"Basking," he said with a grin.

"Ugh," she groaned theatrically. "Fine. Be cryptic. I'll just assume you're cloning dinosaurs, Dr. Wu."

"Much more ethical. And less teeth. Wow, another obscure reference, but I know that too, the doctor in the original Jurassic Park."

"Haha, you are good, maybe a future Jeopardy contestant once you finish your research?" she joked.

He laughed again, then softened. "You've been good for me, you know. You pull me out of my own head."

Her teasing edge dimmed just a little. "You've been good for me, too. It's been a while since... well, since I gave a damn."

They continued to laugh and talk over the last of their ramen. She hasn't felt this unguarded in so long; it scared her, and that told her it was real.

While they walked back towards the lab, silence fell again, charged this time. His eyes were on hers, and she didn't look away.

He reached, fingers brushing hers.

"Amelia."

She didn't pull back.

"Yeah?"

"I want to take you out. A real date. Not just noodles and late-night wandering."

She smirked, but her voice came out softer than expected. "You sure you can handle that much daylight? I thought you were only free at night?"

"Then we'll do dinner," he said. "Or midnight breakfast. Just something where it's not always about a break from the lab. Just you and me."

She swallowed, suddenly unsure. "You keep saying things like that, I'm gonna start swooning."

"Good. I want you to."

The moment stretched. Then he grabbed her by the waist and pulled her in close, without asking, and kissed her.

Not a soft, tentative kiss. A real one. Deep, hungry, honest, and passionate, like the kind you see at the end of a romance movie.

She responded before she even knew she had. Her hand found his collar and pulled him in closer. The taste of him, the smell of him, she could barely remember the last time a kiss had felt this... alive.

When they finally broke apart, breathless, she blinked up at him. "Okay," she whispered. "Yeah. A date."

He smiled, flushed and perfect. "Soon."

He turned and headed towards the building, looking back one more time at the door.

"I can't wait to see you again."

She watched him until he disappeared behind the closing doors. Her heart pounded and her hands trembled. Her lips still tingled. It had been centuries since she felt like this, and that terrified her. She stood, collected herself, and walked out into the alley. The city hummed around her.

"Okay, Devereux," she whispered. "Get your shit together."

She needed air. A distraction. Something familiar.

Get sandwiches and head down to Skid Row, she thought. *Keep investigating the missing. Get real.*

She moved through the streets like a shadow, heart still soaring, a small smile playing at her lips, but behind it all, something inside her whispered.

Don't let it matter too much; it's just a crush.

And still...She couldn't wait to see him again.

What she didn't see were the two sets of eyes glowing faintly in the dark across the street. Tadhg and Edin had been following her for weeks. Memorizing her patterns. Her habits. Waiting for a weakness.

Tonight, they found one.

CHAPTER 32

Skid Row hadn't changed. Still clinging to the edge of the city like an unwanted memory, buzzing with quiet suffering and the scrape of shopping carts.

She stepped out of the alley and into the familiar din. Sirens in the distance. People arguing across tents. The hiss of a propane stove catching flame, but underneath it all, there was something else, something quieter.

The tension was palpable; people saw her and nodded. Some smiled. A few waved like she was some kind of patron saint of lost causes.

I didn't deserve that, and I wasn't here to save anyone. I didn't come with miracles, just sandwiches and bandages.

She approached Lisa first. She sat on her usual milk crate, arms wrapped around herself like she could keep the world out if she just squeezed tight enough. Her hair was pulled back into a knot, her face tighter than usual.

"Hey, Lisa," she said, kneeling beside her. "Peanut still MIA?"

She shook her head, then hesitated. "He's not the only one missing."

She blinked. "What do you mean? Have there been more?"

Lisa leaned in, her voice lowering like she thought the shadows might be listening. "Three more, two men and a woman. All the young ones, I think. They used to crash by the 7th Street overpass.

All gone. Nobody's seen them in over a week. Everyone keeps bringing up the rich guy...Ross or Voss? Something like that. The other night, a guy dropped a card on the ground. At first, I thought it was money, so I waited til he walked away to pick it up. Let me find it," while she shuffled through her things.

"You mean Sebastian Voss?"

"Yeah, I think that's what I heard. Oh, here it is," as she handed it over.

"You don't think they might've just moved on," she said, even though she didn't believe it, and took a closer look at the card.

Her spine stiffened. On the front of the card was VE embossed in gold letters, and blank on the back. She recognized the initials.

Voss Enterprises

Lisa shook her head. "No. They left their stuff. Blankets, bags. And..." She stopped herself.

"What?"

"I saw something. A couple of nights ago. I was walking to look for food behind the deli, and I saw someone standing in the alley. Just standing there. Tall. Still. Watching"

"Watching who?"

"Everyone," she whispered. "He looked right at me. He was real weird, his skin was so pale, and just stared. Manny was with me, and he took a picture of him with his phone. Then he just... disappeared. Like he folded into the wall. We didn't believe it at first, and we had to look at the photo. He was definitely a creep."

She didn't respond right away because she'd seen vampires do just that. "Ok, I'll ask Manny about the photo."

She stood slowly. "Thanks, Lisa. If anyone else goes missing, you find a way to get word to me, okay?"

Lisa nodded. "They're scared, Amelia. Something's changing."

No shit.

She moved through the encampments, stopping at every familiar face until she found them. Manny, George, and Ruthie, and asked the same questions.

"Anyone missing? Anything strange?"

The stories were all the same, glimpses of tall figures in hoods, glowing eyes caught in the corner of someone's vision. Whispers. Silence where there should've been noise and Voss' name...again.

"Manny, I heard you actually got a photo of one of them? Do you still have it?" Amelia asked.

"Yeah, let me see...oh yeah, here it is."

As she pinched the screen to get a better view, there he was. It was that strange lab tech working with Andrew...Elis.

"Thanks, guys. If you see anything else, I'll be back soon. We'll get this figured out. No one's gonna scare my people." Amelia smiled reassuringly. It seemed to put them a little more at ease. She needed to see how Sebastian was involved in all this, and why would he send a lab tech down here?

You better not be turning the homeless Sebastian, or I'll tear down your whole empire.

Across town, nestled deep within Sebastian's top-floor office building. Andrew Lee, in his lab, sat alone perched on the edge of a chrome stool as he peered into the glowing readout of his latest cell experiment. The sleek, surgically clean environment reflected light in clinical shades of blue and white. Equipment he'd only seen in theory papers lined the walls. It was every geneticist's dream.

So why did it feel like a trap?

Andrew leaned back from the microscope, rubbing the bridge of his nose. The weight of the necklace Sebastian gave him felt heavier every day he failed to make progress. Andrew unclasped the necklace and set it on the table, staring at it as though the answers were spelled out on the pendant. He hadn't slept much...again. But it wasn't just the excitement of his research that kept him up. There was a tension in the lab lately. Not in the work, but in the people.

At first, he'd brushed it off. Sebastian had warned him that his private team of technicians was recruited from "exceptional backgrounds." And sure, they fit the bill; they were efficient, intelligent, impossibly calm. Almost...too calm.

He watched them when they moved around the lab. The way they glided through the corridors, spoke in hushed, identical tones. They all looked like they'd walked off the set of some perfume ad with impeccable skin, perfectly symmetrical features, and not a blemish or frown line in sight. Even under harsh lab lights, they glowed.

But there was something else, something colder. None of them ever seemed to blink. Or maybe they blinked less than normal. He wasn't sure, but once he noticed it, he couldn't stop seeing it.

Something's off here, he thought, drumming his fingers on the edge of the workstation. *Am I just sleep-deprived?* His eyes flicked to the far side of the lab, where two of the staff, Elis and Marin, stood near the sequencing bay, backs turned and whispering. They were always whispering. He made a mental note to check Sebastian's staffing records. If Sebastian even kept records. Amelia's voice drifted back.

"Not everything is what it seems. Be careful...."

He turned back to his screen, trying to refocus. Logic first. Always logic. And then he saw it.

The cell line under his microscope had stabilized. Not only that, it had *reversed.* The mutated strand, the very same marker he had isolated in both his gene therapy trials *and* Sebastian's sample, had actually regressed. The cells were reprogramming themselves into healthy tissue...although, only for a short window. Seven minutes and twelve seconds. But still, that was incredible. He had done it!

"Holy shit," he muttered, sitting up straighter. He ran the data again, verifying each marker. Confirmed.

He leapt from his stool and crossed to the sequencing station, pulling up backup logs. He repeated the test in a parallel simulation using more of Sebastian's blood samples. Again, the same reversal, brief but undeniable.

The implications surged through him like adrenaline. This wasn't just progress; this was a *breakthrough.* The gene reversal therapy he'd been working on for years was finally showing real results. And the same approach, that he tweaked slightly, seemed to *temporarily* suppress the aggressive mutation Sebastian had described as his "rare skin disorder."

Andrew exhaled a long and shaky breath. "This changes everything. It was history waiting to be rewritten." But then the high of discovery dimmed, just slightly, as the other weight returned. If Sebastian *really* had a rare disorder...why the secrecy? Why the late-night meetings? Why the endless non-disclosure paperwork and private security? And the staff. The ones that cast odd reflections in the lab windows. He turned slowly, looking behind him. Elis and Marin were gone. No footsteps. No sound. They were just gone. His stomach flipped.

But the data on his screen held him. This was too important. It needed to be catalogued, cross-tested. Sebastian would want to know.

Andrew saved the data to the main servers and a private external drive. Just in case. Paranoia or precaution, he wasn't sure, but instincts didn't lie, and tonight, his gut was screaming in two different directions. He checked the clock on the wall. It was 4:12 am. No wonder he was unraveling.

Grabbing his coat, he tucked the drive into an inner pocket. The lab had gone still. Too still. As if someone had dialed the ambient hum of machines down a few notches. Even the ever-present fans seemed quieter. Or was that just him? He made for the exit.

As he passed the long window facing the sequencing chamber, his reflection glanced back. He was tired, pale with dark circles under his eyes. Then he heard the elevator arrive with a soft ding at the end of the hall. Elis was inside, he was standing *perfectly* still. Staring at Andrew not blinking.

"Going down Dr. Lee?"

"A...yes, Elis," Andrew replied.

"Let me get the button for you." Elis held the elevator door for Andrew to come in before stepping out.

Andrew turned to say something, anything, but Elis was already gone.

"Get some rest," he muttered to himself. "You need to sort fact from fiction." Then the doors closed.

The lab above returned to its perfect, polished quiet. Andrew, with a breakthrough in his pocket and a question burning in his gut, descended into the dark, unaware that the real experiment wasn't in the lab. It was him.

CHAPTER 33

Sebastian sat at the apex of his high-rise office, the city bathed in twilight, gold bleeding into red across the black-glass walls. Behind him, security feeds from his private lab cycled silently across a wall of monitors. He sipped dark red liquid from a crystal tumbler, his expression impassive, but his eyes, ice blue and inhumanly steady, were locked on the screen showing the lab's main corridor.

"Bring him in," he said without turning.

Camille walked in with two vampire guards, dragging Elis. His once-pristine lab coat was torn, blood trailing from a split lip and a gash at the hairline. Elis looked furious, not fearful. He'd been caught making a call, a brief encrypted transmission caught only because Sebastian's head of security, Camille, had noticed the signature.

"Do you know how many eyes I have in my building, Elis?" Sebastian said, standing slowly. "Camille said you smelled wrong... the moment you stepped in."

Elis spat blood onto the floor. "You don't see it, do you? Your empire's crumbling. The young ones are done hiding."

Sebastian stepped closer. "And yet here you are. Caught. Disgraced."

"It's too late," Elis said, voice ragged but triumphant. "They're already on the move. Dr. Lee won't survive the night."

Sebastian's jaw tightened. For a moment, there was silence.

Then, with quiet fury, he turned to Camille. "Find out what he knows and make him know we are serious people."

Camille nodded to the two guards as they dragged Elis out, screams trailing behind them like the echo of broken pride.

Sebastian exhaled and turned to the nearest control panel. He didn't need chaos right now. Dr. Lee was too important. He checked his tablet, scanned through all the security feeds, but Dr. Lee was nowhere to be found.

He reached for the sleek black phone reserved only for his most strategic assets. A direct line.

He dialed.

The safehouse was unusually quiet, the kind of quiet that signaled something was about to go sideways. Reece stood at the window, watching the sodium orange haze of the city lights through the security mesh. His thoughts were a jumble: the burner phone, the ambush at the mayor's office, and the creeping suspicion that someone else was playing a deeper game.

Hot Shot was at the table, fingers dancing across her keyboard, still digging through surveillance data. Marcus cleaned his rifle with slow, methodical movements. Cole sat across from Reece, arms folded, watching him like a hawk.

Then Reece's phone buzzed.

He frowned and answered. "Yeah."

"Good evening, Mr. Drake," said Sebastian Voss, voice calm, deliberate. "I trust you're well."

Reece stiffened. The others looked up instantly. He put the phone on speaker.

"Who is this? How'd you get this number? What do you want?" he rifled off.

"This is Sebastian Voss, and it's not important how I got this number at the moment. I have my access. I'll make this brief," Sebastian's voice came smooth, but urgent. "You need to get to my lab. Now. There's an imminent strike. Someone in my staff was compromised."

"And you're calling us, why? You've got security."

"I don't believe my security is up for this, and because this attack isn't about my building, it's about Dr. Lee. And I don't want to lose an investment that benefits us all. You care about protecting humans. I care about protecting my assets."

Cole straightened. "Who is after him?"

"A vampire faction called the Reign. Unruly and dangerous. I believe they are the same that killed your teammate at the fundraiser. They've been gaining ground, particularly among the city's forgotten population. I intercepted chatter about a hit tonight."

"Why tell us?" Reece asked, eyes narrowing.

"Because frankly, your team's efficiency is a resource I respect, and I would expect you want some sort of revenge."

Hot Shot raised an eyebrow. "Where?"

"My R&D facility in Mid-Wilshire. He left the lab moments ago. The facility has blind spots. My security lost visual."

Reece's jaw clenched. "You're saying they're after him?" But something in his gut already knew the answer.

"Yes, and he will be dead by sunrise if you can't get to him in time. I'll send over the address."

"Don't worry, we know where it is," Reece chirped back.

"Hmmmm, interesting," Sebastian acknowledged.

Then the line went dead.

Cole was already on his feet. "We go now."

Reece hesitated.

"You serious right now?" Cole demanded. "You think he's lying? You think he'd tip us off just for fun?"

Reece turned slowly, jaw clenched. "I think Voss is ten steps ahead of everyone in this city. I think he doesn't do anything without a long-term plan."

"So what? We let Lee die because you're paranoid?"

Marcus chimed in, calm but firm. "He was a bystander in that fundraiser mess, and now if he's a target, we can't sit this out."

Hot Shot stood. "He's got a point, and if Voss is playing us, better we walk into it armed."

Reece hesitated. His instincts screamed not to trust Voss, but

Andrew was a civilian. One who didn't know the world he'd been dropped into. Reece looked at each of them. His team. His responsibility. His gut still screamed that something wasn't right.

He grabbed his gear. "We move now. Grab your gear."

Cole muttered under his breath as he locked and loaded. "About time."

But Reece couldn't shake it. The more Voss offered them clarity, the more Reece felt unsettled about everything. Like a game board, he didn't know he was already on.

Sebastian Voss stood at the window, drink in hand, watching the city flicker beneath him. He couldn't tell if the taste on his tongue was the creeping bitterness of a game turning against him.

CHAPTER 34

Skid Row was different tonight; while it was no stranger to fear, it was heavier. Like everyone could feel something hunting them, but no one wanted to be the one to say it. By the time she hit the edge of the block, she had what she needed. There was a pattern here. A pulse. The vampires weren't looking for easy meals. They were watching. Amelia's mind kept circling back.

How was Voss involved? Was he staking new territory, or was this a way for him to get to me? Wrap me in his web. Or worse, was he turning the homeless for his little empire?

She pulled her phone from her jacket and stared at the screen; an unanswered call from Sebastian.

"Now what are you up to?" She muttered, "I swear I'll drive a stake through your favorite Italian suit if you have anything to do with these people going missing."

Then she noticed it.

Something was moving through the streets, and for once, it wasn't her. Amelia's instincts told her she had to get back to the lab and make sure Andrew was okay, but she stayed longer than she should've.

The air felt off, heavy in a way you don't notice until your instincts scream to move. She'd been around too long to ignore a feeling like that. So she doubled back and slipped through the alleys she knew best, past sleeping bodies and smoldering barrel fires. Somewhere between 6th and Wall, she caught it. The scent in the air. The same smell of cold stone after rain that was etched in her memory. She ducked behind a graffiti-covered dumpster and waited. Breathing shallow and muscles loose.

Then she saw them.

He was tall and hooded. Moving too smoothly for a human and not in that obnoxious confidence kind of way. He was a predator, silent and moving like a ghost. His companion, leaner and smaller, flanked him a step behind. Then she saw it. Fangs with glowing eyes.

Fucking wonderful. They weren't feeding. They were watching. Like a couple of nosy shadows with a blood fetish.

Now she followed at a distance. Close enough to trail, but far enough to stay invisible. He stopped suddenly, lifting his nose like a wolf catching scent.

"Split up," Tadgh growled. His voice rough as though expecting a fight.

Shit. She thought.

Amelia moved fast, darting into the skeletal remains of a condemned building off 7th. Rotten wood groaned beneath her feet. Rebar reached like ribs from shattered concrete. One of them followed. She could hear his light feet and no breath. She waited until he was inside. Then she struck.

Tadgh didn't even get a word out before her dagger found his shoulder. He roared, twisting back with inhuman strength and slammed her into the wall. The brick cracked behind her skull, but she grinned through the impact.

"You'll have to buy me dinner first," she spat, headbutting him square in the nose. He reeled back just enough for her to sweep his legs and drive her knee into his chest.

The other one was faster.

Edin dropped from above like a vulture in combat boots. A feral snarl ripped from her throat as she lunged. Amelia pivoted, barely dodging claws that could've gutted a bear.

Edin raked across her ribs again. Amelia felt the hot pain flashing, but she twisted in and drove her elbow into Edin's temple.

Her head snapped to the side, and Amelia followed up with a blade to the gut. She didn't flinch. Not until Amelia twisted.

"Tell me who sent you," Amelia growled, pinning her against the wall with a forearm to her throat. "You like silence? Let's see how long it lasts with your intestines outside your body."

"You're too late," Edin rasped. Blood dripped down her chin. "He's already marked."

Cold dread hit her. "Who?"

Edin smiled with a crooked look and with blood filling in her throat, "The human. Your pet."

She was talking about Andrew. A cold shock ran through Amelia. She didn't wait for more. Amelia shoved the blade up into her heart. Edin's face went blank before her lips began to scream. Amelia watched her crumble into ash.

The male hissed behind her and lunged, but Amelia was already turning. Already driving the dagger into his chest. He shrieked, clawing at her as he disintegrated, his fingers leaving black smears on her jacket.

Silence returned, but her heart didn't slow.

They weren't just watching. They were hunting. Hunting for me. And this was all a distraction.

"Andrew..." Amelia whispered in desparation to herself.

She stumbled outside, wiping ash from her face with a shaking hand. For all the centuries she'd lived, all the blood she'd spilled, she wasn't prepared for this kind of fear. The fear that comes when someone she cares about might be taken before she figures out what they mean to her.

She pulled out her phone and called Sebastian.

He didn't answer. Her boots pounding the pavement, heart screaming with a rage she hadn't felt in a hundred years, and for the first time, she was terrified she might be too late.

CHAPTER 35

The corridors of the lab were silent as Dr. Lee exited the brightly lit laboratory. His mind buzzed with the break-through he'd just made, a fragile, but thrilling success in his latest round of trials. The cells hadn't just responded, they'd *changed*. It wasn't a full reversal of Sebastian's condition, but it was the closest he'd ever come. A first step. Something real.

As he was heading to the lower floors in the elevator, rubbing his eyes. He checked his watch. It was 4:18 AM.

Time to sleep before I start hallucinating progress, he thought.

When the elevator doors opened into the building's expansive lobby, a strange stillness met him. The usual security guard was absent from the front desk. No hum of late-night jazz on the over-head speakers. No ambient glow of a muted news channel. Just stillness.

Andrew slowed, peering behind the desk. Empty.

Probably on patrol, he reasoned, though unease settled across his shoulders.

He crossed the marble floor and pushed through the doors marked "Parking Garage."

The air changed instantly, cooler, mustier, laced with oil and concrete dust. His footsteps echoed as he descended the ramp toward his parking space. Fluorescent lights flickered overhead, casting shadows that stretched and snapped like rubber bands. He reached his car, but something caught his attention. A dark puddle had formed under the front of the vehicle, slowly creeping outward.

"Come on," he muttered. He opened the driver's door and slid inside, jabbing the key into the ignition.

Nothing. Just the cold, unsatisfying click of a dead engine.

"Seriously?"

He exhaled and stepped out, intending to head back to the lobby and find the guard or *anyone* for help.

That's when he saw it.

A figure in the shadows behind a column stepped out. Still and watching.

Andrew's pulse jumped. He took a cautious step backward, then spotted a second figure, half hidden behind a concrete column. This one had glowing red eyes, or he thought, was he hallucinating again?

His breath caught in his throat. He pulled his phone out, remembering Sebastian telling him if he ever felt unsafe to call Camille, his head of security. He looked down quickly and pulled up her number, and clicked DIAL. No Service.

Damn it! He thought.

He turned and sprinted toward the door he'd come through. Before reaching it, he glanced back. Now three, no, make that four figures had emerged. All silent. All watching.

He slammed through the lobby doors and staggered back into the reception area. The front desk was still empty. His gut twisted. He circled behind the desk and gasped.

The guard was there.

Face down in a pool of his own blood, throat slashed open.

"Oh God..."

Panic surged. Andrew bolted for the elevators, pushing the button, but nothing happened. That's when he remembered, he took off the necklace. The necklace that gave him access to everything in the building, including the elevators. There was only one option, the front doors and into the streets. *People.* Someone had to be out there. Someone could help.

He shoved the glass doors open and stumbled onto the dark streets. A few cars passed, their drivers oblivious to the man waving his arms in desperation. No one stopped.

He ran. Checked his phone. Bars finally. He dialed Camille again. It started ringing, three blocks down, he spotted a corner café switching on its lights. A woman inside swept the floor.

Camille answered, "Where are you. There's..."

"I'm..I ran onto the street heading towards the corner cafe... they're after me!"

Andrew surged forward until a figure stepped into his path from between two trees. It was Kellin. This was his mission. What he'd been waiting for.

"Dr. Lee," Kellin said with a cold smile. "Where are you going in such a hurry?"

Andrew froze. The man's coat hung long and black, his skin pale, his posture regal, but it was the eyes. Those unmistakable glowing red eyes that paralyzed him.

More figures stepped out from the shadows. In a circle, surrounding him.

Andrew's knees wobbled. "No...no, this isn't real..." he muttered, dropping the phone.

Kellin approached, hands in his coat pockets. Then, without warning, he lunged. His hand closed around Andrew's throat, lifting him clean off the ground.

Andrew kicked, gasped, and clawed.

"Let's make it hurt," someone said nearby. Another hissed, "Drag it out."

Kellin grinned, then hurled Andrew into a parked car. The windshield shattered around him as his body crumpled across the hood.

Pain exploded in his ribs. His lungs burned. He tried to move and barely managed to slide off the hood when another pair of hands yanked him backward.

He flew into a trash bin, crashing hard. Pain again. Worse this time. Ribs fractured, maybe more. Blood filled his mouth. From the pavement, he blinked upward, dazed, while Kellin advanced.

Andrew saw the face, inhuman, pale, beautiful, and most of all, monstrous. The glowing red eyes and then the fangs.

"No..." he croaked. "You're not real. You're not..."

The vampire's face twisted into a grin.

"Just a story," Kellin said mockingly. "Until we turn the page."

He raised his hand, claws glinting under the streetlight.

Then...

CRACK.

A gunshot split the air. One of the vampires staggered backward, hissing.

CRACK. CRACK.

More shots rang out from rifles with laser sights, pinning targets. Reece's team had arrived.

"Get him out of there!" Reece barked into his comms.

Marcus swept out of the alley, spraying silver rounds into two more vamps. Cole dropped one with a shot to the heart, finally enough to kill it as it vanished into ash.

"Move, move!" Hot Shot's voice came from above, her sniper position covering the street.

Andrew lay barely conscious, broken and still in shock. Kellin turned from Andrew and faced the advancing team, fangs bared.

"Protect the Doctor!" Reece shouted, drawing twin pistols and diving into the fray.

Blood splattered the street. Ash filled the air. Vampires shrieked as UV rounds ignited their flesh, but Andrew wasn't watching anymore. He was crawling, grasping at anything that could get him away from the horrors and the gunshots. He didn't know who was saving him. Only that monsters were real and he wasn't ready to die yet.

CHAPTER 36

Gunfire thundered through the alleys, ricocheting off the glass and steel of the pre-dawn morning. The vampire ambush had turned into a bloodbath. Reece's team was caught in a full-on battle, with vampires darting through moonlit shadows, using their supernatural speed and strength to push the hunters to their limits.

Reece ducked behind a concrete barrier, his breath ragged. "Cole! Right flank! Marcus, on me!"

Cole fired a burst from his rifle, bullets laced with silver. One vampire shrieked as the rounds tore through its chest, but it didn't go down. It just staggered, snarled, and came at him harder.

"They fed! They're stronger!" Cole shouted.

Reece cursed under his breath and drove a silver blade into the chest of another vampire. Ash exploded in a burst across the concrete.

Across the battlefield, Hot Shot was tucked into a sniper nest on a rooftop, eyes focused through the scope of her rifle. She took out two targets before noticing movement of something fast, an agile figure scaling the opposite building. It was a blonde woman moving faster than she had ever seen.

"Shit," she hissed, shifting her aim. "They've got my position. Reece, I got company."

Her comm crackled and went silent. Reece heard the line die. "Hot Shot?" No response.

High above, Hot Shot turned just in time to see two vampires charging her perch. She took one down with her Glock pistol, but the second tackled her hard. They rolled, claws, teeth, and elbows impacted until she buried a blade in its chest. It went in deep and as it screamed and turned to ash, but then a third vampire, it was Syla, blindsided her.

The rooftop edge crumbled beneath them. They landed on a lower rooftop. Syla grabbed Hot Shot by her bulletproof vest and threw her to the side.

"You just gonna take pop shots at us from the rooftops? Didn't wanna get your hands dirty? Well, maybe I'll bring the game to you then." Syla said with menace.

Hot Shot, slow to get up, pulled out her Glock again, but Syla was on her and with a quick spinning roundhouse kick, knocking the gun out of Hot Shot's grip. Then, with vampiric speed, Syla grabbed Hot Shot again with one hand by her armored vest, reached back with her other to deliver a near-deadly backhand. Hot Shot, barely conscious now, held limp in the air by Syla's ruthless grip, was starting to blackout. Syla was done playing, flicked her off the rooftop ledge like she was tossing trash, and watched her limp body fall out of sight towards the ground.

While falling with her last ounce of awareness, she managed to reach out to grab anything that would break her fall. She snagged two telephone lines on the way down, slowing her fall just enough to crash through a skylight onto an office desk, instead of pavement. The glass and tables broke her fall. Blood pooled beneath her as she gasped in pain. Her leg twisted unnaturally. Her comm crackled faintly.

"...Down... I'm down..." and then she blacked out.

Syla walked over to the ledge and didn't see her at first until she went around and saw Hot Shot's body twisted in a mess of glass and the broken table. She wasn't moving. Syla laughed, short and cold, then vanished back to the battle.

Marcus was already sprinting. "Hot Shot's down," he said into the comm. "I'm going for her."

On the ground, Reece and Cole were barely holding the line. Kellin, the one in the black coat, moved like a blur, his strength augmented from fresh blood. He clawed through the smoke toward Andrew, who was crawling slowly, bloody and dazed.

"No!" Reece shouted, unloading a full magazine into the vampire.

But the creature was too fast. It reached Andrew and grabbed him by the waist, claws sinking deep. Blood poured from the wound as Andrew screamed in agony.

Then they saw his face. Kellin. Skylar's killer. Reece's grip tightened. Cole went silent. For a moment, the battle faded beneath the roar of memory.

Cole flanked and shot the vampire through the neck. Kellin reached for his neck when Reece tackled him. Dropping Andrew, Kellin grabbed him by his vest as they rolled and launched him across the sidewalk. Cole fired multiple rounds through Kellin's side while he stumbled to get up. Reece, seeing the opening, lunged into Kellin, driving a silver stake deep into his chest. Kellin's scream dissolved into ash. Revenge was sweet but short-lived. Reece, barely breathing, looked over at Andrew.

"He's bleeding out!" Cole barked.

"Grab him, GO!"

Reece and Cole lifted Andrew, sprinting through the blood-stained streets back toward Sebastian's tower. As they rushed through the lobby, the lab's private elevator opened and a team of Sebastian's staff poured out, Camille leading the way. They were clean, polished, unnervingly calm, and rushed forward with a gurney. They took Andrew and vanished into the building. Reece and Cole stood in the lobby, soaked in blood and panting. Sebastian appeared out of nowhere. He was in an immaculate suit, his expression unreadable.

"My team will take it from here," he said smoothly.

Reece looked up, breathing heavy. "He's dying."

"Not if I can help it," as he disappeared back into the elevator.

Cole clenched his fists but said nothing. Breathing heavy, they watched as the hustle of Sebastian's staff started cleaning up the blood-stained marble floor. Their comms crackled again.

"Found her!" Marcus said. "She's alive, but she's hurt bad."

Reece and Cole ran to find their teammates.

Upstairs, the lab was in a frenzy of motion. Technicians, perfectly eerie and model-like, worked quickly around Andrew's failing body. Sebastian stood over him, calm in the chaos. "Begin the transfusion."

"But sir, your blood..."

"Do it. Now."

Andrew blinked through the haze. A figure loomed; it was Sebastian. His sleeves were rolled up. He saw his pale skin and blue veins...the fangs. His breath caught. No... it couldn't be..."

Then darkness took him, and the last thing he felt was not pain, but the sinking dread that none of this was an accident.

CHAPTER 37

Amelia's pulse was hammering. Her ribs screamed with every breath, but it didn't matter. She'd killed the two vampires, but not before hearing the most gut-twisting words imaginable.

"You're too late. He's already marked."

Andrew.

She yanked her phone from her pocket with bloodied fingers, thumb trembling as she hit Sebastian's number.

Voicemail. Again.

Her breath caught. Fury surged in her chest like fire in her lungs. "Pick up, you bastard," she muttered. "This is your mess too."

The phone dropped into her pocket as she stumbled toward her motorcycle, mounting it with a grimace. The engine growled to life, and with a snarl, she twisted the throttle and tore into the night.

Amelia skidded to a stop outside the tower and bolted through the lobby doors. She didn't notice a pair of blood-smeared men exiting the side stairwell. It was Reece and Cole.

Cole's eyes narrowed when he spotted her. "That's her."

Reece followed his gaze, his body tensing the instant he recognized the striking woman from the fundraiser. Her dark hair was disheveled, her face bruised. She was limping with a scowl on her face, but definitely unmistakable.

"It is," he murmured.

Reece's hand clapped Cole's shoulder. "We've got our own crisis. Marcus needs us. Hot Shot's down."

He didn't move.

"I'm serious," Reece growled. "I don't care what your gut says. She's not our priority right now."

Cole gave one last glance back in the lobby before nodding. "We'll circle back. She's part of this. I know it."

They raced into the night.

The moment her boots hit the marble lobby floor, she was met with silence. It was too clean, too quiet. One of his sleekly dressed staff stepped forward, expression unreadable.

"I need to see Andrew Lee," she said, voice low with a razored edge.

"I'm sorry, Miss Devereux, but Dr. Lee…"

"Is in this building," she snapped, "and I'm not leaving without seeing him."

Before the staffer could answer, Sebastian appeared from the elevator, rolling down his sleeve with his usual smooth glide. His expression was neutral, but his eyes betrayed that faint glint of calculation.

"Amelia," he said, the name floating like silk. "You look… battle-worn."

"I'm going to give you ten seconds to explain where Andrew is, and why your people are stonewalling me at the door."

Sebastian raised a hand in mild surrender. "He's been attacked, but alive. My doctors are working on him right now. So far, he's unconscious, but stable. He may need to be put in an induced coma for healing and containment."

Without another word, she brushed past him. Sebastian gestured, and two staff members wordlessly guided her toward the private elevator.

Amelia stepped into the sterile chill of the ICU; the hiss of machines and faint rhythmic beeping were the only sounds. A nurse pointed her to a glass-paneled room. She moved to the door, pausing when she saw him. Andrew looked fragile, too pale, wrapped in wires and IVs. She watched as nurses bandaged his abdomen, where they must have just stitched him back together. But he was alive and breathing.

She watched impatiently as they finished stabilizing Andrew. Once the doctors and nurses finished and left the room, she stepped inside. She moved to his bedside and sank into the chair beside him. She took his hand, cold but familiar, and pressed it to her lips.

"I'm sorry," she whispered. "I should've been there. I should've stopped them."

Time passed. Hours, maybe more. She didn't sleep. Just slumped with exhaustion, head resting beside his hand. She never let go. The subtle twitch of fingers broke the stillness. Amelia jolted upright. Andrew blinked slowly, his lips parting with effort.

"Hey," he rasped.

Her heart surged. "You're awake."

He gave a faint smile. "Barely." His eyes scanned her face. "You came?"

"I did."

"You're hurt."

She brushed off the comment. "So are you. Don't change the subject."

"I remember...red eyes. Fangs." He paused, wincing. "And you... standing there. Like a vision."

Probably a hallucination," she said too quickly. "You lost a lot of blood. Probably imagined things?"

His gaze lingered on her face. "Maybe."

She swallowed. "We'll talk more later. You need rest."

"I wanted to say..." He struggled to sit up, but she pressed him gently back down.

"Don't. Just rest."

He nodded, exhausted. "Thanks for coming."

She smiled softly. "I wouldn't be anywhere else."

He drifted back to sleep, and Amelia exhaled slowly, brushing her thumb over his hand. Once she knew he was asleep, she stood.

The moment she left the room, the guilt twisted into rage, and she knew exactly where to aim it. She turned on her heels and stormed out of the ICU, her boots echoing in the quiet hallway. One of Sebastian's assistants moved to intercept her, but she shoved past with a snarl.

"Don't," she barked.

She reached Sebastian's office, threw open the door without knocking, and found him flipping through his tablet, sitting behind his desk, perfectly composed. He looked up slowly, lifting a single brow.

Amelia stalked toward him with his assistant trailing behind.

"You and I," she said, voice low and dangerous, "are going to have a talk."

"It's alright, I've been expecting her," Sebastian said to Evelyn, his assistant. He was calm as a winter lake, without glancing up from the tablet in his hand. He set it down slowly as Amelia stalked in, dried blood still on her brow.

She didn't stop until she was across his desk. "What did you do to him?"

Sebastian lifted his eyes, cool and unreadable. "Amelia," he said with a slow, measured smile. "I was wondering when you'd come storming in."

Evelyn lingered at the doorway.

He gave a single nod. "Leave us."

Amelia paced once, trying to stop herself from putting her fist through his obsidian desk. "I saw him. I *felt* it. He's not just recovering, Sebastian. Something's changed. What the hell did you do?"

He stood, adjusting his cufflink with casual precision. "Dr. Lee was bleeding out. Fast. We had minutes. I administered a transfusion. It was that or let him die. Forgive me for choosing the option that didn't end in a body bag."

She stepped forward, eyes blazing. "What blood did you use?"

He looked at her like the answer was obvious. "Mine, of course."

"You gave him *your* blood?"

"I couldn't trust anyone else's. He needed purity, control. Mine was the safest choice."

Amelia's jaw clenched. "So you could bind him to you? Make him one of your projects? One of your...pets?"

Sebastian's lips twitched. "Now that's a little dramatic, even for you."

"Did you turn him?" she snapped.

"No." He moved around the desk, slowly, deliberately. "It was a clean transfusion. No turning, no siring. Check his neck if you need proof. No bite. No venom. He's not one of us."

"Then what *is* he?" she demanded.

Sebastian paused, then shrugged. "That's the interesting part. He's exhibiting some...traits. Heightened recovery. Sensory shifts, but nothing stable, yet. It's uncharted territory. Revolutionary, really. He may revert. Or he may not."

"You don't know?" She said angrily.

"I saved his life," he replied. "You're caught up in the fine print."

She stared at him, eyes hard. "If anything happens to him, if he becomes something he can't come back from, I will burn this place to the ground with you in it."

"I wouldn't expect anything less," he said, almost fondly.

She turned to go, then stopped short, something else boiling to the surface. She spun back to face him.

"There's something else," she said. "Skid Row. People have been going missing. Your name keeps coming up, and I found this card," as she whipped out the card from her jacket pocket.

Sebastian's smile faded. "Excuse me?" As he reached out and examined the card.

"They're scared. They're saying *you* took them. That you're behind the disappearances and then that weirdo, lab tech guy, Elis has been spotted down there."

A flicker of interest sharpened behind his eyes. "First of all, this is not one of my cards. Do you think I would be so clueless as to leave a calling card? That's not my pattern. You know that. As for Elis," he flipped a couple of screens on his tablet and handed it to her. On the screen, Elis was strapped to a chair, bloodied and beaten, obviously mid-tortured by one of Sebastian's guards while Camille stood over them.

"Elis was found to be the leak that exposed our dear Doctor. He hasn't told us much more, yet..."

A flash of anger passed through Amelia, "What has he told you? Who is he reporting to?"

"Now, now. So far, he's keeping a tight lip, but eventually he'll crack, or die. Camille is also looking into the attack. We will know soon enough, and I'll pass that info along."

"You better," she said. Then, going back to her interrogation, "Why is someone leaving fake cards and whispering your name? I've been in the camps. They're saying someone who *looks like you* has been offering food. Shelter. Then people disappear."

Sebastian's jaw tightened slightly. "Someone's impersonating me."

"Why?" she asked. "Why let the rumors run?"

"I didn't." He walked back to his desk, suddenly more focused. "If they're using my name, it's bait. For you. Or me. Or both."

She stepped closer. "Then figure out who's behind it. Fast."

He nodded once. "I'll have Camille put surveillance in the area. If someone's operating in my shadow, I want them out of it."

"Good," she said. "Because if you're tied to this, if you're using the homeless like livestock..."

"Amelia," he cut in, voice suddenly colder. "You *know* that's beneath me. The Reign, maybe, but not me."

She didn't respond. She didn't trust him, not entirely. But part of her believed him. That was the dangerous part.

"Keep me updated," she said.

"Of course," he replied smoothly. "Anything to keep you close."

She turned and started toward the door.

"And Amelia?"

She paused, glancing back.

"Let me know if Dr. Lee...changes. I'd like to monitor him."

She narrowed her eyes. "You're not the one watching him. *I* am."

And then she was gone, the door snapping shut behind her with a force that echoed long after she disappeared down the hall.

CHAPTER 38

The air in the chamber hung damp and metallic, thick with rot and the memory of blood. Varek stood in silence, arms folded, as the last remaining vampire from the ambush knelt before him. Blood streaked down the younger vampire's temple, drying against the dirt.

"What's this I hear about a hard drive?" Syla asked from behind Varek's shoulder, voice like a knife's edge.

"I saw it fall out of his pocket when he hit the car. He was bleeding and crawling. I grabbed it and ran before the others fell. I don't know what it is, but it's gotta be something we can use."

Varek took the drive, holding it delicately between two fingers. "You're the only one of his men that made it back."

"They killed Kellin, but he was able to gut the doctor," the vampire said, bitterness in his voice. "They tore through us like we were nothing."

"You *were* nothing," Syla snapped. "You followed Kellin, all ego and no discipline. You went in unprepared. You underestimated them. If it wasn't for me taking out that sniper, you all would've been dead as soon as the hunter scum showed up."

"How were we supposed to know the hunters would show?" The young vampire muttered.

"Someone tipped Sebastian off. Anyone hear from Elis?"

Varek's voice was calm. Almost too calm. "We've been losing numbers. Too many to keep up with the pace of this war."

"No, the last we heard, the Doctor was leaving, and then the line was cut off," the young vampire replied.

"Well, he's dead then. We'll start turning more again," Varek said. "Let's focus on the Skid Row plan. Take the vulnerable. Turn them fast, train them faster. Sebastian probably knows we've been dropping his name now that Elis is gone, so that's not necessary anymore. It'll just expose us more. Just focus on building our ranks, even if the humans want to or not."

"And what of Amelia?" Syla asked, as she watched Varek turn the drive over in his hand.

"Have we heard from Tadgh and Edin? Did they complete their mission?" Varek asked.

"They haven't reported in yet."

"I'll assume they are dead then. So we need to keep an eye on her," Varek replied. "Find out what she knows and then kill her."

As he smiled thinly. "Now let's see what secrets Sebastian's dead pet scientist has been hiding."

CHAPTER 39

The scent of antiseptic clung to the walls like bad memories. Reece and his team stood in silence around Hot Shot's hospital bed, the steady beep of the heart monitor a reminder of how close they'd come to losing her.

Hot Shot sat upright in the hospital bed, bruised and bandaged, but alive. A long gash crossed her temple, and her right leg was elevated in a brace. She looked like hell, but her eyes were clear and sharp.

"Glad to see you're not dead," Marcus grunted, handing her a cup of water.

"I told you," she smirked, her voice raspier than usual, "it takes more than a bloodsucking asshole to put me down."

Cole stood near the window, arms crossed. "We went in blind. And came out with nothing."

"Not completely," Hot Shot said, sipping water. "I saw something during the chaos. Might be important."

Reece turned to her. "What?"

"When the doctor was crawling, trying to get away, just before he got grabbed, I saw something fall out of his coat. Looked like a hard drive."

Reece's jaw clenched. "Did they see it?"

"Yeah. One did. Snatched it and ran while the others covered him. Didn't see that one again."

"Shit," Cole muttered. "You sure?"

Hot Shot nodded. "Positive. I hit one of the bastards trying to reach him and saw the other make a clean break with the drive. Never saw him again."

Marcus paced at the foot of the bed. "So that hard drive's out there and whatever's on it, it's worth something to them."

Reece clenched his fists. "Could've been data from his lab. Maybe something he found. Maybe something Sebastian didn't want others to know."

Hot Shot's gaze narrowed.

"That Sebastian's hiding something. The tech we saw...it's military-grade just in the lobby. What else they got up there? And the staff that came out? They were creepy as hell. No emotions, just blank stares, and I swear, I saw one of them not blink the entire time we were in the lobby," Cole said.

"Great," Marcus replied. "Now we're fighting vampires *and* conspiracy science."

Reece stepped back, his mind already spinning. "We need to assume that whatever was on that drive exposed something critical. Something about Sebastian. About his operation."

"And something those vampires have now, too," Marcus added.

Reece nodded slowly. "Whatever it was, they have it and we're already behind."

CHAPTER 40

The lights in Sebastian's private ICU were dimmed to a soft amber glow, mimicking the color of dusk. Machines beeped in a rhythm that no longer made Amelia flinch. She had memorized them now. Each tone, each pause between pulses, marked another moment Andrew stayed alive. She knew the truth would catch up with her eventually. She didn't expect it to be today.

He was awake. Finally.

Barely, but his eyes were still foggy with sedation, had found hers and hadn't let go.

Amelia sat on the edge of the bed, one hand gently wrapped around his. His skin was cold, which shouldn't have surprised her considering what ran through his veins now, but it did.

He tried to speak, and she leaned in close.

"Water first," she whispered. She brought the straw to his lips, and he drank in small, careful sips.

"I saw it," he rasped, once his throat was no longer sandpaper. "Before I passed out. I saw him. Sebastian. His eyes. They glowed. And his teeth..."

She didn't flinch. Didn't lie. She just nodded slowly.

"You're not crazy. You saw exactly what you think you saw."

He recoiled slightly, his back pressing into the raised hospital bed.

"What the hell is going on?" Adrenaline or fear started to course through his veins.

She looked down at their joined hands, then back up, her voice low. "Sebastian Voss is a vampire. So are the ones who attacked you."

"So am I."

The words hung there like a guillotine.

Andrew blinked. His breath caught. He tried to sit up, but winced in pain. "No. No, that's not possible. You're not...You don't kill people. You... you help the homeless. You laugh. You eat ramen."

"Not all vampires are monsters. But the ones who attacked you? They are."

He stared at her like she was seeing a stranger.

"You were dying," she continued gently. "And Sebastian used his blood to save you. It was the only way."

Andrew pulled his hand from hers slowly and started feeling his neck for punctures.

"What does that make me?"

She took a deep breath. "Not a full vampire. You weren't turned the traditional way. No bite, no ritual. Just a transfusion. Which means you inherited some of our... gifts."

"Gifts," he repeated flatly.

"You'll heal faster. You'll be stronger, quicker. But there are limitations. You can't go out in the sun anymore. It'll burn you. This may be temporary, but so far, this is all we know."

Andrew turned his head away. His jaw tightened.

She tried again. "You're not a monster, Andrew. You're still you. But you're... more now."

"I didn't ask for this."

"I know."

"You should've let me die."

The words hit harder than a punch. She didn't flinch, but it left a mark.

She swallowed it down. "But I didn't do this to..."

He turned back to her and looked, eyes red-rimmed but blazing. "How could you not tell me? How could you let me fall for you...without ever telling me what you are?"

She felt that one, too. Deep.

"Because I was afraid," she said quietly. "Because I haven't felt what I feel around you in a very, very long time. And I didn't want to ruin it."

He turned away again. Silent.

The next several days were agony.

He didn't speak much. He ate in silence. He let the medical staff monitor him, allowed his body to recover. But not once did he reach for her hand again. Amelia gave him space. She didn't press, but she was always there. In the chair by the window. In the hallway, pretending to scroll her phone. Just...close.

Finally, on the fifth day, she returned to his room to find him awake, sitting up, staring at the flickering lights of the night skyline through the window. He didn't look at her when she stepped in.

"You told me the truth," he said.

She nodded. "Yeah."

"And you stayed. Even when I didn't want you to."

"I don't give up easy."

He finally turned. His eyes searched hers, softer now. "So what happens to me now? Am I...one of you?"

She shook her head. "You're something new. Something in between. This hasn't happened before," she said. "There's no precedent for what you are now. You're not a turned vampire. Not fully human either. You're...in uncharted territory."

"So I'm a medical mystery."

She smiled. "You always were."

He laughed. It was small. Tentative, but it was real.

"You scared the hell out of me," he said.

"Welcome to my world."

A long pause. Then he reached out, this time willingly. She took his hand.

"I don't know what this means yet," he said. "But I still want you in it. Whatever this is, whatever I am now...I want to figure it out with you."

She let out a breath she hadn't realized she was holding. Her fingers squeezed his.

"Then we figure it out. Together."

And just like that, the storm between them eased. But outside the walls of that sterile room, the real storm was only beginning.

CHAPTER 41

The light in Amelia's penthouse was low, muted by thick velvet curtains and the subtle glow of vintage lamps. Outside, the city buzzed and flickered, but within these walls, time slowed to something quieter, more personal.

Andrew sat curled on the edge of the plush couch, a glass of blood in his hand, chilled and poured into a wine glass, the way Amelia had served it to him with a careful smile. He'd asked for it. He wanted to see what it felt like. It was surreal, but in a way, it felt almost normal? That was the terrifying part. Maybe that was the *most* terrifying part.

Amelia lounged nearby in a chaise, legs tucked under her like a cat, her gaze steady but unreadable. She'd watched him sip, noted the twitch in his eye, the way he blinked afterward like he'd tasted something foreign and forbidden. Which, of course, he had.

"Still not sold on the vintage blend?" she asked, her voice playful and teasing.

He gave her a dry look over the rim of his glass. "It's... fine. Like drinking pennies with a hint of cabernet."

She smirked. "That's the plasma. It adds character."

He set the glass down and rubbed his hands together. "So this is life now?"

Her smirk faded. She leaned forward, resting her elbows on her knees. "Not quite. You're not like me, not completely. The transfusion...it changed you, sure. You'll heal faster, you'll be stronger. You might even live a lot longer than most, but you're still human. Mostly. At least for now."

He looked down at his hands. They didn't feel different, but then, what did transformation feel like? "And the sun?"

"You'll burn. Not immediately, but it won't be pleasant. You won't turn to ash, not like we would, but your skin will react violently. Think third-degree burns after minutes of exposure."

He flinched.

She shrugged softly. "The rules vary depending on the vampire and the bloodline. You're a hybrid now. That makes you something...new."

He stared at her for a long moment. "And the feeding? You said I wouldn't need to..."

"Not like us. You won't crave it. Not unless you start. That door swings one way. Drink from the source, and it gets harder to go back. Blood bags are clean, efficient. No high, no thrill. Just fuel."

He frowned. "But feeding from a person... that gives you more?"

She nodded. "Yes. Strength, speed, and even enhanced perception. It amplifies everything. But it comes with...consequences. And guilt, if you're still the type who has that."

"I am."

She smiled faintly. "Good. Keep it. It makes you dangerous to the wrong people."

"Wait, I saw you...I mean we, we ate normal food?"

"Yes, we can still eat normal food, but we don't get the sustenance like humans. If we don't have blood, our bodies wither but never die. We basically starve to death, forever. It's as painful as it sounds. I don't recommend it."

A silence settled between them again. Not uncomfortable, just heavy with the weight of everything left to say.

Andrew leaned forward. "You said earlier you help the helpless. Is that how you deal with it?"

She nodded. "It's the only thing that still feels real. Humans forget how fragile their lives are. They waste decades thinking they have more time. They wait to say the important things. Wait to love. Wait to forgive. I see them dying a little every day, pretending they're living. I help where I can, remind them someone's watching. It keeps me tethered."

He looked at her differently now, as though the pieces had finally aligned. Not just the beauty or the mystery, but the pain, and the purpose.

"That's why you go to Skid Row."

She nodded. "They don't pretend. They don't have time to lie to themselves. That kind of honesty? It's rare."

He leaned back, processing it all. "And the myths? Stakes? Crosses? Welcoming a vampire into your home?"

She rolled her eyes. "Fiction. Stakes work only if you pierce the heart, but that works on humans, too. Using silver weapons are more effective against our kind. It may have something to do with metallurgy and the purification process of silver. Now crosses, garlic, holy water, that's pure fantasy. The whole welcoming a vampire into your home is the only way for them to cross the threshold? Now I have no idea where that came from, but that just sounds like a Better Homes and Gardens conspiracy. What is true, is sunlight. That's real. The worst kind of real. You've seen what it does."

Andrew's mind was spinning, but his gaze remained on her. "You should be terrifying."

"I am," she said with a smirk. "Just not to you."

He laughed, then sobered. "I don't know how to live like this."

"You don't have to figure it all out tonight. Just breathe. Let it happen. It took me years to draw a line. And mine is simple: I don't kill humans. No matter what. Not unless I have no other choice. But vampires? We've had lifetimes. If we're still hurting people, we've earned the end."

He thought inward as she continued.

"You're not alone, but I do know how you can relate it to your work, the way we are is through a genetic disorder. We're still humans, but some of our cells mutate just like cancer cells. Call it our 'immortal cancer'. You see, most of the myths have a bases in religion pushed from books and media. Vampirism isn't an effect of something religious, it's a mutation in the evolutionary chain. I'm not saying we are the next step, but possibly an offshoot branch."

He stood and crossed the room to sit beside her. She didn't flinch. Didn't move.

"Thank you," he said, voice low. "For telling me. For not hiding it."

"You deserved the truth."

He looked into her eyes and saw no monster. Just someone who'd been carrying the weight of immortality with a quiet grace. Someone who hadn't let it destroy her.

She leaned into him then, letting their shoulders touch.

He closed his eyes.

"How long have you been...this?" he asked.

She hesitated, then looked out towards the window, as though looking back in time. "Three centuries, give or take a decade. Paris, 1720s. I was the daughter of a French noble and a Japanese merchant. My family arranged my marriage to secure some ridiculous trade agreement. I ran the night before the wedding. And then I met him. He promised freedom and adventure."

Andrew didn't interrupt. Just listened.

"He was beautiful, mysterious, everything you want when you're twenty and stupid. I didn't know what he was until it was too late. He turned me because he wanted someone to love him forever."

"Did you?"

Her mouth twitched into something bittersweet. "For a while. Then I realized forever is a long time to love someone who only wants to possess you. So I ran. I spent the next century running. Then fighting. Then surviving."

They talked. For hours. About blood, sunlight, myths, and truths. About centuries and choices. About what it meant to live outside of time, tethered to a world that never stopped changing.

And somewhere between stories of Paris in the 1700s and her

warnings about the seductive strength that came from feeding on humans, their conversation shifted. The space between them narrowed. It was subtle at first, a glance held too long, the brush of fingers as she handed him another glass, the way her laughter curled around his name.

When she leaned in, this time it wasn't to tell a story. Her hand grazed his cheek, knuckles tracing his jaw, and his breath caught. His hand covered hers, holding it there. Neither spoke.

Her lips found his, slow at first, testing. A whisper of a kiss that deepened when he pulled her into him. The dam broke. Months of tension, of longing, of tentative curiosity erupted into a wave of heat and emotion.

They moved together in instinct and rhythm, his hands in her hair, her body pressed against his. She straddled his lap, and they kissed like they had all the time in the world and no time at all.

Amelia's fingertips traced down his chest, sending lighting through him. His breath hitched, and she felt it, felt him responding to every inch of her. He pulled her closer, his hands gripping her waist with reverent desperation.

It wasn't about possession. It wasn't even about release. It was about trust. About finally letting someone see the bruised soul beneath the centuries of armor. And for Andrew, it was about surrendering to something that terrified and thrilled him at the same time.

They melted into one another, not in fury, but in fire. The kind that burned slowly and deeply, the kind that didn't destroy, but transformed.

Later, tangled together in the afterglow, Amelia rested her head against his chest, listening to the rhythm of his heart. Steady and real. Still human, she thought, at least morally.

His fingers traced lazy circles along her back. "I never thought I'd feel like this with anyone," he whispered.

She closed her eyes. "Neither did I."

For the first time in centuries, she didn't feel alone.

"So," he said, voice tired but full of wonder, "what do we do now?"

She smiled, small and secret. "I show you how much I missed this, and tomorrow, I teach you how to spot a vampire pretending to be human."

His eyes opened again, humor creeping in. "That sounds like a terrible reality show."

"It would get amazing ratings."

They lay together like that, two broken people, stitched together by truth and blood. Something neither of them had dared hope for, a second chance.

CHAPTER 42

The first sliver of sunrise burned on the city's edge, bleeding orange across the Los Angeles skyline. Sebastian stood before the wall of UV-protected glass in his office, the city stretched out like an empire beneath him. His sleeves were rolled to his elbows, his hands tucked casually into the pockets of his slacks, but his stillness was deceptive. Inside, he simmered.

Behind him, on his desk, lay a single document, a blood test printout. Andrew Lee's. The results were unlike anything Sebastian had seen in centuries. The transfusion had worked. Better than expected, but his blood was different than pure vampire's blood. It was something else, and that wasn't going according to plan.

The doctor was supposed to be grateful, indebted, and pliable. He became more defiant than before.

Sebastian let out a breath through his nose, slow and deliberate. First, the attack on Andrew had been orchestrated without his knowledge. Then his name was being whispered in the streets by impostors. Finally, the doctor he saved with his own blood wasn't truly appreciative of what gifts he was given. That made it personal. Was his grip slipping?

Evelyn, his assistant, pinged him, "Camille and Damien are here as requested."

"Let them in."

Two figures stepped inside: Camille, head of security and Damien, one of Sebastian's consuls. They stood, postures rigid with their eyes lowered.

"Give me the report," Sebastian said, still watching the pale morning creep across his city.

Camille spoke first. "Street cams and security footage confirms it was a coordinated strike. Eight vampires, all younger, led by Kellin. They all traced back to The Reign...Varek."

"Anyone survived?"

"Six downed by the human hunters, including Kellin. Two escaped, we believe Syla, Varek's number 2, and another vampire."

Sebastian finally turned and asked, "And Elis, the traitor who leaked the doctor's whereabouts to the Reign? Did we get anything else from him?"

"No. He's...no longer with us."

Sebastian nodded once. "Did he suffer before the discreet disposal?"

"Yes, sir."

He approached his desk, fingers ghosting over the blood test. He didn't look at them as he spoke.

"Someone thought they could rip my pieces off the board. They failed, and now they think I'll play defense."

Damien shifted uncomfortably. "With respect, sir...there is concern about Amelia Devereux. Her involvement complicates your connection to Lee."

Silence dropped like a blade. Sebastian's gaze lifted slowly and unblinking.

"Complicates?"

Damien paled. "I only meant..."

"Amelia," Sebastian said slowly, "is not a variable. She is a constant."

No one dared reply.

"Before you go," he finished. "Camille, I need you to check out Skid Row. There's been rumors of individuals speaking my name. Find out who's playing us."

Only when the door hissed shut behind them did Sebastian

move again. He walked back to the window, lifting the blood-filled crystal glass from his side table and watching the sunlight stretch over the hills.

He sipped.

She came for him. Bled for him. Stayed by his bedside. Love is always the first leash. Still is.

He thought of the look in her eyes when she spoke his name now; it was cautious, bristled, but warm in the cracks. Andrew had already begun to burrow into her ancient, tired heart. Good. It meant she could be moved, and if Amelia could be moved, then she could be used.

"Soon," he whispered to his reflection in the glass, red eyes flickering behind the faint sheen of sunrise, "even she will follow the string."

The city blinked and stirred below, unaware of the storm quietly building above, and Sebastian smiled.

CHAPTER 43

The first few weeks of recovery had passed in a blur of whispered conversations and sleepless nights. Andrew's body was healing rapidly and unnaturally so. By the time his wounds had fully closed, he could already feel it, the difference. The edge to his reflexes. The subtle expansion of his senses. Sight, sound, and even smell, they had all sharpened like he was walking through the world with a fresh layer of perception peeled back.

At first, it frightened him. Now, it fascinated him.

Inside the lab, he worked alone, the glow of monitors flickering across his face. His fingers flew across the keyboard, entering new genetic sequences, comparing cellular behavior, tracking mitochondrial anomalies with manic precision. The very thing he had once feared was now living inside his own bloodstream; it was a hybrid state of vampirism. Not fully, he hadn't turned, but he was changed nonetheless.

And now that he could feel the strength surging through his muscles, now that he could move faster, process faster, heal in hours rather than weeks...he didn't just want to cure Sebastian. He wanted to evolve beyond him.

Andrew stepped back from the microscope and rubbed his face. The research had consumed him. The idea of reversing the vampiric condition, not just halting it, but undoing it, was no longer enough. He could feel a new ambition blooming under his skin. If he could isolate the sunlight sensitivity, manipulate the genetic vulnerability to UV radiation, he might not just cure a disease. He might transcend it.

He would be the first of a new species. Human intellect. Vampire power. None of the weaknesses. None of the chains. Although one problem still lingered, and it was a big problem, the sun.

No matter how many simulations he ran, no matter how many models he tested, the sunlight was the wall he couldn't break. His major breakthrough before the attack had shown promise; the vampire cells briefly tolerated a synthesized analog to UV radiation before degrading. It was huge, but not enough.

His hands trembled as he adjusted the Petri dish. Inside, a cluster of Sebastian's hybridized blood cells writhed under the microscope, reacting to controlled UV light. For seven minutes and thirty seconds, they held, but then they died just like before. Andrew leaned back in his chair, heart pounding. "That's it," he whispered. "That's the window I need to keep opening."

It wasn't perfect, but it was something; it was more progress. And progress meant hope. Later that evening, as the lab lights dimmed into evening mode, Andrew found himself summoned to Sebastian's office. He entered without hesitation, the quiet confidence of his enhanced body language showing through the fatigue. Sebastian sat in his chair as usual, backlit by the Los Angeles skyline and the warm amber of UV-protected glass. A glass of crimson swirled in his hand.

"Dr. Lee," Sebastian greeted, smooth as silk. "You're looking stronger."

Andrew offered a polite nod. "Your blood worked. Better than expected."

Sebastian smiled, motioning toward the chair across from him. "You say that like you're surprised."

"Science doesn't favor surprises," Andrew replied, settling into the seat. "But it loves results."

Sebastian's eyes flickered, studying him with interest. "And are you...content with the results?"

Andrew didn't flinch. "I'm alive. That counts for something and making progress every day."

There was a pause. Sebastian tilted his head slightly, as if listening for something beneath the surface. Then he leaned forward.

"Tell me, Dr. Lee...think of something from your past that has a strong emotional connection"

Andrew blinked. "Excuse me?"

"Humor me."

Andrew thinking of the night his mother died. "Okay. Now what?"

Sebastian's smile faltered. Barely. He leaned back slowly, swirling the blood again.

"Interesting."

Andrew watched him. "Is there a problem?"

Sebastian's eyes narrowed, just a flicker. "Not at all. Merely...unexpected. Those who receive the blood of an elder typically form a kind of resonance. A connection. Thoughts, emotions...subtle impressions at the very least."

Andrew's blood ran cold.

"You're saying you can read minds?"

"Not directly, but I can sense truth. Doubt. Loyalty. You, however..."

Sebastian let the words hang.

Andrew held his gaze. "Maybe I'm just harder to read."

Sebastian chuckled softly. "Or maybe you're something else entirely."

For the first time since the attack, Andrew felt truly unsettled.

As he left Sebastian's office, the weight of that conversation echoed in his bones. The lab hadn't just changed him physically. It had set something in motion. Something deeper.

And if Sebastian couldn't read him...it meant Andrew might be the only one playing the game without a leash around his neck.

ndrew hadn't left the lab in nearly forty-eight hours. The sterile glow of the fluorescents made everything feel hyper-real, like he was trapped between brilliance and breakdown.

He moved from station to station with a fevered urgency, analyzing new samples, adjusting serum compositions, and typing notes into his database so quickly the keyboard clicks sounded like a weapon. His body finally healed, no longer requiring rest the way it had before, but his mind had become a tangled wire of genius and obsession.

The breakthrough he'd been making every week had consumed him. The latest serum iteration showed temporary resistance to UV degradation in vampire cells. It wasn't complete, but it was undeniable progress. The next step was clear: he needed to test it on a full vampire host and not just blood under a microscope.

He stood now, staring at the culture tray as the cells wriggled against their synthetic environment. Nine minutes and forty-five seconds. Two minutes longer than the last test. Still not enough, but a new benchmark all the same. It still needed a live host test. He pushed away from the microscope and made his way to Sebastian's office.

Sebastian, ever composed, sat behind his polished obsidian desk, fingers steepled under his chin. Andrew stormed through the office doors with Sebastian's assistant trailing behind. Sebastian nodded, letting her know that it was ok.

Andrew hurried up to his desk and dropped the latest report on his desk, "You need to see this," he said with rushed excitement. His hands shook as he pointed. Not from fear, but maybe exhaustion or something deeper. Something manic. He was pointing to different numbers in the report, wildly waving his arms to accentuate the points of the new numbers.

"You're sure it's stable?" Sebastian asked after Andrew presented the latest data.

"As stable as I can make it without a living test subject," Andrew said. His voice was tight with frustration. "Blood only tells part of the story. I need to test on someone real. Someone turned."

Sebastian tilted his head slightly. "You realize what you're asking? To risk one of my staff on an unproven serum?"

"It won't work without it. You said you wanted results."

Sebastian stood, walking slowly to the glass wall of his office. The Los Angeles skyline burned in gold behind him. "We move with precision here, Dr. Lee. Not haste."

Andrew bristled. "You're protecting pawns when we could be rewriting the rules of the game."

Sebastian turned back, eyes gleaming faintly red in the low light. "Even pawns serve a purpose. And I don't waste my pieces. You want to change the world, Dr. Lee? Then prove your science first. Without shortcuts. Without recklessness."

Andrew's jaw clenched, but he said nothing. When he stormed back to the lab, he found Amelia waiting for him, perched on the edge of his workstation, her arms crossed and expression unreadable.

"You look like you haven't slept in days," she said softly.

He barely looked at her. "I don't need to. Not anymore."

She stepped closer, brushing a hand across his shoulder. "You also haven't eaten. Haven't left this room. I know obsession when I see it."

He pulled away from her touch. "I'm close, Amelia. I can feel it."

"Close to what? Breaking yourself in the name of science? You need to get out of here. Even just for a night. Come with me. We'll go check on the shelter downtown. Hand out meds, and some sandwiches. The world's still out there."

He shook his head, not meeting her eyes. "I can't waste time handing out sandwiches when I'm on the verge of solving a genetic curse."

Her voice cooled. "So what I do is a waste of time?"

He looked up finally, realizing too late how his words landed. "That's not what I meant."

"No? Because that sure as hell sounded like it."

He exhaled sharply, running a hand through his hair. "I just...I need to see this through. If I stop now, I might lose the thread."

"And if you keep going like this, you'll lose yourself."

They stood in silence for a moment, the soft hum of the lab the only sound between them.

Amelia stepped back. "You want to change the world, Andrew? Fine. But if you lose yourself doing it, what's left to save?"

Without waiting for a reply, she turned and walked away, the door sliding shut behind her with a hiss.

Andrew stood alone in the sterile glow, the echo of her footsteps lingering in his chest longer than he wanted to admit.

CHAPTER 45

Amelia didn't answer his messages for almost twelve hours.

Andrew sat at his workstation, a half-filled syringe trembling between his fingers, the unfinished serum catching the cold lab light like a reminder of everything he couldn't control. He hadn't slept. Not properly, and every time he closed his eyes, all he saw was her expression when she walked out of the lab. Disappointed and hurt. It haunted him worse than any nightmare. It was 5 PM, and he couldn't take it anymore. He left the lab.

The Los Angeles sun was starting to make its way down the horizon, and it still glared through the cloud cover as Andrew stepped outside. His face was shielded with a light UV-blocking cream and shaded by a wide-brimmed hat. It wasn't perfect, but it bought him time. Enough to find her. Enough to try. Just after the sunset, he tracked her to Skid Row, the place she always returned to when the world felt too heavy.

She was there, just like he thought. Kneeling beside an elderly man with bandaged hands, offering him bottled water and a warm smile. That smile dimmed when she spotted Andrew.

"Hey," he said, uncertain. "You got a minute?"

She looked him over, then nodded slowly. "Yeah." They stepped aside to a quieter corner between tents and shopping carts. The street noise muffled around them.

Andrew exhaled. "I'm sorry. For what I said. For how I acted. I let the research get to my head. I forgot the bigger picture."

She crossed her arms, not scowling, but not forgiving yet either. "This isn't about me needing an apology. It's about you needing to recognize what matters."

"I do. Now, I do." He stepped closer. "You were right. About taking a step back. About not losing myself. I want to be here. I want to be with you and not just when it's convenient."

A beat passed. Then another. Finally, Amelia sighed. "Then help me pass out these sandwiches. And don't argue if someone asks you for two."

He smiled. "Deal."

They spent the next two hours walking the alleys together. Amelia greeted most of the regulars by name. Andrew kept pace, handing out bags and bottled water, listening to their stories, and for the first time in weeks, he just listened. To stories that didn't end in breakthroughs, but only in survival. To people who had nothing to prove, just something to hold onto. It made everything else feel smaller. They were just being human. Grounded, and he loved her for grounding him.

Back at the Sebastian's office building, the elevator doors to the top floor opened with a soft chime.

Sebastian looked up from his desk as Mayor Billings stepped inside, adjusting his expensive coat with the practiced flair of a politician. His smile was polished, but it didn't reach his eyes.

"Master," Billings said with a shallow nod. "Heard there was a bit of excitement a few weeks ago."

Sebastian closed his tablet, leaning back. "Thank you for coming," he said smoothly. "Just a minor disturbance. My security handled it."

"Ah, of course, but you know how the city gets. Rumors. Whispers. People talk." He took a seat in one of the leather-wrapped chairs. "Some say Dr. Lee was attacked."

Sebastian steepled his fingers. "Some say many things."

"He is, after all, a public figure now. Could be dangerous if someone thought he was a threat. Or valuable."

Sebastian let a pause stretch between them. "It's funny," he said slowly, "I've been wondering who leaked his location that night."

Billings offered a politician's shrug. "Who knows? Do you think someone in your organization would do such a thing?"

"Perhaps. Or maybe someone is trying to play both sides."

Billings smiled, tight and practiced. "That would be reckless."

Sebastian stood, walked to his liquor cart, and poured himself a glass of blood red liquid. "Yes. Reckless."

Billings nodded in agreement, his mind racing. "How's the doctor doing?"

This was the hook Sebastian needed, "he's doing very well considering he nearly bled out. I was able to save his life, you know, through a transfusion, although unfortunately not everything has worked out." Slipping just enough, so if Varek had this information, this would reveal that Billings was the real leak.

He handed the mayor a folder. "Tell your friends at the city council this is the data they'll need for the next vote on housing reform. That should buy us good press."

Billings took the folder, while Sebastian watched him closely. "Thank you for making sure we are always on the right side of the city."

The mayor rose with the folder tucked under his arm. "You always know how to play the game, Master."

Sebastian's smile never reached his eyes. "That's why I never lose."

He watched the mayor leave, glass still in hand.

CHAPTER 46

Beneath the city, industrial lights buzzed against damp stone walls, casting long shadows across the cavernous space. The hum of generators echoed through the halls, powering rooms hastily constructed from stolen equipment.

Varek stood before a steel table in the war room, the hard drive Dr. Lee had lost, clutched in one hand. Syla leaned against the wall behind him, arms crossed, her expression equal parts suspicion and curiosity.

Varek's burner phone buzzed. Unknown number. He answered.

"He's alive," came the mayor's voice, thin and clipped. "Your man failed. Sebastian saved him with a transfusion from his own blood."

Varek's eyes burned red. He didn't respond immediately.

Billings continued. "I've heard he's not a full vampire. Some traits, not all, but he's working in the lab again. Thought you'd want to know."

"Why are you telling me this?" Varek asked coldly.

"Because I still want Sebastian out of the picture, and now the doctor is a variable neither of us controls. Think about that."

The line went dead. Varek turned to Syla, thoughtful now.

"He's playing both sides," Syla muttered, eyes narrowing.

"Feeding us just enough to keep us interested. What's he really after?"

Varek clenched his jaw. "Power. Control. Insurance. He thinks he can pit us against Sebastian, let us bleed each other dry, then take whatever's left."

"So what do we do?"

"We play along," Varek said darkly. "For now. But we feed him misinformation. Something traceable. When it gets back to Sebastian, we'll know for sure. Then we burn Billings, too."

Syla smirked. "Good. I never liked that smug bastard."

"And what about the doctor? We thought he was dead," she said, eyes narrowing. "Kellin's last thing was gutting him, bleeding in the street."

Varek inserted the drive into a terminal. "Kellin was always reckless. He let emotion blind him, and that's why he's dead."

One of Varek's vampires typed furiously on a keyboard, the screen flickered, then burst to life with data logs, genetic sequences, and timestamps. A quiet beep confirmed full access. The screen filled with Andrew Lee's experimental data iterations of serums, blood analyses, and notes scribbled in clipped shorthand.

"This...this isn't just a cure for Sebastian," Varek muttered. "He's trying to reverse it all. A full genetic rewrite. If this works..."

Syla pushed off the wall, coming closer. Her gaze scanned the glowing screen. "Then we wouldn't just walk in daylight. We'd be gods."

"Should we kill him before he completes it?" She asked.

Varek shook his head slowly. "No. Not yet. We let him finish. Let him think he's changing the world. And then we take it."

Syla smirked. "You're thinking long game."

"Always." Varek stared at the data. "Sebastian wants to walk in the light. We'll beat him to it, and when he's vulnerable, we strike."

She leaned in, scanning the data more closely. "If we're serious about this, we need space. A real lab and equipment."

"We'll build it here. Below the city, where no one will find it."

Varek's voice hardened. "We have new rooms needing to be filled. Get the engineers. Start construction tonight on a lab."

Syla arched an eyebrow. "And the doctor?"

"We follow him. Learn what Sebastian won't give him and when the time is right..." He smiled darkly. "He'll come to us. One way or another."

"And if he doesn't?"

Varek's gaze never left the screen. "Then we'll remind him how persuasive pain can be."

In the background, the hum of the generators deepened, as if the nest itself had awakened a beast stirring beneath the city, hungry for the light it had been denied for centuries.

The war wasn't over. It was just beginning, and now, beneath the city, it was evolving.

CHAPTER 47

The breakthrough had come unexpectedly. For weeks, Andrew had meticulously tested each serum variant, pushing the boundaries of cellular resistance to UV damage. After failed batches and small progressions, the latest sample yielded promising results. The tissue didn't degrade; it adapted. It healed faster. It resisted, and it was the closest he'd come.

Andrew stood in front of the wall-mounted display in Sebastian's office, presentation in full swing. Charts, results, and test sequences all scrolled behind him in glowing blue as he spoke.

"This version held for nearly an hour under concentrated UV simulation," Andrew said. "Skin cell degradation was 64% lower. Internal cell temperatures only rose marginally. It's holding."

Sebastian remained seated behind his desk, steepling his fingers. His eyes, unreadable as ever, followed the data, but never wavered from Andrew.

"It's progress," Sebastian said. "But simulation is not sunlight."

"Which is why I need a live subject. I can't go further without real-world testing. The serum won't evolve without it."

"And what happens when your 'progress' sets someone on fire in front of my staff?" Sebastian asked. His tone was mild, but the words bit.

"We adjust. We learn. Science is trial and error."

"We're not in a university lab, Dr. Lee. My people aren't test tubes."

"Then give me just one." Andrew's voice sharpened. "One volunteer. Monitored, timed exposure. I'll take every precaution."

Silence stretched between them.

Finally, Sebastian stood. He walked to the window, sunlight diffused behind the reinforced UV protective glass. "One. Only one. If this fails again, we go back to blood cultures and theory. Are we clear?"

Andrew exhaled, tension finally slipping from his shoulders. "Crystal."

The next day, the test subject, a younger vampire named Malrick, hand-picked by Sebastian for his loyalty and discipline, stood in the observation chamber. The serum had been administered. Andrew paced just outside, flanked by Sebastian and two medical technicians.

"Vitals stable," the tech reported. "No visible reaction."

As the roof pulled back, Malrick stepped into the sunlight. Ten minutes and no burns, but by the fourteen-minute mark, his skin pinked but held. At twenty-two minutes, slight sizzling formed along the forearms, but the healing factor kicked in. The redness faded almost immediately. Andrew watched, stunned. It was working. For the first time, it was working.

Malrick turned and grinned through the glass. "Feels...warm," he said.

Then twenty-eight minutes passed.

Malrick's smile faltered. He blinked rapidly. His hand trembled.

"Something's wrong," the tech said. "Temperature spiking."

Malrick stumbled backward, clutching his abdomen. Smoke curled from his sleeves.

"Get him out of there!" Andrew barked.

The med tech hit the panel. The door hissed open. Malrick stumbled through, and they rushed to meet him, but it didn't stop. His skin blackened. The healing didn't catch up. He screamed, fell to his knees, and the smoke became fire. The flames came from inside, bone-deep combustion. Within seconds, the room filled with choking smoke and the scent of burning flesh. By the time the fire suppression system kicked in, all that remained was a pile of wet ash paste.

Silence fell in the aftermath. Andrew stood shell-shocked, staring at the scorched floor.

Sebastian's voice cut through the haze like a scalpel. "You said it was stable. You told me you were ready."

"We were close. The results were promising."

"Promising doesn't bring back one of my best," Sebastian snapped. "We are not running a butcher shop. This isn't a game of trial and error."

"Science *is* trial and error," Andrew fired back, the frustration finally boiling over. "Do you want perfection or progress?"

"I want results that don't cost me valuable assets," Sebastian said. "Until you can deliver those, you're back to bloodwork and rats."

Andrew murmured. "It should've held. It was holding."

Sebastian advanced slowly, his calm barely containing fury. "You rushed it, and you killed him. You failed the man who trusted you."

That cut him deep. "But science *needs* testing. Setbacks lead to..."

"Not like this," Sebastian snapped. "You don't get to burn my people and hide behind 'process.'"

"Give me another shot," Andrew said. "Not someone important. Just another test subject."

Sebastian's eyes flared. "You think any of them are expendable? You think because you wear a lab coat, you get to decide who lives and who burns?"

Andrew's defiance faltered.

"Until you prove something in blood again," Sebastian growled, "you're done with live subjects. Go back to your cells and simulations. We proceed on my terms."

He turned and stormed out, leaving Andrew standing in the

ashes of his work, the success slipping through his fingers once more, returning to the lab alone. As the roof closed in the observation room with a heavy thud, Andrew stared at the screen. The data, the charts, and everything screamed that he was close. That he could do it. He just needed another chance.

The days blurred into nights and the nights into chemical haze. The only constant was the low whir of lab machines and the slow drip of ambition tightening like a noose around Andrew's throat. He hadn't slept properly in weeks. Not since the serum had almost worked. Not since he watched as a man looked into his eyes in fear as he burned from the inside out like a human torch.

Andrew had stormed back to the lab, the weight of failure and guilt heavier than his rage. He knew what he saw. He knew they were close, but his samples weren't enough. He needed more testing. More exposure. More time.

With weeks bleeding into each other, sleep came in hazy increments. Food was an afterthought. Amelia checked in once or twice. Her presence was warm, grounding, but he was too deep, too obsessed. She didn't push, but maybe she should have. Eventually, something cracked. He couldn't take another night staring at slides and watching cultured blood cells disintegrate, so he left.

The night was cool, the streets damp from a recent drizzle. He wandered down toward Skid Row, thinking maybe he'd surprise Amelia. She'd be there. She always was. Helping the helpless. Reminding him what purpose looked like.

The air shifted as he turned onto the main avenue. He heard the steps before he saw them. Soft, matching his pace. Too rhythmic and too coordinated.

He picked up speed. So did they. His pulse spiked. He turned a corner, and suddenly Varek was there, stepping into the streetlight like a shadow peeling from the wall.

Andrew stopped. The breath froze in his lungs. He reached for his phone.

"Dr. Lee," Varek said, voice smooth, disarmingly calm. "Out for a midnight stroll?"

Figures emerged around them. Three. Four. More behind. All

vampires. Their eyes glowed faintly red, like coals waiting to catch fire. Andrew's fists clenched. He couldn't run. He could fight, but not all of them. Not alone.

"If you're here to finish what..." he began.

Varek raised a hand, almost amused. "Please. If we wanted you dead, you'd already be ash."

Andrew didn't relax.

"We're here because we know what you're working on," Varek continued. "We know you're close. And we know Sebastian is holding you back."

"Who are you? And how do you know anything?"

Varek smiled. "My name is Varek, and we have eyes where it matters."

Andrew hesitated. "What do you want?"

"To help."

"Right. The violent vampires want to *help*."

Varek took a step forward. "You think Sebastian is your ally? He's using you. He wants the sun for himself. You? You're a means to an end."

Andrew's throat tightened. Varek was hitting too close to truths he hadn't wanted to admit.

"I also have what you need," Varek said. "A lab. The equipment, freedom from his oversight. You want to change the world? Come see what that actually looks like."

Andrew looked around. None of the vampires moved. None attacked. It was almost...diplomatic. He felt his thoughts spinning.

Varek stepped beside him and lowered his voice. "Or you can go back. Keep begging for table scraps. Keep watching your breakthroughs burn."

Andrew clenched his jaw.

"One night," Varek said. "That's all I ask. Come with us. See for yourself. Then choose."

Andrew took a breath. Every instinct screamed this was a mistake. But something else, the hunger for answers, for progress that screamed louder.

He nodded, once.

Varek smiled. "Good. This way."

Andrew followed, the night swallowing them both and just maybe, the last part of his conscience with it.

CHAPTER 48

The air underground was cool, dense, and humming with silence, not the emptiness of abandonment, but the stillness of secrets. Andrew followed Varek through the dimly lit tunnel beneath the abandoned warehouse. The sound of their footsteps echoes over damp stone. Torches, yes, actual wall-mounted torches, flickered along the carved stone walls. Not for necessity, the place was wired with advanced lighting and climate control, but Varek had a flair for the theatrical.

"Welcome to the true Los Angeles," Varek said, leading him through a heavy iron doorway. "The one that exists beneath the rot."

The opening revealed a wide expanse that made Andrew's jaw slacken. This wasn't a cave. It was a damn facility. They passed through the cavernous warehouse while vampires built and expanded the nest. Then up to two adjacent tunnels until they reached doorway openings. As they walked through, Andrew saw walls of concrete encased cutting-edge tech: sequencers, mass spectrometers, cryogenic tanks. A lower ceiling than Sebastian's sterile tower, but no less capable, more alive, and definitely more urgent.

"This can be your lab," Syla said, appearing beside them. Her voice was velvet, laced with something sharp. "Everything you need. Everything you've ever wanted, Doctor. No chains. No watchful eyes, just freedom. It's all yours."

Andrew took a few steps in, awe widening his eyes. It wasn't as polished as Sebastian's, but it was advanced and frighteningly so. Some of the equipment he recognized from journals, but had never seen outside of classified government facilities.

"You built this underground?"

"In a world that wants us hidden, we grow roots where no one dares look," Varek said. "We had to be ready. For you."

Andrew turned. "You knew I'd come?"

"We hoped you would," Syla murmured. "But more importantly, we planned."

They continued down the corridor past the lab. A thick steel door with a biometric lock hissed open at their approach. Inside, a row of cell-like chambers lined the wall, each occupied. There were eight in total. The occupants were pale, twitching, and some were sleeping, while others were pacing with nervous energy. Homeless, by the look of them, but something had shifted. Their eyes glowed faintly. Their teeth sharpened.

"Turned recently," Varek said. "They were dying in the streets. Forgotten. We gave them purpose."

Andrew's stomach knotted. "You're using people off the street as your experiments?"

"Volunteers," Syla said. "In the sense that they were already dying. This way, they live. More importantly, they help you succeed."

"You turned the same people Amelia and I are trying to help," Andrew muttered. "We see them as worth saving."

"Well, so do we," Varek replied. "Just differently. You can save all of them, Doctor. Think bigger."

Andrew looked from one chamber to the next. Their eyes met his. Some vacant, some pleading, while others defiant. He looked away. Every success here would be paid in flesh. Could he live with that? He felt his morals begin to fracture under the weight of what he could accomplish here.

"Sebastian denied you live subjects," Varek said, voice low and persuasive. "He fears loss and fears failure. We fear nothing."

"He has a reason," Andrew said, though it sounded weak, even to him. "He lost someone important."

"And what did that loss teach him? Fear. Hesitation. A cage built of glass and control," Syla said, circling him. "You don't need to live in his shadow. Here, we give you light."

"You don't care about them," Andrew said quietly. "These people..."

"We care about progress," Varek snapped, his tone hardening. "And right now, you're the only one who can deliver it. You know that. We know that."

Andrew turned back to the lab, to the hum of machines and promise. It was everything he needed and everything Sebastian withheld.

"What do you want from me in return?"

Syla stepped forward. "Information. Quietly. What Sebastian suspects. What he plans. Nothing overt. Nothing dangerous, just enough to stay ahead."

"And the serum? You'll let me test it on them?"

"Under your full control," Varek said. "We're not here to interfere, only to enable."

Andrew hesitated, the weight of Amelia's voice echoing in his memory. *You're not like them. You help people.* But what if this *was* helping? What if she saw the results? Would she understand then?

"I want full access to your resources," he said. "No restrictions. I work how I want, when I want."

Varek grinned, fangs just barely visible. "Agreed."

They walked him back toward the tunnel entrance. Andrew's heart pounded with a mixture of adrenaline and fear. He had crossed a line, but he was closer than ever. He had to believe that.

Before they parted, Varek rested a hand on his shoulder. "We're not here to control you, Doctor. We want to see you rise. To win. And when you do, we'll be there, ready to walk in the light beside you. You understand that, don't you?"

Andrew nodded, already thinking of formulations. Of adjustments. Of the way Amelia's eyes lit up when he spoke of progress.

He would make this work. He would change their lives. One way
or another.

CHAPTER 49

Reece had always trusted his instincts. They'd kept him alive through desert warfare, black site infiltration, and vampire hunts that left most men twitching in their sleep. But now...they were telling him something he didn't want to believe.

That not every vampire was a monster, and worse, that trusting his instincts might be the thing that breaks his team apart.

He kept to the shadows on the edge of Skid Row, hood up, footsteps soft over the broken pavement. Across the street, Amelia's motorcycle sat parked beneath a graffiti-covered street-lamp, its black frame gleaming under a weak orange glow. Reece's eyes flicked toward the movement ahead.

There she was.

She emerged from the alley like a ghost in leather and boots, a messenger bag slung over one shoulder. No weapons to be seen nor bloodlust. Just her.

He watched, crouched behind a rusted-out van, unsure of what he'd expected. Was she hunting? Is this her feeding ground?

Amelia walked up to a group of huddled tents and knelt beside a shivering man curled in a sleeping bag. She handed him a thermos, then medicine. Touched his shoulder gently, said something that made him smile.

He'd seen a thousand vampire kills. Quick, brutal, and detached. This wasn't that.

She was checking wounds and distributing food. Carrying first-aid kits, moving from tent to tent like a medic in a warzone. Not a predator, but an angel.

Reece stayed rooted, invisible behind the van, watching her finish her route before slipping back onto her bike and roaring off into the night. Reece had spent years painting the world in black and white, hunters and monsters, clean lines and cleaner kills. Watching her now, those lines blurred. That scared the hell out of him.

He didn't follow her. Not yet. He just...stood there for a while, staring at the space she'd just occupied.

This went on for weeks; she wasn't hunting, she was helping. On the last night of surveillance, he crouched down beside the spot she'd left. He found blood here, but it wasn't fresh; it wasn't hers, but still pungent in the air. This wasn't unusual for Skid Row, but his gut tensed all the same. He started checking the edges of the camp. That's when he noticed it. One of the tents, the one with the bright yellow top that said "JESUS SAVES" etched in marker on the flap, was empty; it stayed empty. No signs of struggle, but the bedroll was still there. So were the boots. The blankets. Like someone had just stepped out and never returned.

The next night, two more tents stood empty. Their beds were untouched, and their boots unmoved. No sign of struggle, just the eerie stillness of people who'd vanished without taking anything. It was like they'd vanished into thin air. Reece stood motionless, piecing it together. Amelia hadn't hurt anyone. But someone had, and someone was doing it under the cover of her goodwill. That's when he made his decision.

Back at their hideout, the tension in the air was already thick. Cole was cleaning his weapons on the table, his jaw tight, eyes sharp. Marcus leaned against the wall, arms crossed, his silence louder than any accusation. Reece closed the door behind him as he walked to the table.

"I've been watching her," Reece said, stepping in. "The female vampire from the fundraiser."

Cole's head snapped up. "Finally decided to finish the job?"

"She's not hunting. Not like the others."

Cole scoffed, slamming a clip into his rifle. "Oh, spare me. She's a bloodsucker, Reece. That's the job."

"She's feeding the homeless. Bandaging wounds and giving out medicine. I've watched her for weeks. Each night I see her, she's on the streets, helping them."

"She's using them," Cole barked. "You think this is kindness? It's cover and manipulation. Classic predator behavior, make 'em trust you, then pick 'em off."

Reece slammed a hand on the table. "She's not picking anyone off! People are disappearing, yeah, but not by her hand. Something else is going on down there. I think vampires are abducting the homeless. And we don't know who. That's what I've been trying to find out."

Cole stood, fists clenched. "So now you're tailing vampires instead of staking them? What's next, bringing her flowers? You've gone soft, Reece. What's worse, you've gone blind."

Reece's voice was low and dangerous. "Say that again."

Marcus stepped in. "Alright, both of you, cool it."

"No," Cole growled. "He's compromised. He's lying to us. Taking nights off to watch the enemy, and we're supposed to trust that?"

"I'm doing what you won't," Reece snapped. "Thinking. Asking questions. There's more to this. The mayor's dirty. Someone's feeding vamps intel. And this," he pointed toward his chest, "this isn't about one vampire anymore, it's about the whole damn system."

Cole shook his head, disgust curling his lip. "You're not our leader anymore."

The silence hit like a gunshot. Marcus straightened. "Hold up, now." He looked between them, between Cole's fury and Reece's fire, and said nothing more, but something in Cole's eyes shifted. Quiet and calculating.

Reece didn't say a word. He grabbed his gear from the table and stalked toward the door.

"Where you going?" Marcus called.

Reece paused, just long enough to answer over his shoulder. "Back to Skid Row. To find out who's really behind this." Then he was gone.

Back on the edge of the camp, Reece settled into the same spot behind the rusted van. His boots pressed into broken glass and wet leaves. The street was quiet and empty.

He pulled out his scope, scanning the camp. No Amelia. Not tonight. Just emptiness, but it was a different kind now. As if something darker had come through and scraped it clean, and Reece knew, whatever was coming next was already closer than anyone realized.

CHAPTER 50

Sebastian stood at the windows of his office as his thoughts drifted like smoke, wrapping around a question he couldn't shake.

How is he making progress this fast?

Behind him, the soft tap of shoes approached. Sebastian didn't turn.

"Dr. Lee just submitted another report," said Evelyn, his assistant. "Immunoreactivity in modified samples doubled in three days."

Sebastian finally shifted, glancing over his shoulder. "Three days? He was at a plateau a week ago."

"He claims to have refined the formula using a retroviral binding sequence and something he calls a stabilized ultraviolet conversion protocol."

Sebastian raised a brow. Clever. But this was too fast.

"Thank you, Evelyn. That'll be all."

She nodded and exited the room.

Sebastian turned back to the glass. His suspicions weren't idle. Dr. Lee was brilliant, yes, but science rarely jumped tracks that quickly without some...outside stimulus. He'd noticed the doctor's fatigue. Dark circles, the occasional slip in composure. The man was burning himself at both ends, and Sebastian intended to find out what had lit the second flame as he flicked through screens on his tablet.

Days later, beneath the city, far from sterile walls and biometric locks, Andrew stood in the low-lit lab, trembling hands covered in latex and sweat. The first subject, a vampire barely two weeks turned from a man, who once panhandled on 6th Street, lay still on the examination table. The serum had failed. Not immediately. At first, the signs were promising stabilized vitals, increased energy, but then came the spasms, the convulsions, and finally, the collapse. The body seized, ignited from the inside, and turned to ash before Andrew's eyes.

He didn't speak for a long time. Syla stood beside him, silent and unreadable, her expression oddly reverent. The second attempt was worse.

Another volunteer and another failure. Only this time, the death was slower. More agonizing. The vampire's screams echoed through the concrete walls of the nest, haunting Andrew long after the silence returned. That was number two, he thought. He nearly gave up.

"Skin held up for nearly forty minutes this time," he muttered into a recorder. "Pulmonary collapse began at the thirty-nine-minute mark. Neural tissue showed brief resistance, but succumbed with the dermal layer."

The vampire's eyes were still open when the body turned to ash. He used to say a prayer after the loss. Now he just documented it. He peeled off the rest of the protective gear, wiping his brow with the back of his forearm. The scent of ozone and burned flesh still clung to the air, thick and angry.

He locked himself away in the lab's back corner for days afterward, unable to eat, barely sleeping. He kept seeing their faces. Not monsters, but they were people. Scared, desperate people he once would have tried to save.

"I can't do this," he whispered to Syla. "Not if it means...this."

Syla placed a gloved hand on his shoulder. "You're helping them. You're building a future for all of us. What's a little pain if it means freedom?"

"You want a life with Amelia in the daylight? A cure? Then this is the path. You think progress comes without a price?" Andrew screamed in his thoughts to himself. He refocused with renewed determination to solve the problem.

The third subject didn't die. Not right away. His skin blistered in the UV exposure chamber, but didn't peel. He stood longer than the last two combined. Thirty-four minutes and finally forty minutes passed before the third subject had to be removed from the light.

By the fifth test, Andrew was breaking records. Each host endured longer. Not just sunlight resistance, but they were getting stronger, faster. The serum amplified everything. It was working. But there was a catch.

The mutations were irreversible. Once a vampire received a dose, a second injection would destabilize the cells. One shot per subject. No retests. He needed new bodies...again.

He turned as Syla entered, clipboard in hand.

"That makes five," she said, matter-of-factly.

"I need more."

"There are three left," she said with a curious look.

Andrew paced. "That's not enough. I need fresh subjects.

"Varek says you work with what you have."

He snapped. "Then tell Varek he's sabotaging his own miracle."

Syla raised a brow, intrigued rather than offended. "You're welcome to tell him yourself."

Varek's chamber was colder than the rest of the nest. A psychological design, the kind that made you feel like prey even when you were invited.

"You're killing them," Varek said, lounging in a chair carved from dark stone. "Every time you break through a limit, it costs a body."

Andrew didn't flinch. "And every time I break a limit, we get closer to walking in sunlight."

Varek chuckled. "Spoken like a man with purpose."

Andrew folded his arms. "Let me get more."

"You want to go to your shelter?"

"No, everyone there has been put into the system. There would be too many questions if they go missing, but I know where to find them."

Varek's eyes gleamed. Syla, nearby, watched silently, her lips curling.

"Very well," Varek said. "Bring back what you need. Just remember, Doctor, you're one of us now. Not just in blood."

Later that night, Andrew stood in an alley off Fifth and San Pedro, his hood up, his eyes scanning the rows of tents and makeshift shelters. He had a pack slung over his shoulder containing protein bars, antiseptic, and water. The things Amelia used to bring. He used to watch her do this and admire her for it, but tonight, he was looking for something else.

A man limped by, mumbling to himself. Another huddled near a barrel fire and nearby a younger man, maybe twenty, coughing uncontrollably, blood staining his sleeve. Andrew approached and offered a bottle of water. A blanket. When the boy looked at him with exhausted gratitude, Andrew's expression softened.

Andrew hesitated. Just a second. Just long enough to wonder if Amelia would ever look at him the same way again.

Then he offered the blanket.

"Come with me," he said. "I can help you."

The boy nodded. Behind his eyes, guilt warred with resolve. But the resolve was winning. He had a purpose now. In the shadows, Varek watched from a rooftop.

"He's ready," he said.

Syla's voice was barely a breath. "Soon, he won't even remember what it felt like to hesitate."

Andrew led the boy into the alley, toward the waiting van, and away from the man he used to be.

"Soon," she whispered. "He'll be ours entirely."

CHAPTER 51

Amelia had been floating lately. There was no better way to describe it. After everything they had been through, she and Andrew were finally...good. Actually, better than good. He laughed again. Smiled like he used to, and every smile he gave her was for a reason deeper than science. Now his joy was something else. It was her. It was for them. For their future.

"I ran simulations last night," Andrew said as they sat together at a quiet corner booth in their usual late-night spot. "If the UV resistance markers hold up in secondary trials, we could see real metabolic stability under full-spectrum exposure. Enough to build from."

Amelia smirked around her straw. "Sounds hot."

He chuckled. "You know what I mean. We could walk in the sun, Amelia. Maybe not tomorrow...but someday. You and me, no shadows, no alleyways. A walk in the park, in the sunshine."

She'd rolled her eyes then, teasing, but her heart had been full. The idea that someone could dream like that for her, not about power, not about blood, but about sunlight meant more than he knew.

And it lasted. For a while. Each late-night dinner, each brief touch, each glance, they all built something steady, something bright, and something they could look forward to.

Until the cracks began. It was subtle at first. The way his

fingers twitched when he wasn't holding a pen or a scalpel. The dark circles beneath his eyes, which he brushed off with a joke about too much caffeine, but it wasn't caffeine, and it wasn't nothing. Then one night, during what should have been another dreamy, casual dinner, she saw it. He was distracted, barely touching his food, chewing on the inside of his cheek like he was doing calculations in his head.

"Andrew?" she asked, nudging his foot under the table.

He blinked at her. "What?"

"I asked if you wanted to swing by Skid Row with me tonight. There's this woman, Lucille, I promised I'd bring more insulin."

His jaw tightened. "Amelia, I have work. Important work. I can't just keep playing street nurse with you. Do you get that?"

She blinked, stunned. "Do you hear yourself right now?" The air went still between them. "Playing?" she repeated quietly.

He sighed, immediately realizing his mistake. "I didn't mean it like that. I just...I'm close to something. Really close. And it feels like everything else is a distraction."

Her mouth was a tight line. She didn't argue. She didn't yell.

Instead, she gathered her bag and stood. "Good luck, Doctor." She didn't wait for his apology.

Her mind was still reeling from Andrew's growing distance. She was happy. She *had* been happy, but happiness, she reminded herself, was not a guarantee. It was a moment. A fragile, flickering thing, and if Andrew's flicker was going out, she'd just have to be her own flame.

She hadn't even realized how much she'd been leaning on him until she found herself walking the darkened streets of Skid Row alone again, back to where it all started. This was the place that kept her grounded. Not his experiments or his dreams. This. The air smelled like sweat, and struggle. It wrapped around her like a familiar shroud. She passed by Lisa's camp, still intact. She handed out food and distributed meds with shared smiles. Then she realized she hadn't seen Manny. He was always one of the first to catch her attention. She walked by his little corner and saw his empty chair.

Looking over at Lisa again, she asked, "Have you seen Manny? I wanted to check his bandages again."

"I'm sorry, dear, I haven't seen him since yesterday. He hasn't been back to his chair all day."

"Ok, will you let me know if you see him. With all these folks going missing, I just want to make sure you all are safe."

"Of course, dear, I'll let you know as soon as I see him," Lisa replied as Amelia started her deeper search.

Amelia's boots echoed against the cracked pavement as she moved past familiar corners, eyes scanning for Manny's crooked grin and patched-up coat. He was always here. Always waiting to trade stories for coffee or loose change.

But tonight, the corner was empty.

Her chest tightened. She stopped strangers, asked quick questions, but every shake of their heads only deepened the hollow in her gut. She turned down the alley where he sometimes slept, the shadows thicker here. That's when she saw it: a leg jutting out from under a mound of black trash bags, wrapped in the same bandages she'd changed for him days ago.

"No..." Her voice cracked as she pushed forward, tearing at the slick plastic.

The sight stole the air from her lungs. Manny lay sprawled, eyes glassy and unblinking. His skin ashen and stretched tight. There wasn't a drop of blood left in him. His mouth hung open like he'd tried to call out, but no one had come.

Amelia's hands trembled where they hovered above his chest. This wasn't just another nameless victim in Skid Row. This was *Manny*. A man she'd patched up, fed, and listened to. One of hers. Rage cut through the grief like a blade. The missing weren't statistics anymore. They were her people. And someone had stolen them from her.

She pulled out her phone and pressed Sebastian's number with trembling fingers, pacing the alley as the phone rang. When he answered, his voice was smooth, almost warm. "Amelia. To what do I owe the pleasu..."

"They killed Manny." Her voice was low, edged with fury.

"And who is Manny?" Sebastian's cold voice responded.

"He's one of the men I take care of on Skid Row. They drained him like he was nothing. I want to know who's behind this. Now."

There was a pause on the other end, too long to be hesitation, too practiced to be surprise. "That's... unfortunate," Sebastian said at last. "But people die in that part of the city every day. It's a sad truth."

"Don't do that." Her grip on the phone tightened until the plastic creaked. "You *know* this isn't random. You told me about the price on my head, about the Reign. Are they the same ones who attacked Andrew and are now preying on the homeless? Tell me what you're not saying."

His chuckle was soft, infuriating. "Careful, Amelia. Accusing me of half-truths when I'm the only one willing to give you any truth at all? That's not wise."

"Sebastian..."

"I'll look into it," he cut in smoothly. "But answers take time. In the meantime, stay alive. You're far more valuable breathing than buried."

The line clicked dead before she could reply.

Amelia lowered the phone slowly, bile rising in her throat. He knew more. He *always* knew more. And if he wasn't telling her, it was because it served his plans.

CHAPTER 52

Reece adjusted the hood of his jacket as he leaned against a cold metal dumpster tucked in the shadows of Skid Row. It was past midnight, the quiet hum of the city interrupted only by the occasional rustle of wind or the distant cough of a street dweller trying to sleep. He'd been here for hours. Watching. Waiting, but she wasn't there tonight again. He'd hoped to spot her and maybe ask her what the hell she really was, but the night was silent.

He exhaled, ready to pack up, when movement caught the edge of his vision. A figure. Tall and lean with a confident stride. Reece narrowed his eyes, reaching for the small monocular in his coat. He brought it to his eye.

"Well, I'll be damned," he muttered. "It's Dr. Lee, and he's alive."

Reece felt an odd twist in his gut, a strange blend of relief and suspicion. But then he saw it. A flash. It was faint, but real. Andrew's eyes, they glowed. Not bright, not overtly, but unmistakably red in the shadows.

Reece stiffened.

No way. I imagined that, he told himself. *After everything we've seen, maybe I'm just paranoid.*

Still, instinct took over. He melted deeper into the shadows, following Andrew at a distance. Andrew was smiling as he approached a group of men huddled around a fire pit. Reece crouched behind a rusted-out car, close enough now to hear their conversation.

"Still holding strong, I see," Andrew said to a bearded man bundled in layers of patchy flannel.

"We get by, doc. Thanks for the antibiotics last time. Saved my damn leg."

Andrew handed him a sealed bag. "Some gauze, vitamin D supplements, and protein bars. Share 'em if you can."

He moved to another man who was coughing. Andrew placed his hand against his forehead, "No fever, that's a good sign. You need more of those inhalers, right?"

The man nodded and clutched his shoulder. "You're an angel."

"Hardly," Andrew said with a warm chuckle.

Reece's grip on the camera slackened slightly. *Okay, I was defi-nitely seeing things. Maybe the glow was just a reflection. This guy's helping just like the female vampire.* Reece felt something uncoil in his chest. Maybe he'd been wrong.

Then Andrew moved again. He spotted a large young man, standing nearly 6'6", but slumped forward, obviously showing signs of physical distress, and he curled against a chain-link fence. He was pale, shivering, and clearly sick. Andrew carefully walked up and offered him a bottle of water. "Hey. Are you all right?"

The injured man flinched.

"It's okay," Andrew said gently. "Here. Take this." He pulled a blanket from his bag and wrapped it around the man's shoulders. "You're freezing. Come with me, we can get you somewhere warm."

The man blinked down at him, not sure what to make of it. "Hold on, are you a doctor or something?"

"Yeah. And I have a place that can help. If you trust me?"

The large man hesitated, then nodded. Andrew helped him steady his feet for the walk and began guiding him down the alley. Reece followed. Camera in hand, he snapped a few shots of

Andrew's profile, the blanketed man, their two figures walking into the dark. He stayed back as they turned a corner, out of sight.

Moments later, headlights flickered from behind a low building. Reece darted behind a dumpster and watched as a nondescript white van rolled slowly into view. Two large men dressed all in black with trench coats stepped out and exchanged words with Andrew. Then they opened the sliding door and helped the man inside.

"Well, those guys don't look like orderlies. What are you up to, Doctor?" Reece muttered to himself, "And where the hell are you all taking him?"

As the van began to back out, Reece crouched low, thumbed a magnetic GPS tracker from his pocket, and flung it.

Clink. It stuck.

He bolted for his own car, firing up the GPS receiver. The blinking dot on the screen moved slowly west, then took a sudden turn away from downtown.

That wasn't the way towards the shelter, he thought.

Reece followed, headlights dimmed, keeping at least three blocks back as he followed the blinking dot on his screen. The van passed Downtown Medical Center, rolled through deserted industrial corridors until it pulled into a rundown warehouse district. It stopped outside a building that looked condemned with broken, boarded-up windows and a chain link fence sagging like tired skin. Reece parked down the block, got out, and slinked low behind a row of abandoned crates. He pulled out his camera again.

Andrew and the others exited the van. They slid the side door open and coaxed the man out. His legs buckled. The two big men supported his heavy frame. They approached the warehouse entrance, which had massive steel doors rusted at the seams. Suddenly, they creaked open.

Then one of the men turned and scanned the area. His red eyes glowed through the night; it was clear as day. Reece froze.

Vampires. There was no reflection. This wasn't a mistake.

The man stared into the night. Reece held his breath. After a beat, the vampire turned and followed the others inside as the doors closed behind him. As the rain started to fall, Reece sat in silence, crouched and hidden, his heart hammering in his chest. His eyes stayed locked on that building, even as the camera shook in his hands.

Okay, Doc...what the hell are you doing?

CHAPTER 53

Reece burst through the safe house door just after 2 AM, rain clinging to his jacket in heavy droplets. His jaw was tight, his wet steps sloshed across the hardwood as he tossed his gear on the nearby table. Cole, Marcus, and Hot Shot were still awake, gathered around the monitors tracking drone surveillance footage.

Cole looked up. "You look like hell."

Reece ignored the jab. He grabbed a towel, wiped the back of his neck, and walked straight to the center of the room. "I found Andrew Lee."

Hot Shot blinked. "Wait, the doctor? He still alive? Where?"

"Skid Row. I was surprised myself. He looked like nothing happened to him. At first, I thought he was just checking in on people, handing out food and meds like the female vampire. That's what it looked like. Until I started following him."

Marcus leaned forward, sensing the shift in tone. "And?"

Reece hesitated for a beat. "He took one of the homeless with him. Led him to a van. Three men total. I followed them to a warehouse on the outskirts of downtown. It was a run-down place, no guards on the outside but heavily fortified. One of the men who got out with Andrew...he had red eyes. Definitely a vampire."

Cole stood. "So, what? You're saying the doc's been turned? That he's working with them now?"

"I don't know, but something's off. He's different. I saw his eyes glow, too. Faint, but I saw it."

Hot Shot, still limping, exhaled. "Jesus. And we thought the mayor was the one to keep an eye on."

Reece shook his head. "We can't rule out Sebastian. He's still in the center of this web, but something tells me the doc is being used or he's crossed over."

Cole scoffed. "Or maybe you've gotten too soft. First female vampire, now the doc. You see the good in everyone, while the rest of us are out here watching them rack up body counts."

Reece met his eyes without flinching, but his fists had clenched, knuckles pale under the strain. "I'm seeing facts, and the fact is, the doc is involved, but we don't know how. And the female vampire, like I said, hasn't killed anyone. We all saw her at the fundraiser and I've watched her for weeks in Skid Row. Not a single person."

"You were supposed to take her out," Cole snapped. "That was the mission. Not babysit. Not stalk."

"Enough!" Hot Shot's voice cracked through the room like a whip. "We don't have time to turn on each other."

Reece paced, running a hand through his wet hair. "Here's what we do. Cole, you and Marcus keep digging into the mayor. We know he's connected, and that burner phone number might still have intel."

Cole hesitated, jaw clenched, then gave a terse nod. "Fine. But I'm not dropping that vampire bitch."

"You won't have to. I'll handle that," Reece said. "I'm going back to Skid Row. Too many people are disappearing. I've seen it myself, the young homeless, gone without a trace. They're being taken."

"Taken for what?" Marcus asked.

"I don't know yet. But I'm going to find out."

Hot Shot tapped at her keyboard. "I'll keep drones circulating the area. Did you get a tracker on the van?

"Yeah, I got one on the van," Reece replied,

"Ok, I'll keep track of the van, and if we get movement, I'll ping you." Hot Shot said.

Reece gave her a grateful nod. "Good. Keep eyes on it."

The room fell quiet, and no one spoke. Even the hum of the monitors seemed to fade. The weight of the plan settled into their bones. They all felt it; the war was shifting. Lines were blurring, and allies and enemies weren't so clear anymore.

Reece turned to leave again, grabbing his gear.

Cole crossed his arms. "Where are you going now?"

"To see what Andrew's doing with the homeless, he's taking. And if I find out he's hurting them..."

Reece didn't finish the sentence. He didn't need to.

The door shut behind him with a low, definitive click.

CHAPTER 54

The low orange glow of early evening spilled down the graffiti-tagged alleys of Skid Row, reflecting in puddles and cracked glass. Amelia hadn't made it down to Skid Row in a few days as she moved quietly between the rows of tents and makeshift shelters. With a canvas bag slung over one shoulder, her boots thudded softly against wet pavement as she handed out water bottles, sandwiches, and small bundles of medical supplies to familiar faces.

"You seen Johnny?" she asked an older woman wrapped in a tattered blanket beside a shopping cart.

The woman shook her head, eyes sunken and wary. "He was here yesterday. Had his guitar and everything. Then he just...vanished. Didn't take none of his stuff."

Amelia's brow creased. That made another disappearance this week.

"Anyone else gone missing?"

"Taye, young guy with the red hoodie. And that new girl, Sandy. Same story, but her tent's still here."

Amelia handed her an extra granola bar and moved on, unease curling in her gut. She caught whispers in the alleys, talk of shadows that didn't belong, people who came at night and never came back, but no one mentioned Sebastian's name anymore. That silence said everything. It was clear, someone else was doing this. Her senses were sharper than most, and tonight they buzzed like static under her skin. She paused near the edge of the block, kneeling beside a man who was missing a shoe and wearing a beanie. "Any trouble lately?"

He looked up with glassy eyes. "Sometimes I hear voices. Not the regular kind. Low, like they're trying not to wake the dark. You feel me?"

She did. More than he knew. Ever since she found Manny, more and more people were going missing and Sebastian wasn't giving her any new information. As she stood, she felt it. A prickle at the back of her neck. There was movement, a breath shifted the air behind her. Someone was following her. She didn't turn. Not yet.

Instead, she started walking. At a measured pace, boots scuff against the curb. Her fingers curled loosely near the hem of her jacket, ready if anything turned violent. She let him follow for three blocks before he ducked into a dim alley between two buildings, one with a broken neon sign buzzing like a dying insect.

"You can come out now," she called, voice flat but amused. "Your footsteps are lighter than a thief, but you're not exactly silent."

Reece stepped into view, his hands visible and nonthreatening. He looked worn, jaw tight with whatever he hadn't said yet.

"I didn't come to fight."

"Pity. I was starting to think you'd only ever show up to try to kill me."

He ignored the bait. "I needed to see what you were really doing down here."

"And?"

"I see you're helping people. Like, really helping them. No feeding or attacks. Just...handing out food and medicine."

"Told you I wasn't like the others."

"No, you didn't. You just ran."

A pause. Amelia sighed. "So what now? You stake me for being a good Samaritan?"

"No. I came to talk. Something's going on here, and I'm not sure what it is. My name is Reece."

She folded her arms. "Okay, I'm Amelia, and I'm listening."

He hesitated, then pulled out his phone and flicked through photos. "You recognize him?"

The screen showed Andrew, smiling, handing a blanket to a young homeless man. Her stomach fluttered.

"Yeah, of course I do. What about it?"

"Keep watching."

He showed her another series, Andrew leading the same man to a van. Then another one of the van, pulling up to an abandoned warehouse. Then a grainy shot of red eyes from the shadows.

"This doesn't make sense," Amelia murmured.

"I thought the same. Until I saw it happen. The warehouse is just outside downtown."

She stared at the images, struggling to breathe as Reece told her exactly where the warehouse was. Her heartbeat thundered in her ears, barely registering anything he was saying.

"No. He wouldn't. Not Andrew."

"I didn't want to believe it either," Reece said, softer now. "But I've seen enough people change. Good ones. Smart ones. It doesn't take much to lose yourself in the name of progress, and I don't think he's the same man as he leads us to believe. I don't know what he is."

Amelia stepped back. Her mind raced, the late nights, the experiments he wouldn't talk about, the distant look in his eyes lately. And all the people gone missing. Manny's death. All the cracks she'd tried not to see. Was he somehow a part of all this?

She tried to process what the images told her, but her mind screamed for denial. She wanted to believe in him; she needed to. After centuries of burying love beneath survival, Andrew felt like a miracle. Not just a man, but a reason to hope again. Someone who saw her. Someone who reminded her what love could be. And now...was that all a lie?

No, her heart argued. There had to be an explanation. Maybe

he was doing something to help. Maybe he had no choice. Maybe he was being forced.

But a deeper part of her, the one forged in centuries of betrayal, whispered. *You've seen this before.*

"I need time," she whispered, throat dry.

"You have it," Reece said. "But Amelia...if you find out I'm right, you know what comes next."

She didn't answer. Just turned, walked past the broken neon, and disappeared into the dark. Her boots echoed against the wet pavement, but the sound of her hope cracking was louder.

CHAPTER 55

The sterile, humming silence of the underground lab was broken only by the steady beeping of biometric sensors and the quiet tap of Andrew's fingers against the touchscreen display. He stood before the sealed observation chamber, sweat dotting his brow, his lab coat smeared with dried blood and covered in scribbled notes. On the other side of the glass, a vampire host paced the small cell like a caged animal. Sunlight streamed through a reinforced UV-filtered skylight, mimicking the real thing.

It had been ten minutes since the serum injection. No burns. No screaming. No smoke.

Andrew leaned in. "Vitals steady. Core temp slightly elevated, but within tolerance. Forty-five minutes have now passed."

The vampire inside was lean and twitchy. This was the tenth turned subject from the Skid Row extractions. Unlike the previous test group, these hadn't burst into flames or collapsed, screaming in agony. In fact, all seven current test subjects had responded to the latest iteration of the serum with remarkable resilience. These seven had already endured over an hour of controlled UV light in preliminary trials.

"Increasing exposure," Andrew murmured, voice barely audible. He tapped a command.

The lighting intensified.

Inside, the subject growled low, more animal than man, eyes flashing red for a heartbeat before calming. The restraints on his temper were fraying. Andrew noted the behavioral shift. Stronger and faster, yes, but the cognitive changes were becoming more pronounced.

They're losing inhibition, he thought. *Becoming something else.*

Still, they obeyed. So far, only him though, he thought, and it was probably because of his blood. That was the variable he hadn't shared with Varek, Syla, or even Sebastian. They thought this was just scientific advancements. They didn't know he'd shifted the formula two weeks ago, replacing each turned vampire's blood with small infusions of his own altered blood. The moment he did, the deaths stopped. The vampires stabilized, and they listened to him.

He'd told himself it was a necessity. They needed a breakthrough, something radical. Something living, but now, watching the fourth subject circle the perimeter of his cell like a predator, Andrew felt the unease tickle up the back of his spine. They were becoming something new. They were stronger, smarter, and loads deadlier. His blood was the difference, and it was time to test the final phase on his last subject and then on himself.

He hadn't told Amelia. He hadn't told anyone, but if the serum could offer *hours* in the sun? That was everything. Not just for him but also for her. For them.

He pictured her beside him in Griffith Park, sunlight catching in her hair, her hand steady in his. No shadows or secrets. Just the quiet kind of love people take for granted, but first, he needed to survive the next step.

He turned from the chamber and moved to his private bench. Inside a refrigerated case labeled UV-*Trial-9A*, nestled in foam, were three silver cylinders, syringe tips at the ends with a pale iridescent liquid in the clear side window. The last and final serum.

His fingers hovered over it. Soon, he thought. Then he would be ready to share it with Amelia. From behind him, the vampire in the chamber roared. Not in pain. In hunger. Andrew turned slowly, watching the subject slam against the glass with enough force to crack it. He didn't flinch. They obeyed him, at least for now. He looked up. Seventy-eight minutes, and the vampire was still alive. The clock glowed like a verdict. The serum had held. No more trials. No more excuses. It was time. This was the moment.

223

CHAPTER 56

Mayor Walter Billings adjusted his cufflinks as he stepped out of the black SUV idling beneath a broken streetlamp. The alleyway reeked of stale oil and city runoff, a far cry from the polished marbled corridors of his office, but power often moved in shadows, not in press briefings.

Syla was already waiting, leaning casually against the hood of a matte-black classic sedan, her silhouette sharp under the flickering streetlight. Her eyes tracked him like a predator weighing a meal.

"You're late," she said flatly.

"I just left Sebastian's office," Billings replied, stopping a few feet from her. He glanced once over his shoulder and saw no tails. Good. He smiled. "Besides, someone like you doesn't wait unless it's worth it."

Syla didn't smile back. "Why the in-person meeting? You've never risked that before."

Billings reached into his coat pocket and pulled out a silver cigarette case. He flipped it open, withdrew one, and lit it slowly. The orange flare briefly lit his face. "I needed to make sure you understood the stakes."

"We know the stakes. He clings to power. We're here to rip it from him." Syla said.

Billings exhaled a plume of smoke. "Then consider this a favor...or a warning. Sebastian's been making moves. Quiet ones.

But expensive ones. He's ordered military grade sensors under shell companies. Last-minute construction in his office building. Some sort of 'containment system' in the east wing. Not in the plans and not on the books."

High above the alley, from the rooftop of a condemned building across the street, Marcus adjusted the zoom on his scope. Cole ducked as a gust of wind stirred debris across the rooftop.

"You think they made us?"

Marcus kept his eye on the scope. "Not yet. But we won't get a second chance if they do."

"That's that blonde vamp bitch that attacked us on the streets," he said, his voice low and grim into the comms. "No mistaking her."

Cole, crouched beside him behind a vent shaft, swore under his breath. "I think that's the one that almost killed Hot Shot."

Marcus continued recording through the scope's camera. Down below, the Mayor and Syla stood close, their body language unmistakably confidential.

Syla narrowed her eyes. "You sure?"

"They came across my desk," he said, tapping his temple, "through the cracks. Not addressed to him, of course. But I've been watching him long enough to recognize his fingerprints. He's also sending Camille, his security chief, and his personal guards down to Skid Row tonight based on an anonymous tip I happened to drop from my office. I knew it would get to him. I overheard them planning when I was at his office. He'll be exposed and vulnerable tonight."

She folded her arms. "Why tell us?"

"Because if I were you," Billings said, stepping closer, lowering his voice, "I'd want to know that he's not just waiting. He's preparing. Maybe for defense. Maybe for something more...proactive. Either way, he's not sitting idle."

Syla held his gaze, trying to peel back the layers. Lies were easy to spot when they were clumsy, but Billings has been playing this game for a long time. This was careful manipulation.

"And what do you want in return?"

He smiled. "Peace. Order. A balance of power where I stay out of the splash zone."

She raised an eyebrow. "And if you're lying?"

Billings shrugged. "Then you ignore me, but if I'm right and you wait too long, he'll burn your nest to the ground while you're still sharpening your fangs."

The two stared at each other for a long moment. Then Syla nodded once.

"We'll take it under advisement."

"Well, if you take action, you'll need this," Billings pulled out an access card from his pocket. "This will get you through the service entrance and elevators. I took it from his assistant's desk when she was in his office."

She grabbed the card, turned, and walked back to her car without another word. Billings stayed in the alley, watching until her taillights disappeared into the misty night. Then, and only then, did he smile. He didn't need them to believe him. He just needed them to act on it.

"That confirms it," Marcus muttered. "The Mayor doesn't just know about the vamps, he's working with them."

Cole clenched his jaw. "Reece needs to see this."

They both watched as the two figures broke apart and disappeared in opposite directions. A long, heavy silence lingered.

"So what now?" Cole asked.

Marcus didn't look away from the empty street. "Now we start preparing for war."

Shortly after, across town, Mayor Billings entered his penthouse suite and poured himself a generous glass of scotch. He stood at the window, watching the lights of Los Angeles blink and shimmer beneath him. He walked back to his desk, grabbed his phone from the top drawer, and pressed his most recent number on the phone. It rang nearly four times before the other side picked up.

"Master," the Mayor said.

"Billings," Sebastian's smooth voice came through the line, warm and polished.

"I thought you should know, my sources say Varek's people are planning a move. They think Dr. Lee might be...more flexible than you thought."

A pause that was just long enough. Sebastian's tone cooled. "Do they?"

"Let's just say they've been watching his comings and goings. You might want to double-check where his loyalties lie."

"I'll handle my own." There was steel under Sebastian's silk.

"Of course," Billings said, all innocence. "I'm just trying to keep the peace. We don't need another bloody incident in the middle of my city."

He ended the call before Sebastian could respond. He sat for a moment, staring out the window as the sky went fully black. Two sides. One war. He didn't need to know who would win. He just needed to make sure he was the one holding the match when everything went up in flames. Let them scramble. Let them tear each other apart. When the smoke cleared, he'd be the last one standing.

Back in the subterranean heart of their nest, Syla stepped through the heavy metal doors and into the chamber Varek used as his command center. Varek sat at the head of a long stainless steel table, half-draped in shadows. He didn't look up when she entered. "What did he say?"

Syla approached and tossed the access card on the table. "Billings says Sebastian's gearing up for a strike. Military-grade surveillance, new reinforcements to his building, something about a containment wing, that his personal elite team is heading to Skid Row, and then he gave me this access card to the building."

That caught his attention. Varek's sharp eyes snapped to her face. "Access? For us?"

"That's the implication." She leaned on the table. "But it felt...rehearsed. Too clean. He wanted me to believe it."

"He's always wanted us and Sebastian to collide," Varek muttered. "That's how he survives riding the blast wave just far enough not to be burned."

Syla nodded. "He might be pushing us to act first. Hoping we weaken each other and leave him to sweep in with the remains."

Varek sat in silence for a beat, digesting the layers. Then he stood. "It's a gamble, but what if he's telling the truth? What if Sebastian is preparing for war?"

"Then we strike first."

Varek looked past her, toward a dark corridor that led to the upper nest. "Wake the strongest. The old blood. I want a strike team ready tonight. We hit Sebastian's tower before dawn. He'll be vulnerable then, his familiars won't be enough to stop us."

Syla stepped closer, her tone cautionary. "If this is a trap, and Sebastian retaliates while you're gone..."

Varek turned, smiling darkly. "Then I expect you'll be ready."

Syla remained quiet for a moment, watching Varek as he paced past the map-strewn table. "You're really going for it, then. The tower?"

Varek gave a slight nod. "Sebastian thinks himself untouchable, but he's grown soft. Surrounded by glass, steel, and sycophants. His power is old and overfed; it's bloated, not sharp."

"What about the doctor and the key to the sunlight serum?" Syla asked carefully. "We risk losing the very thing that could tip the scales."

"He won't be, he's been in our lab," Varek said, firm. "The doctor is ours. We made sure of that. But I want Sebastian alive long enough to see what we've become. I want him to understand that he didn't just lose a weapon, he created his replacement."

Syla folded her arms. "You think the doctor's truly with us? That he won't break when the blood thickens around him?"

"He's breaking already," Varek said. "You saw it. The experiments, the hunger, the quiet justifications in his eyes. Every subject makes him stronger and makes him ours."

Syla leaned forward slightly. "And what if he doesn't turn? What if his humanity or Amelia pulls him back?"

A flicker of something passed through Varek's expression. It wasn't doubt, but a calculation. "Then we isolate him. Keep him working. Keep him proud. If need be, we bind him. But we do not let him go."

Syla's lips thinned. "So while you storm the glass tower, I play nursemaid and guard dog?"

"You sit on the throne while I'm gone," Varek corrected. "If Sebastian is fool enough to strike while I'm in the open, make sure he regrets it."

"And the mayor?"

Varek's eyes hardened. "If he tries to use this to consolidate power, if he dares pit us like beasts in a cage, I want his blood spilled across city hall steps. Let him believe he's the puppeteer a little longer."

Syla gave one short nod. "We'll be ready."

Varek's voice dropped low and sharp, "so will I," as he grabbed the access card and walked out of the room.

CHAPTER 57

The door to the safe house clicked open as Reece stepped inside, his shoulders dusted with the grime of the street and his jaw clenched tight. His mind was still tangled with what he'd seen: The doc walking a homeless man into a van and disappearing into the mouth of what might be a vampire nest. But more than that, he couldn't get Amelia out of his head. Her silence and what he saw as pain.

Marcus and Cole were already inside, fresh from their own hunt. They looked up from the table where a tactical layout of the city was spread wide. Hot Shot sat nearby, her laptop open, drone feeds flickering across the screen in a cold, blue light.

"Good," Marcus said. "You're back. We need to talk."

Reece dropped his gear with a tired grunt. "You first."

Cole didn't hesitate. "We followed the mayor. Tracked him leaving his downtown office to Sebastian's office and then to a random street with abandoned buildings for an "off the books" meeting with that blonde vampire bitch that attacked us in the street."

Reece stiffened. "You're sure?"

"I watched the video. I got her face burned into my memory," Hot Shot chimed in. "Same vampire that almost gutted me. No mistaking her."

"They talked in an alley for a few minutes. Body language was tight. Then he handed her something. We got the footage."

Hot Shot turned the laptop toward Reece and tapped a few keys. The video played, blurry and taken from a rooftop across the street, but the mayor and Syla were unmistakable.

"That confirms it," Cole said. "The mayor's in bed with the vampires. Probably feeding them intel. Might've been the one who tipped them off at the fundraiser and had us bugged."

Reece ran a hand down his face. "And we don't know if Sebastian's in on it."

"We don't know anything about Sebastian yet," Cole shot back. "Except he's rich, dangerous, and knee deep in all this shit."

"That makes two of us," Reece muttered, and then paused. "I found something, too."

They looked at him.

Reece inhaled sharply. "I tracked Amelia, the female vampire. She was in Skid Row. Helping the homeless. Same as always. But...I confronted her."

Cole slammed his fist on the table. "You *what*? You know her name now?"

Reece didn't flinch. "I talked to her. Showed her the footage of the doctor."

"You should've put a bullet in her! We agreed! Every vampire..."

"She's not like them!" Reece barked, stepping toward Cole. "She was just as shocked about the doctor as we were. She's helping people, not feeding on them. She's saving lives."

"They're monsters! That's what they do! They lure you in, make you doubt, and then they kill you when your guard's down."

"You weren't there," Reece said through gritted teeth. "You didn't see her face."

"I don't care! You're breaking the mission. You're protecting her. That makes you a liability."

Reece took another step with jaws clenched. His hands hovered near his sidearm, but he didn't draw. Cole rose to meet him.

"Enough!" Hot Shot snapped. Her voice cracked through the room like a rifle shot. "You two want to pummel each other, do it *after* we stop the nest that might be turning the homeless into foot soldiers."

Marcus stepped between them. Cole glared, nostrils flaring, but backed down.

Hot Shot spun the laptop back around. "Van hasn't moved. GPS still active. Warehouse outside Boyle Heights. But no traffic in or out. It's just abandoned."

When suddenly, Reece's phone rang.

UNKNOWN NUMBER.

Everyone looked at him, knowing who was calling.

He picked up, "Let me guess...Sebastian."

"Hello, Mr. Drake," Sebastian said with his veiled voice.

"What tip do you have for us now? Your last tip almost got us all killed."

"Well, isn't that part of your job?" He paused for theatrics." Either way, I have an address for you to check out if your team is interested in payback."

"Just give us the address."

As Reece hung up the phone, he had that feeling in his gut again. How was Sebastian always one step ahead of them?

"Hey guys, that address is the same as the warehouse where the vans at." Hot Shot said, looking up from her tablet.

"Then it's our best lead," Reece said, voice still tight.

Cole exhaled, tension leaving his frame like steam. "We need to hit it tonight. Full sweep. We go in expecting a nest. Heavy opposition."

"Hot Shot, you run overwatch and drone support from the mobile unit," Reece added.

"Copy that," she responded.

Reece nodded slowly. "Alright then. We go quiet. We go hard. And we don't stop until we know exactly what they're doing in that warehouse, and we bring the whole thing down."

He looked to Marcus and said, "Bring everything."

Marcus paused in thought, going over a mental armory check-list, then gave one stiff nod. "Let's finish this."

As Reece slides a blade into his boot, outside the night crouched over Boyle Heights like a loaded weapon, and it was ready to fire.

CHAPTER 58

Sebastian stood at the towering window, arms folded behind his back, his reflection etched in moonlight and the cold, electric blue of Los Angeles below. The skyline glittered, unaware of the chessboard war brewing beneath it. Unaware of the blood and betrayal threading through every deal made in the shadows.

He'd received the mayor's message hours ago. A coy little warning about Andrew. That he might be slipping out of Sebastian's control, getting cozy with "another party", the kind of vagueness that reeked of misdirection. Sebastian had listened, of course. He's always listening, but he didn't trust him.

He didn't need the mayor's games to know the direction the wind was shifting. The scent of ambition was always the same, bitter and desperate. If the mayor truly thought he could pit Sebastian against Varek with whispers and implication, then the man was more foolish than he let on.

Still, there was a kernel of possibility in the message. Andrew had grown more elusive, his advances in the lab both rapid and oddly timed. Too rapid, even for someone of his brilliance. The success he reported with UV resilience had come suddenly and almost unnaturally. Sebastian had long suspected there was more going on than what the good doctor shared, but there were more pressing matters.

Sebastian turned from the window and strode to his desk.

With a flick of his hand, the embedded console came to life. He pressed a single key, one of the dozens set to discreet communication protocols, and spoke evenly into the speaker.

"Have the mayor brought to my office tonight, and no aides or press. Tell him I expect him at midnight."

The voice on the other end acknowledged and cut off. He thought midnight was perfect; it was just enough time to set the stage.

As Sebastian poured a glass of bloodwine and settled behind his desk, the sleek surface reflecting his perfectly composed expression, but inside, his mind churned with calculations.

The mayor had finally played his card, and whether it was out of fear or ambition, it didn't matter. Sebastian now knew the truth he needed, not about Andrew's loyalties, but about the mayor's.

He took a sip, savoring the copper sweet warmth. He would let the mayor speak his lies in person. Let him offer up another breadcrumb and see how far he'd go to cover his tracks, and when he was finished, Sebastian would know exactly how to use him or how to dispose of him.

The pieces were aligning. The old order had never been so threatened. If Varek wanted chaos, he would get it, but Sebastian would be ready. He always was.

CHAPTER 59

The team moved like shadows, silent and practiced, pulling up in their unmarked black van, two blocks from the warehouse. The building was a relic of L.A.'s industrial past, concrete bones, rusted steel beams, and broken windows. The white van was still parked out front. Reece raised his hand and motioned for the team to move.

"Still here," he muttered.

Hot Shot scanned the perimeter through her drone feed. "Motion cameras. Four minimum. One by the entrance, another on the northwest corner, third over the loading dock, and a fourth rotating on the back side."

"They're not amateurs," Marcus said, tightening the straps on his chest rig.

"No," Reece agreed. "Which means there's something worth protecting inside."

They fanned out. Hot Shot tapped into the cameras, looped the feeds with a timed delay. Reece and Cole moved through blind spots with practiced ease, staying low and hugging the walls until they reached the biometric locked side entrance.

"Let's make this quick," Cole whispered.

Hot Shot connected a portable device to the panel. Her fingers flew across the tablet. "Give me ten seconds...okay, bypassing biometric filters...rewriting the access protocol...and..."

A green light lit, and the lock clicked. Reece and the team slipped in.

The inside smelled like mildew, dust, and the faint chemical tang of industrial solvents. Empty crates lined the walls. Broken shelves sagged under the weight of rusted tools. A few lightbulbs buzzed overhead, but most flickered or were dead entirely.

"This is it?" Marcus asked. "Just some graveyard for junk? That Sebastian guy really tipping us off to empty sheds?"

Cole shook his head. "No. This was staged. Look at this," he said, pointing at a cluster of crates in the center of the room. "Dust is different. Marks on the floor and...trip wires."

Reece crouched down, running his fingers just above a taut length of wire attached to a series of pressure triggers.

"Explosives," he confirmed. "And there's more than one. Someone didn't want this place explored."

Hot Shot disarmed the traps while Marcus took rear watch. The room grew darker, heavier with each breath. Reece moved toward the largest crate near the back wall. It looked newer than the others.

"No dust on this one either," he said. "Slide marks."

They pushed. It didn't budge.

"Locked from the other side?" Cole guessed.

"What other side? It's against the wall." Marcus chipped back.

Then they heard it, barely at first, then the sound of soft footsteps and muffled voices rising from below the crate. Reece motioned everyone to cover. With a low mechanical groan, the crate slid aside, revealing a hidden staircase exposing a flickering concrete shaft. Two deathly pale men, vampires for sure, emerged from below. One held a clipboard, the other a rifle slung low.

Reece didn't hesitate. With two silenced shots through their hearts, two bodies turned to ash. Hot Shot and Marcus moved fast, dropping into the stairwell. Reece and Cole followed behind. Once they got to the bottom of the staircase, it led to a torch-lined, long tunnel with a lighted opening. They slowly made their way through the tunnel in silence.

Reece peeked into the opening quickly, "We got multiple contacts inside".

Cole took a quick look as well and whistled. "Jesus. It's a damn vampire metropolis."

"There's a few vamps over there. Find cover," Marcus said. "They've been here a while and looks like they are still expanding."

Hot Shot looked up. "There's a catwalk system across the ceiling. I'll sneak up there and get eyes from above."

"Good," Reece said. "Cole, Marcus, keep out of sight and take the left corridor. I'll take the one on the right. Stay comm-linked. Don't engage unless it's life or death. We need to know what we're up against. Set your C4 on any supports, we'll bring this whole place down on them."

"Copy that," Cole and Marcus said in unison.

Hot Shot was already climbing the metal scaffolding like a quiet spider as Cole and Marcus moved. Reece turned into the right-hand corridor, every step taking him deeper into enemy territory.

This was no outpost. This was a nest. A big one, and they had just found its heart.

CHAPTER 60

Amelia sat cross-legged on the floor of her penthouse. She hadn't felt this heavy in decades. Reece's footage played over and over in her mind. Andrew. Her Andrew leading a homeless man into a van, disappearing into what Reece claimed was a vampire nest. She didn't want to believe it. She couldn't, but she also couldn't unsee the look in Andrew's eyes. That mix of purpose and... detachment.

"I need to see it for myself," she muttered, strapping blades to her thighs. "Maybe Reece doctored the footage. Maybe this is a setup or maybe Andrew's trying to help in his own way."

But the doubt clawed at her.

What if it wasn't? What if he was...really gone?

She zipped up her Saint Laurent combat boots and stood, moving to the wall-length window that overlooked downtown L.A. The city sparkled, oblivious to the rot festering beneath its skin. Her reflection in the glass stared back, her eyes shadowed, lips tight, and hair twisted back into a no-nonsense braid. She looked like the woman she used to be. Before him.

She closed her eyes.

What if I get there, and it's all true? That he's turning people? That he's become the kind of monster I swore I'd fight until the end of time?

The thought struck her like a punch to the gut, and worse, what would she do about it? Would she kill him? Could she?

"I can fix this," she whispered. "I just...have to get him out. Away from all of this. If it's not too late."

Hope was a dangerous thing, she knew, but it was also the only thing keeping her from falling apart. When suddenly, she heard her phone ring. Checking it, she saw on the screen: Sebastian Voss.

"Sebastian," she clipped. "Unless you got something for me, I'm too busy to deal with your riddles."

"I do, Amelia. I have the location of the Reign's nest. This is where you'll find them," he said. "The Reign move often, but this...this is their current location."

"Send me the address."

"I believe these are the vampires who attacked Dr. Lee and have been taking your friends from the streets."

"I'll deal with this myself," she snapped back, annoyingly.

"I wouldn't expect anything less. Good hunting my dear."

The line went dead.

That's when it hit her. The address Sebastian just sent over was the same as the location Andrew was taking the homeless. Like a rock tumbling in the pit of her stomach, her dread of what she would find was nearly unbearable. But she needed to know the truth. She checked the blades one last time before she left.

Out on the street, the city hummed with life and decay. The classic Mercedes purred to life. The engine snarling like a beast eager for violence. She revved once, dropped it into gear, then tore through the streets, weaving past drunks, dreamers, and the damned.

The Boyle Heights warehouse district waited silently and full of ghosts. The old building loomed ahead, all rusted siding and broken glass teeth. The kind of place hope went to die.

Amelia killed the engine two blocks out and coasted to a stop behind a loading dock overgrown with weeds. Stepping out, her boots crunching on shattered asphalt as she pulled her hood up.

The air here was thick, not with smog, but something heavier. Dread.

Oh Andrew, how are you wrapped up in this?

She moved like a shadow between the crates and rusted out cars, her eyes scanning every rooftop, every alley. There were signs of life, faint footprints, fresh cigarette butts, and something that was dragged. Maybe someone. Her nostrils flared. Blood, it was old, and it was human.

She ducked behind a container. Her chest tightened. She crept closer to the warehouse Reece had shown her in the footage and saw the white van parked nearby. Then she noticed the footstep imprints in the dirt leading up against the walls of the warehouse. Maybe she wasn't the only one investigating. The biometric locks were lit green, and no security around. Something was definitely up here; was it an invitation or a trap?

She slipped inside. The air was cold and sour with the faint humming of power from deeper within. Her boots barely made a sound as she crept past stacked crates and broken-down machinery. Then she saw it, a clipboard and a rifle lying atop two piles of ash.

Well, I'm definitely not alone, she thought.

Then along a far wall, a large crate was pushed off the wall with a dim light flickering from below. Only her vampiric vision would've noticed, but it was something she needed a closer look. Stepping up to the crate, she discovered it led to a staircase. She walked down the staircase into the long tunnel and stopped before entering the large cavern. Taking a peek into the expansive space, she noticed other vampires moving about, moving crates, working on expansions, so she decided to stay out of sight.

She took the right tunnel down a dark corridor. Rooms lining either side. A flicker of a shadow inside a room sneaked out, something low to the ground. Then she heard it, a soft moan. She crouched beside one of the doors and peeked through a rusted slit.

A man, young, disheveled, clearly once homeless, now pale and twitching. His eyes were sunken. His fangs barely formed. He looked...wrong. Not turned completely, but definitely not human.

He was halfway to hell. She swallowed hard and backed away, pressing herself against the wall.

No. No. Andrew wouldn't...

But she already knew. Her gut twisted. More moans echoed from deeper in the building. Some cried. Some begged. One was laughing low and mad, like his mind had already burned out.

She forced herself forward, heart hammering in her chest. Another corridor. Another door and then...the lab. She froze. Steel tables and scattered medical equipment. Cooling units lining the walls. Vials of blood, all labeled, perfectly organized on the stainless steel table, and stacked neatly were notebooks. At least a dozen of them. She flipped through the top one, and it was filled with Andrew's handwriting. They were test logs with dosage ratios, exposure times, and notes about cellular changes with their burn rates. At the bottom of one page, a line stood out in bold ink.

Host #7 Initial resistance promising. Increased aggression noted. Obedience limited to donor's signature. Need more.

"Donor signature?" she whispered. Then her eyes scanned the line above it.

Injected with donor: A.L.

Her fingers curled around the page. She stared at the letters, heart sinking. There was no denying it now.

A.L. Andrew Lee. He used his own blood...

Her throat went dry. This wasn't just about science anymore. He was becoming something else. Creating something else. With parts of himself. She staggered back, her breath catching. The truth was all around her, not just scribbled in ink, but leaking from the walls, soaking into the floor. Andrew was doing this; maybe he had started with good intentions, maybe it had been to save her. Maybe even to save himself. But this...this was monstrous.

She turned and slipped back through the corridor, faster now, heart pounding in her throat, and her hands were shaking.

What have you done, Andrew...?

She stepped back, hand over her mouth, nausea rising. Her

mind reeled, every piece of her fighting the truth clawing into her chest, then she heard something. First it was the boots, then the voices. She ducked into the shadows beside a support beam and pressed her body flat against the wall. In the distance of the hall, she saw flashlights sweeping across the floor. She reached for her blade, just in case.

CHAPTER 61

Reece crept down the right-hand tunnel, every footstep calculated. The deeper he went, the more the rough concrete gave way to reinforced panels and surgical lighting overhead. This place wasn't just a hideout; it was a lab. A living, breathing operation.

Just as he reached a cross section, movement to his left made him freeze. A shadow peeled from the wall, fast and graceful. Too graceful. He raised his weapon.

"Nice to see you too, soldier boy."

Reece narrowed his eyes. "Amelia?"

She stepped out of the darkness, arms crossed, fangs just barely visible beneath her lip, though not bared, but there.

"What the hell are you doing here?" he whispered.

"I could ask you the same. This isn't exactly a neighborhood watch beat."

His jaw flexed. "I thought you were gone. Out of the city."

"Yeah, well," she said, shrugging. "Things change when your boyfriend might be experimenting on homeless people."

There was a beat of silence.

"You believe what I showed you then?" he said quietly.

Amelia's expression faltered for a split second. "I don't believe it. Not all of it. I needed to see for myself."

"And what if I told you I was here to confirm exactly that? He's down here, Amelia. Running something."

She glared at him. "Then we both better see it for ourselves before you shoot him in the heart."

Reece hesitated, then gave a sharp nod. They moved together, side by side now, down the corridor. Tension crackled between them like static.

They turned the final corner into a long hallway sealed off with glass. Inside was a stark, white laboratory. Stainless steel tables, floor-to-ceiling screens of molecular data, rows of blood bags labeled with strange symbols, and in the center, Andrew.

He stood at a medical station, his lab coat stained and open, scribbling something furiously in a notebook. Around him stood seven vampires; they were lean, silent, and waiting. One enormous vampire lay on a surgical table in the center of the room, thick veins dark against his skin, with an empty silver cylinder lying beside him. Reece pulled Amelia into the shadows before they could be spotted.

"I count seven standing. One on the slab."

"They're...waiting for him," Amelia murmured. "He's not speaking, but it looks like they're waiting for him."

Reece shifted his weight, instinct prickling. "This isn't just blood work. This is something deeper."

Meanwhile, elsewhere in the nest, in a dark, low-lit room filled with flickering surveillance monitors, Syla leaned over a terminal. Her eyes scanned the feed, sharp as blades.

Hmmmm, one of the outer perimeter cameras had gone dead. That's not from a malfunction, that's...a precise loop job. Someone disabled it.

She tapped a few keys, pulling up heat maps and motion triggers. More movement. Multiple signatures.

"Shit," she hissed. Then, with one hard slam of her hand, she struck the massive red button on the control panel. Sirens flared to life. She grabbed the wall-mounted comm beside the console and barked out an order.

"Security breach detected. Lockdown initiated."

The lights in the tunnel corridor turned crimson. The nest pulsed with mechanical panic doors sliding shut, magnetic locks snapping into place, red strobes bathing everything in a warning glow.

Andrew froze for half a second. Then turned to the standing vampires, gave a single nod, and without a word, they turned and bolted from the lab with terrifying speed. Each peeling off in a separate direction, disappearing down adjacent corridors like trained attack dogs unleashed. Amelia and Reece stared, wide-eyed.

"You saw that, right?" Reece said. "He didn't say a damn word."

"But they *heard* him," she added, voice low. "They obeyed him."

"Telepathic control?" Reece asked. "Is that even possible?"

"Not unless... he's their sire," she said slowly, dread blooming in her gut.

Reece pulled his weapon a little higher, just as Amelia stepped out of the shadows and into the lab's doorway.

As Amelia stepped into the light, Andrew looked up, startled. His eyes locked on hers, and something in him cracked. A flicker of relief, swallowed by dread.

Not now. Not like this.

"Amelia, you shouldn't be here," he said.

"No kidding," she snapped. "What the hell have you been doing?"

Behind her, Reece stepped forward, gun low but ready.

"And you better start explaining fast, Doc. Because right now, you look like the villain in your own Frankenstein story."

Andrew's face went pale and not in the usual vampire way. Outside, the alarms screamed louder. They were out of time.

CHAPTER 62

"What are you doing here?" His voice was tight, clipped, and more surprised than angry.

Amelia stepped forward, jaw set, her eyes flicking over the sterile lab, the strapped-down vampire on the surgical bed, the scattered vials and blood smeared charts. Her voice trembled, not with fear, but with fury. "I could ask you the same thing."

Andrew looked from her to Reece, then back. "You brought him?" he asked, like a jealous accusation.

"I didn't bring anyone," she snapped. "We both came here for the same reason because something didn't add up."

Andrew's face flushed with a strange mix of pride and frustration. "I'm doing this for us, Amelia. For *you*. I'm this close to curing our weakness. I've found a way to walk in sunlight. Together and without hiding."

Amelia's eyes widened in disbelief. "You think this," she gestured to the vampire on the slab, hooked to IVs and restraints, "this is a cure?"

"They volunteered," Andrew insisted. "I'm giving them strength. Power. A future outside the dark."

"No," she said, voice low and shaking. "You're using them. You took people who already lost everything and turned them into test subjects. You promised me you were different."

"I *am* different," he said, stepping closer. "I've done what no other vampire has. This," he motioned to the lab, "this changes everything. No more shadows. No more hiding. I did this for *us*."

Amelia hesitated, hurt cutting through her usual armor. "You don't even see what you've become."

Reece stepped forward, the tension in his shoulders visible. "She's right. You've gone too far, Doc. This isn't helping people, it's making monsters."

Andrew bristled. "You don't understand what's at stake."

But before Reece could respond, the large vampire on the operating table stirred. The restraints hadn't been fastened back after the last test. He rose in a slow, ominous movement, every muscle rippling beneath taut, grayish skin. His eyes, red and shining, locked onto Reece.

The vampire tilted his head as if waiting for something.

Andrew gave a single, subtle nod.

Without a word, the creature stepped down from the table, ripping the IVs from its arm and began stalking toward Reece, each footstep heavier than the last. It was clear now, Andrew didn't need to speak. His serum had given him more than physical power. He had command.

Reece raised his weapon and stepped back. "You controlling him?"

Andrew didn't answer. The vampire bared his fangs and kept advancing.

Amelia stepped in front of Reece, eyes on Andrew. "Stop this."

Andrew looked torn. "He won't hurt you."

"That's not the *point*," she snapped. "You're letting him hurt *others*."

From somewhere in the cavern, the sounds of gunfire echoed through the air, the short, silenced bursts and the sizzling sound of vampires turning to ash.

Reece tapped his comm. "Cole? Marcus?"

Only static. Suddenly, Marcus's voice cut in, ragged and

breathless. "We're in deep. They're everywhere. We're getting cut off!"

The comm crackled again, and Hot Shot's voice hissed through. "I'm pinned above the catwalk. We've got movement coming from *every* tunnel!"

Reece's gut twisted. "Damn it."

The vampire charged. Reece ducked, rolling behind a table as the creature's massive arm smashed through a rack of vials, sending glass and blood flying. Amelia launched herself forward, slamming her shoulder into the creature's chest, knocking him off balance just long enough for Reece to recover.

"Andrew, *call him off!*" Amelia screamed.

"No! I won't do that!" Andrew shouted, his voice cracking. "Not now, we are too close!"

Reece fired three silenced shots, each hitting center mass, only to hear the sound of bullets hitting metal plates. The vampire staggered but didn't drop. Andrew also knew about vampire weak spots, and for each of his made vampires, he implanted a steel plate over the heart to make them harder to kill.

"Nothing's working!" Reece yelled.

"I told you," Andrew shouted, panicked. "They're stronger and faster. I've made them better. They can *adapt.*"

"You mean *you made them like this!*" Amelia spat.

The vampire charged again. Amelia and Reece split, darting to opposite sides of the lab as the creature tore a surgical table in half. Reece grabbed a silver-tipped knife from a fallen tray and waited.

The vampire monster lunged for Reece with a predator's shriek, but before it could close the distance, a flash of silver cut through the air. Amelia was already moving, twin blades drawn. She launched herself across the lab, slicing upward through the creature's forearm, then dragging a second blade deep across its ribs. Dark, coagulated blood sprayed as the vampire reeled back, snarling in pain. But it wasn't finished.

With a guttural roar, the creature snatched Amelia mid-movement and hurled her like a ragdoll across the lab. She crashed into a console with a sickening crack, sparks flaring from a monitor as her body slumped to the floor.

"Amelia!" Andrew cried, rushing to her side.

Reece didn't wait. The monster had a blind spot now, a weak side where its ribs had been shredded. As it turned its focus toward Reece again, fangs bared and red eyes glowing, Reece drew his silver-edged combat blade and sprinted forward. The vampire lunged, arms outstretched.

Reece dropped to one knee, letting momentum carry him into a sliding dash. He zipped under the vampire's grasp, slicing the tendon at the back of its right ankle as he passed. The vampire shrieked and buckled to one knee, clawing the air in rage. Reece came up behind it in a low crouch, eyes locked on the shifting point just beneath the left shoulder blade.

"Got you," he hissed in the monster's ear.

He drove the blade into the gap between the third and fourth rib, angling upward toward the heart. The vampire roared, a sound of fury and shock as Reece twisted the blade hard. Ash exploded around him like a black sandstorm; the force of the vampire's death smashed outward in a violent burst. Reece staggered back, coughing, eyes darting through the smoky ash.

Andrew was kneeling beside Amelia, cradling her. She stirred with a soft groan, blood trailing down the side of her face. Her eyes fluttered open, dazed. "Andrew...why?" she breathed, voice barely audible.

Andrew froze. Reece stepped closer, eyes narrowing. "How many more like that are down here?"

Andrew didn't answer. He looked up, and his face was no longer the same. His pupils thinned to slits, his irises glowing red hot. His skin paled, and the veins crawled across his neck and face like black roots. His expression warped with anger, twisting every feature as his lips peeled back over lengthening fangs. He stood slowly, like something uncoiling. Power hummed off of him in waves. Whatever part of Andrew was still human, still good, was being swallowed, and Reece could see it. Andrew was changing.

Reece tightened his grip on the blade and took a step back, heart pounding. This just got worse. Andrew's anger was growing with each moment, opened his mouth to scream, but then the lab lights flickered and a new alarm began to scream. This one from the heart of the facility itself.

251

Across town, in the rain-slicked shadows of mid-Wilshire, two blacked-out SUVs rolled slowly down a service alley behind Sebastian's corporate tower. Inside sat Varek, stone-faced and silent, with eight of his deadliest vampires, every one a couple of centuries old, each chosen for their unwavering loyalty and skill in combat. The air inside the SUVs was thick with anticipation. No one spoke. No one needed to.

As the SUVs slowed to a crawl, Varek reached into the breast pocket of his tailored leather coat and retrieved the plastic access card. On it, the seal of Voss Enterprise gleamed faintly beneath the streetlights.

"Mayor's gift," he said, his voice like gravel and smoke. "At least he's good for something."

Varek, no fool, still suspected the mayor of double-crossing, but for tonight, if the access card got them through the service elevator unseen, then it was worth playing along.

The SUVs stopped. Varek and his crew exited in complete silence, their movements ghostlike. One vampire hoisted a duffel and followed Varek to the security door tucked behind a row of delivery crates. Varek swiped the card. A green light blinked. The door unlocked with a soft click.

"Welcome to the back door of power," one of the vampires muttered. Inside, they moved fast. Down a maintenance corridor, past empty offices, until they reached a junction. Varek turned to two of his men.

"Breaker room," he ordered.

Without a word, they split off, racing toward the building's electrical hub. Thirty seconds later, the lights above flickered once and then died. The building shuddered into darkness, every circuit, camera, and security feed going dead. Only red emergency lights pulsed low along the baseboards.

Varek and the remaining six vampires continued, navigating by scent, until they reached the back elevator that ran on backup generators, which led directly to the executive level. His other two vampires met up as they entered the elevator.

35 floors above, inside Sebastian's office, the lights flickered and died. Emergency panels illuminated the space with a soft orange glow. Sebastian stood at the far end of the room, unmoving, his hands clasped behind his back. Across from him, nervously pacing near the window, was Mayor Billings.

"What? What's going on?" the mayor said, breathless. "Your system's down, security's compromised", he said with fear.

Sebastian raised an eyebrow. "And you thought you'd what? Assist in my evacuation?"

The mayor licked his lips. "I told you. Varek's planning something. He's moving on you, and I... I wanted to prove my loyalty."

Sebastian slowly stood from behind his desk and paced, each step measured, calm. "You mean you wanted to cover your tracks. If Varek fails, you're here to swear you warned me, and if he succeeds, you get to say you tried."

Billings stiffened and coyly walked up to Sebastian as a child who was hoping to hide his fear. "That's not..."

"I've known men like you for centuries, Billings," Sebastian said. "Survivors. Bottom feeders. You think aligning with power is the same as wielding it."

As the elevator hummed softly as it ascended to the final floor, where Sebastian's private office was. Inside it, Varek stood with eight of his most dangerous vampires, centuries old, brutal, and loyal only to him. Their eyes glowed faintly in the emergency lighting that had kicked in since the power was cut minutes ago.

"Human guards will be waiting. Make sure you feed before we get to Sebastian's office," Varek murmured.

"They'll fall and be a quick meal," one of his lieutenants hissed, cracking his neck.

The elevator dinged. The doors slid open.

They stepped into a wide corridor, shadowed and still. The emergency lights flickered overhead, painting the hallway in intermittent red glows. A human guard turned the corner and raised his weapon too slowly. One of Varek's vampires moved like a blur, grabbing the man's neck, the vampire bit viciously into him, pulling quarts of blood from his body, then snapping the man's neck before he ever realized what happened. His body dropped silently to the ground.

They advanced.

Another hallway. Three more guards. Gunfire erupted, but the vampires moved like shadows through the hail of bullets. Within seconds, the guards were dead, two drained, one torn open. More bodies followed. Blood smeared the walls. It was an execution, not a battle. Still, Varek's eyes narrowed while fresh human blood pulsed through each of the vampire's veins. Strength growing with each step.

"That was too easy," he muttered. His eyes scanned the hallway. It was too quiet. *Sebastian's never this careless.*

They turned a final corner and stood before the massive steel door to Sebastian's office. No one at the assistance desk. No guards. No sounds. Just the quiet, heavy hum of reinforced security locks.

One of his men stepped forward. "It's locked."

Varek examined the console. The locking mechanism was far beyond biometric; it was reinforced by an old vampire cipher code and magnetic shielding.

"Then we use force," Varek growled.

From a satchel, one of his lieutenants pulled out a coil of deck cord. They quickly wound it around the seams of the door, attaching small detonators to the cord at each corner.

They took cover in the hallway.

"Blow it," Varek ordered.

A sharp *pop-pop-pop* of charges followed. The deck cord ignited in a bright white flare, and a split second later, the door exploded inward with a thunderous boom. Smoke billowed into the room beyond. They rushed in.

From inside Sebastian's office, before Billings could respond, the explosion rocked the building.

Dust rained from the ceiling. Sebastian didn't flinch. Varek glided in, his leather coat flowed like a cape behind him, eyes blazing red, leading with his heavily armed vampire guards following quickly behind him, fanning out to cut off anyone trying to escape.

Sebastian smiled. "You should've just knocked."

CHAPTER 64

Chaos ruled the vampire nest. The gunfire from Cole and Marcus echoed off the stone walls as they cut through the oncoming horde. They moved like twin hammers, firing round after round into the onslaught of vampires bearing down on them from the dark tunnels. Shell casings clattered across the cement, mixing with the snarls of vampires and the echoes of gunfire. Their precision was clinical, first headshots, then center mass, but the sheer number of enemies was overwhelming. Suddenly, a piercing screech ripped through the tunnels.

It was Syla's voice. The vampires halted, like puppets whose strings had been cut. An eerie silence followed. Cole and Marcus crouched behind a toppled metal shelf, panting.

"What the hell was that?" Marcus asked.

Before Cole could answer, the tunnel darkened with shadows. Seven figures stepped into view; they were taller, broader, moving like liquid muscle. Their eyes glowed crimson, and their skin was leathery, slightly charred in places, like it had been partially burned and healed over. These weren't ordinary vampires.

Marcus muttered, "What the hell are *those*?"

The enhanced vampires let out low, guttural growls. One cracked its neck, the pop echoing like a gunshot. Another leapt forward without a word, crashing into the steel support beside Cole and denting it like paper.

"Don't know, but they're juiced," Cole said, stepping back and drawing his blade.

As the first one sprinted down the tunnel toward them, Cole raised his rifle, firing two center mass shots with silver rounds. They impacted hard into the vampire's sternum but didn't penetrate; the vampire didn't stop. The creature snarled, blood spraying from its mouth, and lunged.

Marcus dove forward and to the right, avoiding the impact. Cole dropped his rifle and rolled, drawing his silver-edged long blade in one hand and a short dagger in the other. He met the charging vampire mid-leap, ducking under its swipe and jamming the dagger into its clavicle. The vampire howled, teeth snapping wildly. Cole twisted and drove the long blade up under its ribs, piercing the heart. It exploded into ash that covered him in a choking cloud.

Another was already on Marcus. He grunted, barely avoiding a set of claws that carved through the air. The vampire moved with jerky, unnatural speed. Marcus ducked low, slicing across its thigh, then surged forward to slam a punch with his silver knuckles into its solar plexus. The creature doubled over, just long enough for Marcus to grab the back of its neck and ram his knife up through the base of its skull, then down the top of its sternum into the heart.

When two more charged, Cole and Marcus pivoted, standing back to back in the tight corridor. A snarl from ahead, then another from behind.

"They're surrounding us," Marcus hissed.

"Good," Cole muttered. "Means less chasing."

The one in front leapt first, arms wide. Cole ducked under the pounce and drove his blade into the side of the creature's stomach, spinning it mid-air and slamming it into the tunnel wall. The force cracked the concrete. Marcus met the other, slashing across the chest before delivering a crushing knee into the creature's sternum. It buckled but didn't fall.

A new vampire rushed from the rear, tackling Marcus to the ground. Cole turned to help, but another brute slammed into him from the side, pinning him to the wall. The claws dug into his shoulder, drawing blood.

Cole snarled and headbutted the vampire hard enough to stagger it. Then he twisted his body, slicing open its throat with his short blade. The creature gurgled, but didn't die.

"Why won't they go down!?" Cole yelled.

"They're stronger than normal. These aren't the vamps we're used to," Marcus shouted, kicking the one pinning him backward.

They regrouped, side by side again. The five remaining vampires formed a loose semicircle, snarling, eyes glowing.

Cole spat blood. "Plan?"

"Kill faster."

And then they moved. In a blur, Cole dove low, sliding beneath the swing of one vampire, slicing at its Achilles. Marcus moved up and over, launching off the wall to bury his knife into another's throat. The corridor became chaos, silver flashing, fangs snapping, snarls and grunts echoing off stone.

Cole rammed his shoulder into one of the enhanced vampires, forcing it back toward the narrow mouth of the tunnel. The brute punched him, sending him spinning, but Marcus appeared behind it, jamming his blade between the creature's ribs. As it turned to face Marcus, Cole stabbed upward through its lower back. It burst into ash.

Another leapt on Marcus, tackling him hard to the ground. Its fangs sank deep into Marcus's forearm.

"Shit!" Marcus howled.

Cole roared and charged, driving both blades into the vampire's back. It let go just long enough for Marcus to twist beneath it and stab upward through the sternum.

Ash exploded over them both. Only one left. This one was smarter. Bigger. It backed off, crouching low and waiting. Cole and Marcus circled. Breath ragged. Bloodied and bruised. Then, without a word, they moved.

Cole slashed wide, herding the creature left. Marcus rolled low and around, flanking. It worked. The vampire turned just in time to see Marcus spring to his feet behind him. Cole surged forward, blade leading.

Marcus drove his knife through the creature's spine, while Cole rammed his blade into the chest, twisting hard, both blades meeting at the heart. The creature screamed an unearthly sound before disintegrating into ash.

They stood there, chests heaving. Covered in grime and blood and soot.

Cole spat. "You good?"

Marcus winced, wrapping his forearm. "Bastard took a chunk. But yeah."

Both hunters stood panting, bruised and bloodied.

"Jesus," Marcus said. "What the hell were those?"

Cole wiped his blade. "Hopefully something we don't run into again."

At the same time, in the control room above, Syla stood over the security console, watching her faction disintegrate. Her red lips twisted into a sneer. The lab was lost. Varek's experiments had outgrown her control.

"Time to bury the mistake," she muttered.

She typed in the failsafe code, fingers flying across the dusty keyboard. On-screen, a countdown appeared: 10:00... 9:59... 9:58... She turned on her heel and left the room as a secondary alarm began to blare.

Above, Hot Shot stayed tucked into the catwalk scaffolding, rifle steady. Her breath caught as she spotted movement below.

"Contact," she whispered into her comm. "That blonde bitch just entered the warehouse with a half dozen vamps."

She squeezed the trigger. One shot. Syla sidestepped effortlessly, the bullet sparking at her feet.

"Shit! She saw me," Hot Shot hissed.

Syla pointed skyward, barking orders. Her vamps hissed and began climbing like lizards up the steel columns. Hot Shot fired again, dropping two. But more kept coming.

Then Syla stepped forward, smiling. "I thought I finished you on the rooftop, little hunter. Guess I'll have to rip your pretty little head off to make sure this time."

She began to climb faster than any of the other vampires. Hot Shot's heart pounded. She reloaded, fired twice, but missed both.

"Cole! Marcus! I really kicked the hornet's nest over here. I really could use a little help!"

They were already sprinting across the tunnels, following the sound of chaos. Below, the remaining vamps spotted them and gave chase.

"Shit! Out of ammo," Cole growled, drawing his blades again.

"Same," Marcus said, slipping back on his silver knuckles. "Let's make this count."

Blades met flesh. Bodies collided. Ash and blood filled the air.

Above, Syla bounded onto the catwalk landing with a solid stomp of her boots. Hot Shot faced off with Syla with only four rounds left. Two connected into her shoulder and stomach. Syla staggered with each shot and fell to her knees, but she rose, grinning through the wounds, her eyes glowing brighter.

"Last dance," she whispered, lunging.

Her hand wrapped around Hot Shot's throat. Hot Shot gasped, clawing at Syla's wrist. Her gloved fingers flicked, and twin silver daggers sprang from her sleeves. She slashed. Syla screamed as her hands detached, flopping to the catwalk floor.

"You bitch!"

Hot Shot hurled herself forward, driving both blades into Syla's chest. She was able to position herself on top of Syla as the momentum carried them off the catwalk. Syla landed hard onto the boxes below, smashing apart beneath them. Lying atop her enemy, Hot Shot gasped for breath.

"Not today, bitch," she whispered, shoving the blades deeper.

Syla's mouth opened in a scream, but she never finished it. Her body exploded into ash. Hot Shot collapsed beside the smoking remains. Cole and Marcus rushed in. Cole hauled her upright.

"That was badass," Marcus breathed.

They barely had time to laugh.

A massive rumble tore through the cavern. Cracks split the walls. The ceiling groaned.

"Reece, come in. This place is coming down. You gotta get outta here." Cole sparked into his comm.

But there was no response.

"Reece, come in..." Again, no response.

"We gotta move!" Cole shouted.

Marcus grabbed Hot Shot. Cole led the way. Behind them, the vampire nest began to collapse.

"I guess we didn't need that C4 after all." Marcus chipped as they rushed up the staircase.

CHAPTER 65

Sebastian stepped around his desk with the controlled grace of a man who had seen centuries of war, his hands behind his back, his expression unreadable.

Varek's eyes narrowed. "You knew we were coming."

"Of course," Sebastian said calmly. "I'm glad the mayor finally found his courage to pick a side... even if it was the losing one."

The mayor shifted, suddenly unsure if standing behind Sebastian was still the safest place to be.

"You always were dramatic," Varek sneered. "Sitting there, thinking your empire would never fall. I expected more from you."

"And I expected you to wait until daylight, when most of my staff was down for the count," Sebastian replied, walking slowly toward the center of the room. "But here you are, so eager to strike that you couldn't even wait for the sun to rise."

"We're done playing by your rules, Sebastian," Varek said. "No more blood taxes. No more hiding in the dark. The serum changes everything, and Andrew will give it to *us*."

Sebastian tilted his head. "Ah. So this isn't just a personal vendetta. It's desperation."

"You're the one clinging to the old ways," Varek growled, stepping closer. "You had your time. But this world is ours now. And when Andrew perfects that serum, we'll rule it under the sun."

Sebastian chuckled softly. "You think a few broken minds in lab coats will outmatch centuries of discipline?"

"No," Varek said. "But I think a monster who rules by fear has finally lost his grip."

One of Varek's vampires shifted, his fingers tightening around the hilt of his blade.

"Careful," Sebastian warned without turning. "We still have time to talk. I'm not ready for this room to be painted red yet."

Varek's fangs showed. "I didn't come to talk. Your security was an afterthought. Human guards and weaklings," Varek sneered. "You're losing your edge."

Sebastian stood unmoved, eyes narrowing. "Or maybe I wanted you to come. Maybe I needed to clean house. You see, I knew about all your little attempts at misdirection. Dropping my name in Skid Row so it would paint a target on my back with Amelia. Then, convincing my doctor to come experiment on your vampires because he wasn't getting them here. I needed to know where you're nest was. What do you think that little necklace he wore every day was? Just an access key to my facility? It was both a GPS tracker and a mic. And once I knew where he was going, it was easy to figure out where your nest was. I even tipped off the human hunters where it is, and right about now, your nest should be infiltrated with them."

"You think you've got everything figured out then? Well, it still leaves you alone and surrounded."

"Hahahaha." Sebastian laughed manically. "You think I'm alone? Let me guess, Billings told you that my guards and security were at Skid Row?" Sebastian looked back at the mayor, then looked back past Varek, and on cue, Camille with her katana in hand, followed by his personal elite guards entered and surrounded the room."

Billings looked stunned to see Camille and the guards, "but... but I overheard you saying..."

"You overheard exactly what I wanted you to hear," Sebastian cut him off. "I wanted to confirm that you were working with Varek, so I had you overhear Camille. Just a little breadcrumb to lure Varek into making his move. Why else would I allow you to steal Evelyn's access card."

Varek's eyes flicked to the mayor. "Your house has rats."

Sebastian looked toward the mayor, who was now pressed against the wall, sweating profusely. Sebastian moved in a blur towards the mayor, his hand lashed out with unnatural speed. He seized Billings by the collar and yanked him forward.

"You mean this rat?" he said, holding the mayor up like a broken doll.

"Wait! Master, I swear I only told Varek what you needed me to. I never thought they'd come. I..."

Sebastian pressed a finger to the mayor's lips.

"Shhh."

He turned, smiling at Varek. "Say what you want about us, but at least you know your place in the food chain. Humans like this one... they forget. They think they're players."

The mayor's eyes widened. "W-wait...Master, I did what I thought you would want! I kept Varek close..."

"Enough," Sebastian snapped, his voice low and sharp. "You've already said too much."

Then he looked back to Varek, that thin, cold smile returning.

He tossed Billings to two of his guards. They caught him effortlessly, holding him in place. Fangs sank into his neck. Billings let out a strangled cry as they drained him, his arms flailing. Sebastian spoke calmly as the mayor's body was passed to two more guards.

"Varek, you believe vampires are apex predators. We agree on that. But loyalty matters."

As the last two guards drained him of the last of his blood, the Mayor's body was torn in half with grotesque efficiency, and what remained hit the floor in two wet thuds. Sebastian looked down at the steaming remains. "Humans who betray one side often betray the other."

The guards wiped their mouths, their eyes glowing with renewed strength. They turned to Varek's group with lethal focus.

"If you want my empire, you'll have to take it."

Varek drew his blade. "My pleasure," he sneered. And with that, chaos erupted.

The room exploded into chaos. Fangs and blades flashed. Blood sprayed across the marble floor. Varek fought with a feral, relentless fury, decapitating one of Sebastian's guards and skewering another. A vampire shrieked as a bullet caught his jaw and sent him tumbling across the desk. But Camille and Sebastian's guards were ancient. Stronger and faster. One after another, Varek's vampires were cut down and shattered into ash.

Only Varek remained, wounded, held in place by Camille and an elite guard.

"You hide behind others," Varek spat. Blood streamed from his lips.

Sebastian raised an eyebrow. "No, Varek. I outlive others."

"You're not strong enough to lead."

Sebastian chuckled and nodded to Camille. She threw her katana to his open hand. Then released Varek and pushed him forward.

"Prove it."

Varek lunged, scooping a fallen blade, poised to attack, only for Sebastian to vanish. In the next breath, he was behind him.

A sickening sound echoed as Varek's body split cleanly from skull to scrotum, both halves falling in opposite directions before collapsing into ash. Sebastian stood still, bloodied katana still in hand.

"Older vampires don't get weaker," he said to the silence. "We only get stronger. It's too bad you never lived long enough to find that out."

He turned to Camille. "Call housekeeping, make sure that rat's blood doesn't stain my floors. And someone fix the damn door."

Flipping the Katana over and handing it to Camille, he walked away, humming softly to himself with a wicked smile on his face.

CHAPTER 66

"Stop!" Amelia's scream cut through the din like a blade, sharp and panicked.

Andrew froze at the sound, the shadows of madness flickering in his eyes as he turned toward her. In his hand, a glass injectable cylinder shimmered, the golden hue of his final serum catching the light. His expression, manic and desperate, shifted as he looked at her, softened with longing.

"Amelia," he said, breathless. "This is for you. For us. Don't you see? I've done it. I can fix everything. You won't have to hide in the shadows anymore. We can walk in the sun together. We can be free."

Amelia stood her ground, trembling with equal parts fury and heartbreak. Her voice cracked. "This... this is not freedom, Andrew. You're experimenting on the very people you swore to protect."

"No!" he barked, shaking his head violently. "I'm saving them. I gave them strength. Purpose. I gave them a chance. And you, Amelia...You said you felt lost. That life had no meaning, but with me, with this, we can make meaning."

She stepped closer, eyes glistening with tears. "You think this will make us human again? You think a syringe can erase centuries of pain and blood? You're becoming the thing you always feared."

His gaze flickered to Reece, still standing just behind Amelia, weapon lowered, body tense.

Andrew's face darkened. "Is that it? You care for *him* now? He's human. You think he'd ever understand you like I do?"

"This isn't about him," she whispered. "This is about you. And me. And the monster you're becoming."

Andrew took a step forward, voice strained. "I did this for *you*."

Reece cleared his throat. "Yeah, well, hate to break up the romance, but you've gone too far, Doc."

Andrew's face contorted. A deep, guttural sound tore from his throat a scream of anguish more than rage started toward Reece.

Reece instinctively raised his weapon, but Andrew was already charging. Amelia stepped between them, slicing at Andrew with her blade, catching him across the ribs. He snarled, grabbed her by the arm, and threw her into a bank of lab equipment. Metal crashed and glass shattered as she crumpled onto the floor once again.

Andrew turned his gaze on Reece again. His eyes glowed red. Reece dodged, weaved, barely keeping pace, but Andrew was faster and stronger, enhanced by Sebastian's transfused blood. It was beyond anything Reece had ever faced.

The lab descended into chaos as they clashed, every surface becoming a potential weapon. Sparks flew from consoles. Chairs splintered and monitors cracked. Reece landed a solid blow, only to be grabbed by the throat and lifted off his feet. He gasped, struggling. His hand latched onto the necklace around Andrew's neck, Sebastian's lab key, and ripped it free.

Andrew roared and hurled him across the room. Reece screamed as a jagged table leg pierced through his thigh. Blood sprayed as he went still.

Amelia stirred, blinking against the pain. Her vision swam as she saw Reece impaled, barely breathing.

"Andrew!" she cried. "Please!"

Andrew, chest heaving, stomped toward Reece, his rage blinding him. "I did this for *you*! For *us*! Why can't you see that?!"

"Because this isn't love," she said weakly, pushing herself to her feet.

He picked up a heavy console, lifting it overhead with supernatural strength.

Reece, semi-conscious, looked down at the lab key in his hand. His breath hitched. He finally recognized the symbol.

That symbol, the same one from his wife and daughter's murder scene.

"Sebastian..." he whispered, and his world faded to black.

Andrew screamed and prepared to bring the console down. Then a sharp crack. A jagged chair leg burst through his back. Amelia, shaking and covered in blood, stood behind him, her face streaked with tears. "Stop."

Andrew dropped the console at Reece's side. He turned, mouth open, gasping.

"We could lead them," he rasped. "Together. Rule them all."

"I loved you," she whispered.

She plunged the stake into his heart. His scream was cut short as his body dissolved into ash.

Amelia dropped to her knees, sobbing. Overhead, the alarms continued to blare. She turned to Reece. Still alive. Barely. Impaled and fading fast. She saw the serum on the ground. This was it. She could leave him. Take the serum herself. Finally walk in the sun and be free.

He opened his eyes, barely a whisper. "Get out of here. This is where I'm supposed to be." Then it all went black.

Amelia stared at the syringe and made her choice.

CHAPTER 67

Cole, Marcus, and Hot Shot stepped into the towering glass-walled office atop Sebastian's private high-rise, the skyline of Los Angeles burning orange behind them in the setting sun. The room was sleek, sharp, and clinical, just like its owner. They hadn't said much during the elevator ride up. None of them had, really, since the collapse. They assumed that Reece died in the collapse. They were on edge and grieving, so being called to some rich, arrogant businessman was the last thing they wanted to do.

Sebastian stood behind his desk, closing the drawer where a silver cylinder rolled. His hands clasped behind his back, watching the security feed looping on a wall-mounted screen. When he turned, his eyes were calm and calculating. "Thank you for coming on such short notice. I know the last few days have been...difficult."

"What are we doing here?" Cole snapped, ignoring the decorum. His jaw clenched. "You said it was urgent. This better be good."

"It is," Sebastian said, gesturing toward the screen. "I wanted you to see something for yourselves."

The video began playing. The grainy footage was from inside the vampire faction's underground nest. It was the security feeds from the different cameras.

The battle with the mutated vampires Cole and Marcus dealt

with, Hot Shot and Syla, and then there they were, Reece, Amelia, and Andrew in the lab. The argument they had, the chaos, and the fight.

They watched as Reece and Andrew clashed. The furious blows. The monstrous strength of Andrew. The room being torn apart, and then the final blow. Andrew turning into ash.

"Jesus," Marcus whispered. "He's dead."

"Wait," Hot Shot said, pointing at the screen. "Look. There."

Amelia crawled to Reece's broken body. Blood everywhere. She lifted something, a syringe.

Cole's face twisted. "No. No, no, no."

They watched as Amelia injected Reece with the serum. They saw her pull the jagged debris from his thigh. They watched his leg seal itself almost instantly. Then came the clip from the exterior camera. Amelia lifted Reece into a car as the building collapsed behind them as they drove off.

"As you can see, he's still alive, in a way," Sebastian said dryly. "While you all were all still inside."

Cole muttered, almost to himself, "I knew something was up. He's a fuckin' vampire now."

Marcus stared, stunned. "But... why would she do that?"

Hot Shot leaned forward, still watching. "To save him."

"Or to recruit him," Cole spat.

"How do we know this is real? How did you get this footage?" Hot Shot piped in.

"I have my ways, and it shows all of you as well. You should remember what happened."

Sebastian let the silence hang just long enough. Then, smoothly, he stepped around the desk and faced them directly. "I brought you here because it's time we all saw the truth."

"And what truth is that?" Cole asked, arms crossed, already scowling.

Sebastian tilted his head. "That you and I now have a common enemy."

"Reece?" Marcus asked, voice laced with disbelief. "You're saying Reece is the enemy?"

"I'm saying he made a choice," Sebastian replied. "Amelia, too. They have something...dangerous."

Hot Shot narrowed her eyes. "You didn't call us here to just *show* us this. What do you want?"

Sebastian smiled, the kind that never reached his eyes. "I want your help."

Cole's hand twitched toward the blade at his hip.

"Not to kill him," Sebastian added, measured. "Not yet. First, we bring him in. Get answers. And if he won't come willingly...then yes. We do what we must."

Marcus looked between the two. "And what if he still thinks he's on our side?"

"Then he'd better prove it fast," Cole growled. "Or he goes down with the rest of them."

Sebastian folded his hands, satisfied. "Then we understand each other. Now, if you will excuse me," as he gestured the three hunters to his door, just as his assistant knocked and opened the door.

"Your meeting with the new acting mayor is here," she says.

As they stepped out of Sebastian's office, Cole, Marcus, and Hot Shot exchanged a silent look, one heavy with doubt and questions. Whatever loyalty or clarity they once had was gone. One thing was certain: Reece was a vampire now, and if they wanted answers, they'd have to find him before anyone else did.

CHAPTER 68

Amelia sat in a plush armchair across from the bed, legs crossed, one of Andrew's notepads opened on her lap. She wasn't reading. Her eyes drifted across the page, lost in memories she couldn't shake. The hollowness in her chest echoed like an old wound. One she'd carried across lifetimes from each lost love.

Was it the guilt for killing him? Or grief for what might've been?

She'd asked herself a thousand times and still had no answer. Maybe it would take another lifetime to figure it out. Her gaze flicked to Reece lying in the bed, then back to the notepad in her hands. Anything to quiet the ache for a moment longer.

As the light filtered faintly through the drawn drapes, casting a warm, golden haze around the edges of the room. Outside, it was morning or maybe the afternoon. Reece had no idea how long he'd been lying in this bed, but he was awake now. And there was no pain. Not in his ribs. Not in his leg. Not anywhere.

At first, the numbness unsettled him. He tried to move, expecting to wince or feel some stabbing reminder of what happened, but there was nothing. Just smooth motion beneath the soft blankets. He shifted again and caught the sensation of fabric brushing against his legs. His legs were both still there. His heart thudded in disbelief. Then he saw her. Amelia.

She looked up, met his gaze, and smiled softly.

"Well, good afternoon soldier," she said, folding the notepad shut. "I see you're starting to feel better."

Reece blinked. The memories were sluggish at first, but as soon as he saw her, they came rushing back like a dam had broken: the vampire nest, the lab, the console raised above him, Andrew's twisted face, the key, the symbol.

His throat tightened. "What...what happened?"

Amelia set the notepad on the nightstand. Her smile faltered. "You blacked out," she said gently. "The last thing you told me was to leave you. That it was where you were supposed to die."

He stared at her. Her tone was calm, but there was weight behind her words. A heaviness on them.

"So why didn't you?" he asked. His voice was rough and hoarse.

Amelia hesitated. Her eyes flicked to the sunlight bleeding around the edges of the curtain. "Because I made a choice. One I didn't want to make. But the cave was collapsing, and...you were bleeding out. There was no time."

He felt it before she said it.

"I injected you with the serum," she whispered. "Andrew's serum. The one he made...for me. I didn't think it would work. Not on you. Not that fast, but it did."

Reece said nothing. Just stared ahead, eyes dull. The silence stretched between them like an abyss.

Amelia spoke slowly, carefully. "It bonded with your blood instantly. That's the only reason I could pull the table leg out. Your body started healing immediately. I got you back here. You've been unconscious for three days."

She waited. Reece just stared. No anger. No shock. Just a blank stillness as the weight of it settled over him.

Finally, he spoke. "So I'm a vampire now. A blood-sucking, sunlight-hating creature of the night."

Amelia stood without a word and walked to the window. She gripped the edge of the curtain.

"Not exactly," she said.

And yanked it back quickly. The sunlight exploded into the room as she stood off to the side in the shadows.

Reece flinched out of instinct, not pain. The light struck his face, warm and radiant. Not a burn. Not even a sting. He blinked. Felt the sun on his skin. His eyes widened.

"I don't...understand," he said.

Amelia stayed just outside the reach of the light. Her face softened. "Andrew didn't just make a vampire serum. He made *the* serum. One that lets vampires survive the sun...at least for a little more than an hour."

She let the curtain fall back into place.

He was quiet again. Processing everything and searching for a feeling to latch onto.

Amelia stepped closer. "You still have to drink blood, but you don't have to lose who you are. There are ways to do that without hurting anyone."

Reece stared at the blanket. His hand curled into a fist. Then he looked up at her, eyes steady.

"What do I need to know about being a vampire?"

Amelia tilted her head, confused. "Why?"

His jaw tightened. "Because I have a score to settle."

And his eyes, now tinged with a faint unnatural glow, burned with purpose. Outside, the sun dipped below the horizon, and the city turned to shadow. The final hunt had begun.